MW00815418

BUFFALITO BUFFET

Lawrence M. Schoen

FOR MARK,
LIFE'S A BUFFET,
WITH OR WITHOUT
THE FLATULENCE!

HADLEY
RILLE
BOOKS

All rights reserved. No part of this book may be reproduced or transmitted, in part or whole, by any means, electronic or mechanical, including photocopy, recording, or any information storage and retrieval system, without permission in writing from both the copyright owner and the publisher.

BUFFALITO BUFFET
© 2012 by Lawrence M. Schoen

Cover art © Rachael Mayo

Hardcover ISBN 978-0-9849670-9-4
Trade paperback ISBN 978-0-9849670-8-7

Published by
Hadley Rille Books
Eric T. Reynolds, Editor/Publisher
PO Box 25466
Overland Park, KS 66225
USA

COPYRIGHT ACKNOWLEDGMENTS

"Introduction" copyright © 2012 by Howard Tayler.

"Buffalo Dogs" first appeared in *Absolute Magnitude* magazine in 2001, copyright © 2001 by Lawrence M. Schoen.

"Buffalogenesis" appeared as a complete book in 2006, copyright © 2006 by Lawrence M. Schoen.

"A Buffalito of Mars" first appeared in the anthology *Visual Journeys*, in 2007, copyright © 2007 by Lawrence M. Schoen.

"Requiem" first appeared in *Absolute Magnitude* magazine in 2005, copyright © 2005 by Lawrence M. Schoen.

"Barry's Tale" appears for the first time in this collection, copyright © 2012 by Lawrence M. Schoen.

"Telepathic Intent" first appeared in *Buffalogic, Inc.* in 2003, copyright © 2003 by Lawrence M. Schoen.

"The Matter at Hand" first appeared in *Aliens And AIs* in 2005, copyright © 2005 by Lawrence M. Schoen

"Yesterday's Taste" first appeared in *Transtories* in 2011, copyright © 2011 by Lawrence M. Schoen.

For Irvin Green, who entrusted me with everything.

ACKNOWLEDGMENTS

The problem with a single author collection is the illusion that it's all the work of one person. Nothing could be further from the truth. The stories contained herein span more than a decade and many many people have contributed to one or more of them, knowingly or otherwise. It's not possible to name them all, and trying would only result in embarrassment and dismay when I inevitably left someone out.

And yet, appreciation and thanks must be expressed, and so I hope you'll linger on this page a while longer and say aloud the following names. Start if you would with James Gunn, whose writing workshop produced the line of dialogue that set everything else in motion.

Like many authors, I have a day job that bears little relation to anything in this book. I would be greatly remiss not to acknowledge Pat Palmer, Dr. Minda Magundayao, and Armand Magundayao for providing me an occupation that allows me to also pursue my vocation.

Various editors and publishers have liked what I've done with Conroy and Reggie enough to print their adventures in magazines and books. Warren Lapine was the first, Steve Miller the most persistent, and the late Colin Harvey from the greatest distance. I thank you all. Most importantly, I thank Eric T. Reynolds, who has allowed me to take my characters to the next level, and who gives me the room to explore them further.

To Walter Jon Williams and Nancy Kress I owe an incalculable debt for tearing down and rebuilding everything I thought I knew about writing. And thanks too to Carrie Vaughn who provided a catalyst that resulted in a blazing moment of clarity. Their gifts to me ripple outward into words that are planned but yet unwritten.

Arthur (Buck) Dorrance, Cathy Petrini, and Tim Burke and have provided moral support, social commentary, and critical feedback for as long as I've been writing about my favorite fictional hypnotist. Their fingerprints are all over every story in this book.

All the best parts are surely the result of their good intentions, vaster experience, and individual suggestions.

Howard Tayler is a mensch and an inspiration. Being around him always reminds me of the best possibilities we are all capable of. Knowing that he is my friend is more than enough to make me feel extremely special.

At the end of all acknowledgments and expressions of gratitude and appreciation must come my wife, Valerie. If we're all part of some grand karmic cycle of death and rebirth, then surely I must have racked up an insane quantity of bonus points in a previous life; I can think of no other way to account for the unimagined good fortune that brought her into my life. I am, quite simply, blessed. Serendipity is a word that defines my existence, and the very best is that I get to share every day of it with her.

And now comes the part where I tell you that, despite all the help from all the people I've named (as well as the ones I didn't mention), any mistakes, malapropisms, plot holes, purple prose, and/or god-awful acts of fiction are all my own responsibility and fault. But if I've learned anything about hypnosis in writing these stories, then let's hope the suggestions I've embedded in the text will work their way into your unconscious mind and cause you to overlook all such errors and instead buy an extra copy of this book for a friend.

Ah, if only it were that easy.

June, 2012
Blue Bell, PA

CONTENTS

INTRODUCTION

"An alien, a hypnotist, and an oxygen-excreting omnivore walk into a bar . . . "

One hallmark of good science fiction is a blending of the familiar and the strange, that marriage of an ordinary idea and something out of left field. Most of us have no shortage of ideas, and even the weird ones tend to grow pretty close to the more fertile parts of our experience. Pile a bunch of fertilizer in one place, turn the mental soil a bit, and the story seeds will start erupting with fecundity.

Lawrence M. Schoen has a Ph.D. in psychology with a focus on cognition and linguistics. We can see exactly where the fertilizer has been piled, high and deep, but even knowing that, none of us could have predicted the emergence of heist tales featuring a stage hypnotist and his furry, oh-too-flatulent pet.

Any writer worth his or her saltpeter (it's a fertilizer . . . I'm playing to the metaphor here) can tell you that the ideas are not what they're getting paid for. Coin of the realm goes to those who execute on the ideas, those who turn them into tales with engaging characters, lively dialog, and perhaps a plot twist or two. I love the Amazing Conroy stories, and like most fans of Lawrence M. Schoen's fiction, I want a pet buffalito. This isn't because "hypnotist + space caper + buffalo-shaped, dog-sized alien" is a recipe for instant literary acclaim. It's because Lawrence M. Schoen writes very, very effectively.

Many writers could harvest a punch line or two from a hypnotist and an oxy-excreting omnivore. Lawrence has reached past the low-hanging fruit and plucked an entire universe.

—Howard Tayler
July 3rd, 2012

BUFFALO DOGS

Back in 1998 I had the good fortune to attend James Gunn's two-week writers' workshop in Lawrence, Kansas. It was wonderful and grueling and electrifying and exhausting. In short, it was everything a writers' workshop should be. On the last night, weary and barely conscious, I was celebrating with the other members of my cohort; we had survived, and the next morning we would all go our separate ways. During a lull in the festivities, a phrase popped into my head and rushed out of my mouth before I could stop it. For no apparent reason I suddenly proclaimed, "Put down the buffalo dog and step away from the bar!" And then, silence. Everyone was staring at me, wondering what the hell I was talking about. If I could have stepped out of myself, I would have stared too. I hadn't a clue what I'd said, where it had come from, or what it meant. And yet . . . as the silence dragged on I found myself vowing to one day create a story that included that profound line of dialogue.

That day came in 1999. Out of the blue, I get the glimmering of an idea for a story where I can use that line that has been plaguing me for years. I begin writing. A thousand words, two thousand, three thousand. . . At first, I'm pretty happy with the story, I like the characters, I like the conflict, I like how it's all coming together. But soon, none of that matters. Soon, all I can think about is getting to a point where I can type those critical words and set down this burden. Four thousand words, five thousand, six . . . and then, finally, nearly seven thousand words into the story, it happens. I type that phrase, and a sensation of such joy descends upon me that mere words cannot describe. I bask in it a while. I wallow in it. I let the feeling that has been years in coming soak into my every pore.

And then, ever so slowly, a glimmer of horror breaks through to my awareness. I'm not done. I still have to finish the story. I'm on the brink of the big confrontation scene; I have to go back to work. I have to find a way for Conroy to win and come out on top. And I still have that damn dénouement to write. . . Of course, I did these things, but it was tough, my friends, I'm not going to lie. And you know, I'm really glad I did because otherwise, not only would that story never have been finished, but I wouldn't have been inspired by that character to bring him back again and again, in the other stories in this collection, in the novels that

I've already written, and in the ones that I'm still planning to write. And all of it because those random words came out of my mouth all those years ago. I still marvel at the serendipity of it, and wonder what prompted them in the first place. I'll probably never know.

Getting arrested a few days before I was to head back to Earth was the last thing I had in mind. I'd been working the *Li'l Doggie*, the only spaceport lounge on Gibrahl, for the past three and a half weeks. My contract called for two shows a night, with an additional matinee on Saturday. I had Sundays off. A day on Gibrahl runs near enough to twenty-four hours as not to quibble, but the weeks last for eight of them instead of seven. My agent back on Earth hadn't bothered to look into the extra day issue before booking me into a contract that paid by the week. It meant that the two shows I was required to do on Gibsday were freebies; all the work for none of the pay.

The marquee out front read "THE AMAZING CONROY, MASTER HYPNOTIST" and cycled through a googol of colorful hues in a blatant attempt to remain eye-catching. It worked. My smallest audiences were decent, and the large ones packed the place. Venues like Gibrahl are always hungry for any kind of entertainment, and a stage hypnotist can make a good buck.

The humans in my audience were all on Gibrahl for the same thing. Every one of them was in some way involved in the buffalo dog trade. The buffalitos were the only resource on Gibrahl, the single commodity responsible—directly or indirectly—for bringing people here. It was a colony world, and it wasn't our colony. Gibrahl belonged to the Arconi, and the human presence was limited to a single square kilometer base. The Arconi laid down the rules, and as long as they had something Earth wanted we abided by them like good little humans. Which is why I got arrested.

Earlier in the day the Arconi had arrested a buffalo dog courier for attempted smuggling. The Terran consulate insisted it must have been a paperwork snafu, but the Arconi possess a limited psychic faculty concerning truthfulness and discovered otherwise. Arcon justice is as swift as it is certain. The man had been tried, convicted, and executed before the end of my dinner show.

Everyone needed a distraction, and for better or worse I was it. I began with a few jokes to break the tension and put people at ease. Seeing a hypnotist, even as entertainment, tends to make some folks nervous, as if with just the lift of an eyebrow I could make men reveal their darkest secrets or women throw themselves into my arms. Don't I wish. They say Anton Mesmer could do that sort of thing centuries ago. More likely he just had a better agent than I do. Me, I need a compelling induction and a good five minutes of relative quiet, not to mention a waiting car if the thing doesn't work. Hypnotic blackmail and seduction may make for good vids, but in real life sticking to the script is a lot safer. That's not to say I never dabble or dally, just never during a show. Later on, that's a different matter. I always install a post-hypnotic backdoor when I'm performing; you never know when it might come in handy. Even after a week's time I can whisper the magic key phrase and presto, you're back in a trance and wonderfully open to suggestion. What can I say, I love my work.

That night there were several tables of Arconi present, as there had been at all of my performances. Fifty shows, and none had ever laughed, never so much as cracked a smile. And they could smile, I was fairly certain of it. The Arconi look like tall, stretched humans, like something in a funhouse mirror. Their skin tone runs through a range of whitish shades, from eggshell to ecru, and their body hair is generally the blue-black of comic book heroes. They have mouths and lips and teeth, and as far as I knew they used them for all the same things we did, but I'd never seen them smile. It wasn't that they didn't enjoy the show, they just couldn't understand it. It was that truth sense of theirs. Arconi always know whether or not they're being told the truth. Among themselves they never lie; they simply can't. It's a small thing, but when you start to work out the incidentals you discover just how ubiquitous deception is in human history.

Arcon society has almost no crime. Sure, they have crimes of passion, same as us, but anything premeditated gets nipped in the bud when the local magistrate asks you if you did it. For the Arconi, the concept of lying didn't come up until they started dealing with humans. They find us fascinating, utterly bizarre. It's like knowing how gills work, a nice safe objective knowledge that you know doesn't apply to you but that opens up interesting theoretical possibilities just the same.

Quite a few Arconi had put great value on seeing a hypnotist make people believe things that were obviously false. They'd flocked to the human district to catch my shows every night since I'd arrived. The first two nights I brought a few up to the stage. They went under just like humans. I had no trouble getting them to cluck like chickens, but they couldn't accept any suggestions that violated their objective reality. They couldn't believe they'd actually become chickens. No imagination, totally grounded. Bottom line, they made for a dull show, and I stopped taking them as volunteers.

Anyway, I was doing my usual show for the last week of a gig. Ten minutes into the performance I had two young secretaries, an elderly bank loan officer, and a middle-aged security guard on stage with me, all of them deeply entranced. I'd told the secretaries they were Arconi diplomats and had them explain the Arcon plan for human enlightenment. There's no such thing of course, but neither secretary/diplomat knew that, and they elaborated and expounded on all sorts of made-up nonsense with great sincerity while the human portion of the audience hooted and laughed.

The secretaries finished their presentation and received thunderous applause from the humans in the audience. I thanked them and escorted them back to chairs on the stage which I'd already assured them comprised the lush Arcon embassy back on Earth. I returned them to a deep trance. They'd done a great job, surprisingly original and clever, and the audience was breathless to see what would happen next. I turned to the security guard and, after a wink and grin at the audience, began her instructions.

"Butterscotch Melpomene," I whispered to her, using the key phrase I'd implanted at the start of the show. Her posture changed, not so much a movement as an attitude. Though completely relaxed she was now almost painfully alert. I turned back to the audience and waved them in, as if inviting them along for the gag.

"You're a native of Gibrahl," I said in my stage voice, all mellow tones and booming resonance. "You're intelligent and articulate, educated and urbane." The security guard sat up straighter in her chair, her face composed and confident, her eyes still closed. "I'd like you to tell us about Gibrahl from your own unique perspective, if you don't mind. Would that be all right?"

She nodded, licked her lips, and raised one hand in the start of a gesture.

"That's fine. You'll begin to do so when I count to three," I said. "Oh, and one more thing. You're not human, you're a buffalo dog. One . . . Two . . . "

"STOP!" An Arcon at one of the rear tables was on his feet. I recognized him. He was a real regular; he'd come to at least one of my shows each day since I'd arrived, always sitting at the same table, always watching with rapt attention. He'd even been a volunteer, a pretty good subject for an Arcon. His name was Loyoka, and he stood pointing a weapon at me. Most of the audience laughed, assuming it was part of the act. I knew better.

"Everyone on the stage is under arrest," he continued. "Do not move. Cooperate and you will not be injured."

Loyoka made has way to the stage, those long long legs allowing him to mount the platform without effort. I'd frozen as soon as I saw the gleam from his laser sight. He approached the security guard, squatted until they were on the same level and asked, "Are you a buffalo dog?"

There was a ripple of laughter from the audience; most still thought the Arcon was part of the act. The woman didn't answer him. She couldn't answer. The only voice she could hear at the moment was mine. Loyoka figured this out pretty quickly and turned to me. "Why won't she speak? You indicated she was articulate."

"I haven't finished counting," I said. "She won't follow the instructions until I do."

"Three!" said the Arcon, his eyes fixed on the security guard. Nothing happened. More snickers from the audience. "You say it," he said to me, without turning his head.

"Three," I breathed, and the guard opened her eyes, smiled brightly, and nodded into the Arcon's face scant inches from her own.

"Are you a buffalo dog?" repeated Loyoka.

"Oh my, yes," agreed the guard. "I was born here on Gibrahl, and let me tell you, it's not an easy life. It's a wonder I'm still here at all. I've seen all of my litter mates and all of my childhood friends shipped off to other planets by you Arconi. Shameless, I tell you, just shameless."

She rambled on and on, confabulating a complete history as an alien creature with a brain no bigger than a walnut. The Arcon's jaw dropped lower and lower as he listened, his psychic faculty assuring him that the human believed every word of it, that despite appearances she *was* a buffalo dog.

Ten minutes later I was in Arconi custody and sitting in a detention cell. My four volunteers were no longer entranced and as far as I knew were being similarly 'detained' by the authorities. My out-system visa had been confiscated. The *Lil Doggie* was closed, pending the outcome of the investigation. The management lodged a complaint with my agent, and filed a lawsuit against the interstellar stage performers' union. There's no business like show business, especially when it comes to blackballing. Even assuming I got out of the current predicament it was highly unlikely I would be able to get work anywhere off Earth again. For the moment though, that was the least of my problems.

Hours passed. I spent the first few going over the show in my mind, again and again, trying to figure out what had pissed off the Arconi. I couldn't think of anything. I dozed, off and on, and jerked fully awake when the door to my cell finally opened and Loyoka entered with two other Arconi, each dragging a short stool. They perched on the stools, feet flat on the floor, their long legs bent, knees at shoulder level. It left them at eye level with me as I sat on my bunk. They stared intently, all of them.

"Tell us . . . a lie," said the one on my right.

"A lie?" I asked. My gaze moved from one stern face to the next. Their eyes looked just like human eyes, but it wasn't comforting.

"Yes, Mr. Conroy, tell us something you do not believe is true. Do it now," he said.

My mind went blank. The only thing I could think of was the aborted show.

"I'm an Arconi diplomat," I said. "I have a plan for human enlightenment."

The two newcomers frowned at that. Loyoka recognized the line from tonight's show and the corners of his mouth turned up ever so slightly. They could smile.

"You are lying," said the one on the left, his frown deepening.

"You told me to lie." I shrugged.

"Yes, and we know you are lying. In your performance, you tell other humans to do things. These things are not lies."

I shook my head. "I'm sorry, I'm not trying to be difficult, but I really don't understand what you're getting at."

"Are you a smuggler, Mr. Conroy?" asked Loyoka.

"Am I what?"

"Are you a smuggler of buffalo dogs? Please answer 'yes' or 'no.'"

"No!" I said, feeling a growing dread.

"But you turned that woman . . . " Loyoka glanced at a small palmpadd, "Carla Espinoza, into a buffalo dog. It was truth. I saw it in her mind."

"But, she wasn't really a buffalo dog!" I grinned. This was all some sort of joke, right? I stopped. They looked deadly serious.

"She was. I saw the truth myself. She was a buffalo dog. An unlicensed buffalo dog, Mr. Conroy." He frowned then, making a complete set of them. "Do you understand the severity of this crime? There are allegations that you are attempting to export a stolen and fertile buffalo dog to Earth."

My mind reeled. The buffalo dogs were one of the few lifeforms native to Gibrahl, and unlike anything else in known space. They looked amazingly like American bison rendered at one fiftieth scale. They were adorable creatures with cute woolly heads and tiny blue tongues that stuck out when they bleated. They could eat anything, anything at all, and thrive. And most amazing of all, they farted enormous volumes of pure, diatomic oxygen, which made them incredibly useful to terraformers. Not to mention the significant dent they were making in problems of landfill and toxic waste sites back home on Earth. On any given night at the *Li'l Doggie* fully one quarter of the people in the audience were couriers, slated to return to Earth on the next ship out, a thin portfolio of transfer licenses under one arm and a buffalo dog tucked under the other. The Arconi controlled the only source of the beasts, and exported them, infertile, at ten million credits a head. At that price smuggling the little guys had become quite attractive, and several sterile pups had been stolen. Not surprisingly, the Arconi government had responded with extreme prejudice. Even suspicion of involvement with black market buffalo dogs could bring a death sentence. I was in deep buffalo chips.

"But she wasn't a buffalo dog," I protested, half rising from the bunk. "She wasn't, not physically."

Loyoka brought a hand down on my shoulder, pushing me back. "I know what I saw in her mind. She *was* a buffalo dog. On Gibrahl, if a human is in possession of a buffalo dog he is either a smuggler or a courier. I can see the truth in your mind, Mr. Conroy. You are not a smuggler."

He paused and looked to either side at his companions. A silent confirmation passed among them and all three rose to their feet.

"We are very troubled by all of this, Mr. Conroy. We take even the suspicion of crime very seriously. While you've been waiting we've done a full search of all registered facilities. None report any missing stock; you're not being charged with theft. The only reason that you have not been prosecuted and convicted on the remaining charge is that Carla Espinoza is infertile."

It was just getting weirder and weirder. "How would you know that?" I asked.

Loyoka barely glanced at me. "We did a complete examination of her. Any human in possession of a fertile buffalo dog is instantly guilty of a capital offense. But, as I said, she's incapable of conception. Infertile buffalo dogs may be transported by licensed couriers. That just leaves the matter of clearing up the paperwork. We have gone ahead and tagged Carla Espinoza and drawn up the appropriate paperwork for your license."

One of the other Arconi presented me with a palmpadd and stylus. I glanced at the document and signed. They'd transferred the bulk of my earnings on Gibrahl out of my account to cover and placed a lien on future income for twice that amount, the balance due for my license. I was now an authorized courier.

"Congratulations, Mr. Conroy. You've acquired a buffalo dog without paying the usual ten million credits." There wasn't a hint of sarcasm in his tone. He really meant it.

"But she's not a buffalo dog now, right?" I said. "She's out of the trance, she knows who she is."

All three Arconi frowned again and fidgeted nervously. The other two left, taking the stools with them, leaving Loyoka to bestow a few parting words. "We admit there is much about your abilities which we do not understand," he said. "While it is clear to me that your subject tonight knew she was a buffalo dog, it is equally obvious that in some ways she was not. This is new territory for us, Mr. Conroy. We'll be watching you closely for the remainder of your stay. I'd advise you to be quite careful.

"You're free to go now," he said, holding the door open for me. "Speak to the clerk at the front desk. He'll return your visa and provide you with a hard copy of your licenses. You can pick up Carla Espinoza there as well." He pointed me to the right and sent me on my way. He headed off to the left and vanished around a turn in the corridor.

Carla Espinoza sat on one of a bank of interlinked chairs in the lobby. She was a bit pale but otherwise appeared unharmed. Dangling from her left ear was a two centimeter disk of bright red plastic. She'd been tagged for transport. There was an angry look on her face, diffused at first but quickly focusing when she saw me approach. I started making apologies as soon as I was close enough to be heard.

"Ms. Espinoza, Carla, please, I'm terribly sorry. I had no idea any of this was going to happen, you must believe me."

She rose to her feet and glared. She was a head shorter than me, and twenty years older. I had no doubt she'd spent most of that time bouncing from one security position to the next. She outweighed me by a good ten kilos, all of it muscle. The look in her eyes made it clear that she could beat the crap out of me without breaking a sweat.

Her hands lifted, tugging at her ear lobe and the plastic tag. It unclipped and she threw it at me. "If this was Earth I'd sue you and your next three generations for everything you had," she said. "You're lucky the Arconi don't permit lawyers here."

I caught the tag and put it in my pocket. It was an expensive souvenir. I handed her my credit chip. "There isn't much left in there, but you're welcome to it. They took most of what I had to cover license costs."

"License costs?" she said.

I gave a weak smile. "They determined that since I was in possession of a buffalo dog, and I wasn't a smuggler, that I obviously had to be a courier and charged me accordingly."

Her anger melted away at this and she laughed. She'd been on Gibrahl long enough to know just how expensive a courier license was. That seemed to satisfy her. She pocketed my credit chip. "I'm going to let this go," she said, "provided I don't see you again.

Otherwise I'm going to tear you a new hole. You'll be hurting so bad that a walk in vacuum would feel like a welcome relief. Are we clear?"

I nodded, trying hard not to flinch. She gave me another look up and down and stormed out. The clerk seated behind a desk at the back of the lobby had watched the entire scene without comment. He looked pale, even for an Arcon. And why not? He'd heard her every word, and knew it was all true. I collected my hard copy and left.

Judging by the position of Gibrahl's wan star high overhead it was nearly noon. I had nothing to do, no money to spend, and a full day before my ship back to Earth left. I started making my way back toward the spaceport proper, hoping to bum a meal and some crash space in exchange for a few hypnotic parlor tricks when a men in a painfully new suit locked step with me. My first thought was that the manager of the *Lil Doggie* wanted a piece of me, but the fellow was too small to be a goon, too preppy. He was a polished, clean-cut, silver spoon archetype who doubtless had an MBA from some prestigious Ivy League university's online degree program. I'm not a tough guy, but compared to me he was a weenie.

It took a moment, but I recognized him from a show. I'd hypnotized him. He was a corporate type, a middleman in the transfer of buffalo dogs to Terran business concerns. He had been at the *Lil Doggie* during my opening show, part of a larger party of still more corporate suits and prospective clients. I'd hypnotized half the people at the table. The clients had been marvelously entertained and this fellow had arranged a generous tip to show his appreciation. Even a small percentage from Gibrahl's buffalo dog traffic translated into vast amounts of cash. He could afford to tip big and to wear new suits.

"Mr. Conroy," said the tipper, "I apologize for contacting you so crudely, but I very much need to speak with you. I have a proposition."

Just when you think things can't get worse, corporate hustlers show up. Great. "I'm sorry, but I'm tired and I'm hungry and I'm really not in the mood for whatever it is you're selling," I said.

He persisted. "Mr. Conroy, my name is Jensen. Please, just hear me out. Why don't we get a nice comfortable table at *The Prairie*. My treat, of course. You can have a nice meal, relax, and after you've listened to my proposal if you're still not interested, well, that will be it."

That stopped me. *The Prairie* was the only five star restaurant on Gibrahl. That put it two stars above everything else in the kilometer city. The cost of the appetizers alone would have wiped out a week's salary. I slipped an arm around his shoulder and mustered up a tired smile. "Mr. Jensen, if lunch is on you, I'm all ears."

He look relieved and escorted me to *The Prairie*. The maître d' fitted me with an appropriate jacket, and in short order I was sitting at an elegant table enjoying an *amuse-guele* of potato cornets layered in crème fraîche, salmon, and caviar and sipping the most delicate wine I'd ever imagined. My cares evaporated but I kept a wary eye on my host. The other shoe was about to drop.

True to his word, he had let me get comfortable before he started his pitch. I was well into the first course—black-eyed peas arranged with antelope sweetbreads, mushrooms, and wild raspberries—when he reached into his breast pocket and withdrew a palmpadd.

"Mr. Conroy, allow me to be direct. My superiors at the Wada Consortium are aware of your recent change of fortune, and the juxtaposition of circumstances that put you there, all through no fault of your own. We'd like to help, if you'll let us. We want to hire you."

I almost choked on my wine when he said that. I set down my glass and wiped at my mouth with my napkin. "You need a hypnotist, Mr. Jensen?" I said.

"No, Mr. Conroy, we need a courier. The corporation we represent is scheduled to transfer thirty-two buffalo dogs off Gibrahl on tomorrow's ship. All of them have already been sold, and we've guaranteed their delivery. The Arcon government allows only a single buffalo dog per licensed courier, and at present we have only thirty-one couriers available."

I gave him a puzzled frown, "then why did you schedule thirty-two buffalitos?" I slipped another forkful of sweetbreads into my mouth.

Jensen sighed. "Because until yesterday afternoon we had thirty-two couriers, Mr. Conroy."

Which was about the time I remembered the execution of a smuggler. I put my fork down. My appetite vanished. That thirty-second pup was worth ten million credits to someone back on Earth, and the penalty for nondelivery was going to cost Jensen's company at least half that much.

"I'm a hypnotist. I don't know much about buffalo dogs or being a courier," I said.

"There's not much to know, Mr. Conroy. The buffalo dogs themselves require minimal care. All a courier does is carry the creature onto the ship and stay with it in his stateroom. For the duration of the voyage to Earth you simply monitor the room's atmospheric regulators to prevent excess oxygen buildup. Upon arrival you carry it off. I'm sure that's well within your talents."

"Why don't you just run someone else through the licensing procedure?" I asked.

"It takes five years to apply for a license, Mr. Conroy. Quite frankly, we're amazed you've acquired one, but we won't question it. For whatever reason, the Arconi suddenly consider you a courier, and they're the only ones we have to please to get that thirty-second buffalo dog to Earth."

He slid the palmpadd across the table. A contract glowed up at me. "I'm prepared to offer you compensation in the amount of one hundred thousand credits in exchange for you acting as our courier."

That was a lot of money, especially since I was broke and soon to be blacklisted. Still . . .

"Is that the standard rate for a courier?" He nodded. I paused, pretended to read over the contract while I wracked my brain, trying to remember that very first show I'd done on Gibrahl. I looked at the sweetbreads on my plate and it came to me. Spicy Egyptian. I leaned forward and whispered, "Jalapeño Osiris."

Jensen slumped back in his chair, his eyes closed. I reached a hand into his jacket and found his wallet. I flipped through it, and checked his corporate ID to learn his first name, as well as the balances on his corporate and personal credit chips. Ken had a lot of credit at his disposal.

"Can you hear me, Ken?"

"Yes, I hear you."

"That's good. We're very good friends, you know. We tell each other everything. There are no secrets between us, Ken. No secrets at all. Do you understand?"

"Yes," he murmured.

"Tell me, what's the standard fee for a courier? One who's carrying a buffalo dog from Gibrahl to Earth for your company?"

"Five hundred thousand credits," he said. No hesitation at all.

"And yet you offered me only a fifth of that, Ken. Is that any way to treat a friend? Why'd you do it?"

Jensen shrugged, looking embarrassed despite his closed eyes. "We figured you wouldn't know any better and were so far down that you'd jump at a hundred."

"You're probably right, Ken. It hasn't been my day. But things are looking up. When I count to three you're going to have a change of heart, Ken. You're going to decide that you really don't want to screw me like that. You realize that I'm saving your ass, and you're going to rewrite this contract for the full five hundred thousand. Plus you're going to throw in your corporate credit chip, just so I have some walking around money until it's time for me to leave. Do you understand?"

"Yes, I understand."

I returned his wallet to its proper place, sat back, and counted to three. Ken Jensen blinked rapidly and sat up straight, acting like a man who had briefly dozed off and looks around to see if anyone noticed. I was staring down at the palmpadd, pretending to study the contract and shaking my head. "I just don't know . . . "

"Let me have that back," he said. "I think I can sweeten the deal. You're really getting us out of a bind, so why don't we call it five hundred thousand, instead?" He made the changes to the contract and slid it back to me. His company credit chip was sitting on top of the palmpadd.

"Mr. Jensen, you've got yourself a courier." The look from across the table was one of relief and satisfaction. I tried hard to keep my face from showing the same emotions.

Jensen left me to enjoy the rest of my meal, but not before he outlined the plan. I was to present my courier license at any of the Arconi registered facilities, where I'd be free to select the doggie of my choice. Before boarding my ship home I would again show my license and be questioned by an Arcon customs officer. Then, presto, five hundred thousand credits upon arrival on Earth.

I confess, I lingered over the remaining courses. I'm enough of a gourmand to know that proper appreciation requires a respectful span. Jensen had already paid for the meal, and I used his corporate chip to add to the tip before leaving. My new profession beckoned. I was off to begin life as a courier.

It didn't matter to me where I got the buffalo dog, though most couriers have all sorts of superstitions about such things. My ship departed at 1:00 a.m., leaving me nearly ten hours to kill. I took my time, decided to enjoy a good walk after a great meal. Pedestrian traffic was light. I passed several other couriers, identifiable by the doggies tucked comfortably under one arm. Eventually I found my way to the facility farthest from the space port's customs gate. I stopped in front of a kiosk and a short, bored looking Arcon regarded me from within.

"You're a courier?" he asked, barely glancing at me.

"You bet," I answered, and he waved me through, the truth of my statement as obvious as daylight.

There was a brief flight of stairs down to the holding area and sheer chaos waiting at the bottom. Thousands of bleating, yipping, scampering buffalo dogs filled a shallow area the size of an Olympic pool. Holographic signs projected warnings of extreme combustibility and the sounds of exhaust fans provided a constant background of white noise. The buffalitos cavorted, none of them able to climb up the two foot height of their pool, though they could see the area surrounding it. They eagerly approached anyone, human or Arcon, who drew near the perimeter. The humans, a dozen or so, were couriers. I watched as they reached in to lift up one creature after another. The selection process appeared to involve hefting the buffalo dog under consideration, tucking it under first one arm and then the other, peering into its eyes, and checking the shade of its blue tongue. Superstitious ritual, but conscientiously observed nonetheless. Eventually, each courier selected a doggie and carried it over to an available Arcon for processing.

After witnessing several variations on the process I followed the example. A very enthusiastic doggie spied me as I approached the edge of its enclosure and plowed through the nearer pups, desperate to reach me. I picked it up. Cute. Adorable really, but for five hundred thousand credits it could have been ugly as sin and I'd have done the job.

"C'mon, little darling," I said to it, barely resisting the urge to use baby talk, "you'll do as well as any other." It farted some oxygen, bleated at me from out the other end, and stuck out its tiny tongue. Cerulean. Fine with me. I looked around for one of the Arconi that wasn't busy, found one, and walked up to her.

"You are a courier?" she asked, her tone only slightly less bored than the fellow at the door.

"I'm a courier," I said, "The Amazing Conroy, Master Courier, at your service." She didn't look the least bit amused.

"And this is the buffalo dog you've selected?"

"Absolutely," I said. "Do I get to name her?"

She shrugged, "That is the custom sir. I'll prepare her tags once I verify the animal's health and administer a sterilizing agent." She took the doggie from my hands and pressed a medical scanner deeply into fur.

"Then I'm going to name her Regina. Regina Catherine Aloysious Nantucket Bitter Almonds St. Croix. What do you think, is it too much?" What can I say, I was on my way to being a half-millionaire, well fed, and in a great mood.

The Arcon frowned. "I would recommend a more masculine name, sir. You've selected a male. He is in excellent health, but if you'd prefer a female instead you are free to put him back and bring up another for verification and sterilization."

I shrugged, "What's in a name? No, this one is fine, I'll just call him Reggie. Go ahead, you can sterilize and tag him."

She shook her head. "I'll be happy to tag him for you, sir, but only the female buffalo dogs are sterilized." She handed the doggie back to me. "If you'll come this way, I'll prepare Reggie's tags."

Five minutes later I exited with Reggie tucked complacently under my left arm, the blue plastic disk of his new tag hanging prettily from his left ear. The entire process had taken barely a quarter of an hour. It was a long walk back to the port, and more than once I had the feeling that someone was following me. I made my way to customs and immediately recognized the officer on duty. He was the fattest Arcon I had ever seen, and for that reason alone I'd had him up on stage as a subject during my first week. He'd gone under easily and loved the experience. After the show he came back stage and shook my hand, something the Arconi simply never did. He did it again now when it was my turn at the customs gate, and added only the second smile I'd ever seen from an Arcon. I was in the presence of a fan.

"Mr. Conroy, I was so sorry to hear about your recent problems with the authorities," he said. In the little kilometer square city rumor traveled at the speed of light, and buffalo dog gossip maybe even a bit faster. "But you've bounced back nicely, I see. I'm delighted to have the privilege of clearing you. This is your first trip as a courier, isn't it?"

I searched my memory again, using the same mnemonic tricks that let me remember thousands of individual key phrases and their respective hypnotic subjects. "Thank you, and my last, I suspect. I'm a hypnotist, really. Sergilo, wasn't it?"

He beamed, standing a bit taller and straighter as if I'd just made him godfather to the Prince of Gibrahl. "That's right, Mr. Conroy. I'm flattered you remember. Well, let's get you processed and cleared without delay. I just have a couple quick questions and you'll be free to board your ship. Ready? Are you a licensed courier? Did you obtain this buffalo dog in the prescribed and lawful manner? And is this the only buffalo dog you'll be transporting? Just answer 'yes' or 'no,' please."

I replied yes three times. The Arcon kept eye contact with me and nodded at each answer, confirming the truth in my mind. I grinned and asked, "Aren't you going to ask me if the critter's sterile?"

He shook his head, "There's no need, Mr. Conroy. You've got a male there."

"How can you tell under all this fur?"

"Blue tag. Blue for males, red for females."

"Handy system," I said.

He glanced at my visa and consulted a schedule. "Your ship doesn't leave until one this morning, so you've got plenty of time to settle in. I'm on duty here till midnight if you need anything. And if I don't see you again, well, you have yourself an enjoyable trip home, Mr. Conroy."

A few minutes later and I was in my cabin on the good ship *Bucephalous*. The economy class cabin I had shared with three other travelers on the trip in had been upgraded to the more spacious and private accommodations typically used by couriers, courtesy of Mr. Jensen and the Wada Consortium. It included a separate pen and restraining couch for Reggie as well as special atmospheric controls to ensure his flatulence didn't cause any problems.

My luggage had been impounded when the authorities closed the *Lil Doggie*, and apparently released when I was. Jensen had arranged for its transfer and everything was right where it should have been in the cabin. Reggie settled into his pen, bleating happily, and I laid back on my own couch to go over recent events. I was about to be wealthier than I had any right to be, though I was still probably blacklisted from ever performing again. That irked me. I'd just told an Arcon that I wasn't going to remain a courier, I was a hypnotist. Still, at five hundred thousand per doggie it was tempting. *But*, I asked myself, *was it any kind of life for a hypnotist?* I held up two images in my mind, courier and hypnotist, comparing and contrasting. An idea bloomed. It was risky, a gamble, but it combined the best of both worlds, if I didn't end up executed.

I got up from my couch and checked on Reggie. He had curled up on a blanket in his pen and fallen asleep. I slipped into the cabin's tiny bathroom, regarded myself in the mirror. I created a new trigger phrase and started to implement my idea.

A half hour before midnight I left the Bucephalous and quickly made my way to the nearest registered facility. Barely a block from the space port, this one was even larger than the last I'd visited. It was like a vast buffalo dog warehouse with humans and Arconi scurrying about. I tried not to look nervous, and figured as long as I didn't lie I'd be fine. I presented my papers at the door, confirmed that I was a courier, and was in. Time was short and I wasn't very choosy. There were dozens of smaller pens, with the doggies in each assigned by particular combinations of height, weight, tongue color, and so on. I looked for one that was more or less the same size as Reggie, scooped it up and headed for the an available Arcon on the far side of the pens.

"You are a courier?" he asked, and I nodded an assent. "This is the buffalo dog you've selected?" Again I nodded. "Fine, let me have it." He wielded his medical scanner with professional boredom, studied the readout and turned back to me. "You've made a fine choice. She's in perfect health. Give me a moment to administer a sterilizing agent and you can take her."

"A female?" I said, trying my best to look disappointed. "I'm sorry, I wanted a male. It's a Friday, you know, unlucky day for females. I'll just carry this one back."

The Arcon dismissed me with a shrug, likely having heard far stranger courier superstitions. He didn't spare me a second look as I carried the doggie back toward the pens; there was plenty of other work for him. I made my way past the pens of doggies but didn't stop to replace the female. Instead I walked toward the exit, trying hard to keep my pace natural and unhurried. No one stopped me and I was back out onto the street without incident. I was now a smuggler.

The trip back to the port was the longest block I'd ever walked. That feeling of being followed returned, and as I rounded the corner I caught a glimpse of two Arconi in my peripheral vision. The trigger phrase leapt to my mind, but it was too early to use it. It was useless until after midnight. Instead I took the red tag out of my pocket and affixed it to the buffalo dog's left ear. According to the tag she was now Carla Espinoza. I entered the space port and detoured into a small pub with an elaborate exhaust system and took a seat at the bar. Most of the clientele were couriers, each with a buffalito tucked under one arm. It was common for couriers to enjoy a drink before boarding the ship home to Earth. Say one thing for the Arcon psychic faculty, it made clearing customs efficient and quick. We'd all be able to get through in under ten minutes. Well, maybe not all of us. It was still a bit before midnight and Sergilo, my fat and friendly Arcon was still on duty and sure to recognize me. I ordered an overpriced beer, put it on the Wada Consortium chip and settled in for a half hour's wait just to be safe. I was on my second beer when four Arconi entered the pub. One of them was Loyoka.

"Put down the buffalo dog and step away from the bar!"

There were other couriers in the room and none of them seemed the least bit alarmed. Those at the bar were all setting their doggies down and keeping their hands in plain view as they moved away. I did the same, sliding a bowl of peanuts under Carla Espinoza's woolly beard to keep her happy. This was it. "Spumoni Heimdahl," I whispered to myself. I blinked and almost stumbled. Something had happened, but I wasn't sure what.

Ignoring the other couriers, Loyoka came for me. "I told you I'd be keeping an eye on you, Mr. Conroy. Is that your buffalo dog?"

"Yes," I said. His gaze never left mine. "Though technically I suppose it belongs to the Wada Consortium. I'm just the courier."

"The same Wada Consortium that recently employed a courier found to be a smuggler? Don't you find that a bit of a coincidence, Mr. Conroy?"

"Not really," I said. "That courier was executed. They needed another one fast and I was available. I don't see anything coincidental about that at all."

He pushed past me to the bar and picked up the buffalo dog, studying the tag on her ear. She gave a bewildered bleat as he pulled her from her bowl of peanuts.

"And this is Carla Espinoza?" His eyes narrowed.

"Yes, she is," I said, giving him a quizzical look.

"This is the woman you had on stage during your performance last night?"

I laughed. "No, this is a buffalo dog I selected from one of your registered facilities. I just named her after that woman."

He grunted then, and thrust the buffalo dog into my arms. "Then let's get you safely through customs, Mr. Conroy, I wouldn't want you to miss your ship." He nodded to the other Arconi who lined up to either side and behind me and together we all marched over to clear customs.

It was after midnight and the customs officer was a short and attractive Arcon, almost human looking. The name Sergilo came to me as I waited in line, but I couldn't place why. I was fairly certain I'd never met her; not *all* the Arconi had come to my shows. When it was my turn I presented my courier license.

She glanced at it, at me, and then at Loyoka and his friends. Loyoka moved to stand next to her, the better to see me. "Mr. Conroy," she said, reading my name from the license, I have just three questions for you. Please respond 'yes' or 'no.' Are you a licensed courier? Did you obtain this buffalo dog in the prescribed and lawful manner? And is this the only buffalo dog you will be transporting?"

"Yes, I am a licensed courier. Yes I acquired this doggie appropriately, and yes, this is the only buffalo dog I'm transporting."

Loyoka stared at me, his face bore a look of surprise and stunned amazement. The customs officer nodded and waved me through, but Loyoka stopped me as I tried to go past, turning me back to him with a hand on my arm.

"One extra question for you, Mr. Conroy, if you please," he said. His eyes burned into mine. "Are you a smuggler, Mr. Conroy? Yes or no."

Irritably I pushed his hand away. "You've asked me this before. I am not a smuggler."

He blinked and then turned to the other Arconi he had brought with him. Three other heads gave slight shakes and Loyoka returned his attention to me. "My apologies, Mr. Conroy, I appear to have misjudged you. Please, no offense intended."

"Right, you were just doing your job. Fine. Are we finished?"

"Completely. Safe travels to you, Mr. Conroy." With that he turned and left, the other three Arconi leaving with him. The customs officer gave me a perplexed look and signaled for the next person in line. I turned, and with Carla Espinoza safely under my arm, boarded the ship.

I proceeded to my assigned cabin and let myself in. My first impression was that I was in the wrong place. Or perhaps some other courier had mistakenly claimed my cabin. For whatever reason there was already a buffalo dog in the room, secured to a makeshift acceleration couch in a pen. I spun around to leave and saw a hand made sign I'd missed before because it was pinned to the back of the door. SPUMONI HEIMDAHL it read in large thick letters. I blinked, felt a moment's dizziness, and realized I was in the right room after all. I locked the door and moved to reset the cabin's atmospheric controls.

Many hours later, long after the *Bucephalous* was on its way back to Earth, one of Gibrahl's registered buffalo dog facilities discovered it was missing a doggie. Reggie and Carla were getting along fine, enthusiastically doing their part to ensure the first litter of buffalo pups born off Gibrahl. To his courier, Reggie was worth five hundred thousand. To a smuggler, plucking an extra buffalito was worth ten million. But I'm a hypnotist, and I was coming away with Earth's first fertile and soon-to-be pregnant buffalo dog. I figured I could set my own price. That's show biz.

BUFFALOGENESIS

If you're reading through this collection in order, or at least read the first story, then what I'm about to tell you will make sense. If not, stop what you're doing right now, and go back and read "Buffalo Dogs." I'll wait...

Ready? Okay, so here's the thing. When I wrote that first story, I had no idea I was starting a franchise. I had no intention or expectation that I would ever take up the Amazing Conroy and Reggie again. But, as they say, the author is always the last to know. Years passed, and I wrote several more stories: The next one to get published was "Telepathic Intent," which takes place about three years after the events in the first story, when Conroy has begun building his corporate empire (having broken the Arconi monopoly on buffalitos) and he and Reggie are off having adventures while making some business deals. Soon after that story appeared a reader contacted me and cried "Foul!" How could Reggie be with Conroy? According to the events described in "Buffalo Dogs," Conroy should have turned Reggie over to the Wada Consortium and gone off to build his fortune using the pups from his smuggled buffalito, Carla Espinoza. Whoops! This is what happens when you don't pay attention to your own creations. I'd gotten it wrong, wrong, wrong. Here's the moral: when you paint yourself into a corner, always remember you can jump out a window. "Buffalogenesis," the novelette that follows, was my window.

One moment I was having a very enjoyable dream involving a gorgeous reference librarian and an inappropriate repayment plan for some late books, and then the girl, the books, and the library itself all faded away, leaving me standing in an abattoir. It was all concrete, bad lighting, and meat hooks. The heavy odor of industrial cleaner hung in the air, but failed to mask the scent of blood that had me on the edge of retching with my first breath.

"Well, well, well," said a voice behind me, "if it is not Amazing Conroy. Come home like hypnotist prodigal son."

Even if the setting hadn't clued me in, I would have recognized that voice by the second syllable. Deep and gravely, with a thick

Russian accent, it made me realize that I was dreaming and a rogue telepath had just invaded my unconscious mind. The very person I'd left the planet to avoid had found me already.

I turned to face him, a giant of a man, big as any Russian bear and twice as mean. Close-set, piggy grey eyes glared down at me from the maniacal face of Gregor Ivanovich Skazhitski, dream tracker and professional enforcer for a Russian black market beef tsar. The butcher's whites he wore bore innumerable blood stains. Wet flecks of red speckled his face and beard, his hands and arms. It was real only in so much as it reflected his image of himself. The man wasn't big on subtlety; he planned to slaughter me.

"Gregor," I said, "What a surprise! But you didn't have to go to all this trouble. You could have just sent a card. Or flowers, flowers are always nice."

One of Gregor's ham-like hands clapped me on the shoulder and nearly drove me to my knees. "Conroy, Conroy, do not be so comical. I think I detect nothing amazing about you. Perhaps you are victim of, how do you say? Misnomer? I expect you be amazing. I expect you have my money and buy back shame you have brought my sister."

I winced. I'd managed to forget the particulars of why I owed Skazhitski. During my last performance on Earth I'd mistakenly allowed Gregor's sister to be among my volunteers. I'd been booked into a seedy club in Kansas City, a private, after-hours function for some movers and shakers in town for a cattle industry convention. The teenage girl had snuck into the room, but nonetheless her brother blamed me. After all, I'd pulled her up on stage and hypnotized her.

Although well within the bounds of decency, some of the antics I'd put her through had not set well with her devoted and protective sibling. Gregor had accompanied a Russian beef syndicate leader, and earlier in the day quite literally ripped off the arms of the opposition during an "accident" and "misunderstanding." The local authorities had been bought off, but it wouldn't do for Gregor to maim someone else so soon, especially for a personal matter. Instead, he had visited my dressing room after the show and offered to let me buy back the insult to his sister. I'd agreed. It seemed better than the alternative. Gregor had named a huge sum, but I didn't have anything approaching that kind of money. He took what cash I had and my marker for the rest, tacking on interest at a rate that redefined usury. Self-preservation being the better part of valor, I skipped town, skipped Earth, skipped the solar system.

"I learn you are courier now, Conroy. It is buffalo dog work that brings you back. I learn this two hours ago when your ship land and its passenger list go online. I drop my other work. I take leave of absence so that I may come see you personally."

"How is work? Still in the enforcer business?"

"I am still deciding which part I like best, hunting a man down in his dreams, or hurting him while he is awake. It is good that I get to do both."

"So rare to find someone who enjoys his work," I said. "Speaking of work, I probably ought to be waking up about now. I have to turn over that buffalo dog you mentioned."

"Yes, is why I am visiting you. Surely you planned to contact me and repay debt you owe for insulting my sister."

Acutely aware of my arms and how pleasantly they remained connected to my torso, I nodded. "I should have half a million credits this morning," I said. "More than enough to cover what I owe."

Gregor's face broke out into a huge grin showing rows of perfect teeth that were surely the pride of Russian orthodonture. "Conroy, Conroy, always you are making with funny ha ha. That is not enough money for debt."

"What? Half a million more than covers the original marker."

"Da, but the interest I am charging you, it compounds daily. Plus, my sister fills with distress when she learns you leave planet without repaying insult to her honor. To ease her remorse I add punitive charges, malfeasance charges, liability charges. Then when you do not return for more than year, I add interest charges on other charges. They compound too."

"Your sister's honor has compounded interest? Okay, how much are you saying I owe?"

"Two million four hundred thousand nine hundred eighteen credits," said Gregor. "You promised to pay for insult to my sister. But then you run. I give you last chance to honor your word."

"That's crazy, I don't have that kind of money."

"If you do not honor your word, I make you pay in other way. And do not think you can go missing again. I will find you when you sleep. I will catch you in your dreams."

I know a thing or two about the human mind. I looked around the slaughterhouse and thought about other nightmarish scenarios he could conjure and keep me in, and quickly put the thought out of my mind. "I'll get you your money, Gregor. But I'm going to need more time."

"See, now you are amazing. I have every confidence you will figure it all out quickly like genius man."

Gregor stepped even closer to me, one hand still clamped to my shoulder. "Genius man, eh? Okay, Amazing Conroy, I will give you till noon tomorrow to find money you owe me. Maybe you can convince bosses you are now working for to give special bonus, or advance for next several jobs. I do not care. You buy back insult in one day, or I will track you down. I will avenge the dishonor you did my sister, Mister Amazing Conroy. I will pluck your arms off like butterfly wings. I will butcher you like calf and leave meat for crows and wolves and other creatures who will grow fat eating meat of man who breaks his word. Bye bye."

Gregor released me, pivoted around on one foot and began walking away. I called after him.

"If, I mean, when I get the money, how will I find you?"

"Do not worry of finding me. In one day, I find you. As soon as you go to sleep, I find you. Bye bye."

And just that simply the dream ended and I was lying in bed, chilled to my bones with a buffalo dog licking my face.

I'm not really a buffalo dog courier. Prior to this trip I'd been making my living, such as it was, as the Amazing Conroy, stage hypnotist. I've never been an animal lover. It's hard to make a fast exit from a seedy spaceport lounge when you're dragging some leashed beast, ten kilos of kibble, and assorted squeak toys. Yet here I was, sprawled on a couch in a luxury cabin feeding treats to an alien critter. Oh, I'll admit he was cute. Picture a bison from the North American plains, scale it down to the size of a breadbox, give it the kind of large, soulful, liquid eyes that you find on those velvet paintings hanging in your better art museums and you're pretty close. The particular fellow on my chest I'd named Reggie, and I was being paid five hundred thousand credits as a courier to deliver him into the care of some suit from the Wada Consortium.

Part of what makes buffalo dogs so valuable is that they fart oxygen. Another is their ability to consume anything. For the last day and a half I'd been feeding Reggie the disassembled pieces of a tenor saxophone I'd acquired from another courier in a poker game a week before. He ate the keys and the levers and particularly liked the pads.

The trip from Gibrahl, the Arcon world where all buffalo dogs came from, ran about three weeks. I'd started trying to teach Reggie some tricks, but the buffalito wasn't holding up his end of the bargain. I'd dangle spare nuts and bolts treats to get him to beg or roll over or play dead, but it was pointless. The only trick he learned was to shake, and he wouldn't even do that on command. Sometimes he'd just wake up from a nap, race over and haul up short. Then he'd extend one tiny front hoof for me to shake. There you have it; Reggie was just incredibly cute.

The same could not be said for the second buffalo dog in my care. With a little self hypnotic misdirection I had accomplished the impossible and smuggled a second buffalito off Gibrahl. The Wada Consortium owned Reggie, my lawfully acquired courier package, but according to the registration papers I'd forged, I was the sole owner of Carla Espinoza. I had named her, after a security guard, and like her namesake she was mean. Where Reggie cavorted and yipped with delight, Carla sulked and stewed. Reggie would delicately accept saxophone bits from my fingertips, but after almost losing several fingers, I fed Carla from a dish. Sweet tempered Reggie slept with me in my bunk each night, happily curling up in the crook of my arm, his soft fur smelling faintly like burning leaves and lazy afternoons. Vicious Carla stayed in the sonic-walled pen that came standard in all couriers' cabins. That suited her fine, and she snapped at me if I even hinted at trespassing into her space.

Reggie would net me half a million credits. If Carla had been sterile, as her papers stated, she would have been worth twenty times that. But the papers lied. On more than one occasion, when returning from the mess or an evening card game, I'd found Reggie had breached the sonic barrier and gotten into Carla's pen. The attention didn't improve her disposition any, but it did prove she wasn't sterile. Days before the *Bucephalous* entered the solar system, Carla Espinoza, my smuggled buffalo dog, the one I was sole owner of, was very pregnant. Did I mention that the Arconi maintained their monopoly of buffalo dogs by sterilizing all female buffalitos before allowing any off Gibrahl?

My fellow couriers had instructed me on the particulars of clearing customs. The only reason anyone ever went to Gibrahl was for the buffalo dog trade, and the *Bucephalous* and everyone onboard it worked for the Wada Consortium. All I had to do was walk through a security arch, hand over my buffalito, and collect my payment chit. I intended to carry Reggie tucked under one arm, but that wouldn't work for Carla. Instead, with great care I stuffed the wooly mommy-to-be in my carpet bag, nestling her amidst my meager possessions. Carla did not approve. Once inside the bag she immediately began taking bites out of everything, beginning with a bottle of alien whisky I'd picked up in the duty free shop. An aroma of minty bourbon drenched my spare clothes and wafted from the bag. But the vapors seemed to calm Carla, and she snuggled up and went to sleep. Closing up the carpet bag I grabbed Reggie and left the ship.

As the newest of the couriers I stood dead last in the line to clear customs. We waited patiently, each with luggage in one hand and a doggie squirming under the other arm, bleating and panting (the doggies, not the couriers). Every now and then *my* carpet bag would jerk as Carla Espinoza shifted in her sleep, but no one seemed to notice.

I'd been watching the other couriers, and the procedure seemed pretty routine. One by one each set his doggie in a wheeled, ceramo crate marked 'biological sample' that automatically weighed and measured the animal. A customs official then checked the encrypted ID tags against the paperwork. Any personal possessions were set on a belt and run through a scanner, while the courier walked through a security arch.

Beyond the arch I could see an armored car bearing the logo of the Wada Consortium, accompanied by half a dozen security guards. A licensed surrogate stood nearby, a meter and a half of gleaming metal and ceramo shaped like a headless ballet dancer with a display panel embedded in its chest. The drone was a stand-in for some Wada executive, linking in via satellite because he was too important to show up in the flesh. Alongside the drone and only slightly taller than it, stood a young, Asian woman in an impeccable business suit. She seemed to be checking off each courier on a clipboard and, at a signal from the drone, handing out credit chits.

It had been about eight o'clock, local time, when I'd awoken from my dream visit with Gregor. I'd gotten in line with the other couriers about nine, and when my turn finally came the morning was well on its way to noon. If I wanted to keep my arms neatly attached to my shoulders, I had only twenty-four hours to get hold of more than two million credits. Time for the first hurdle.

I stepped up to the custom's agent with a big smile on my face. I winked, and handed her Reggie's paperwork, then set the little fellow in a waiting crate. He whined when I let go, and his big liquid eyes locked on mine, imploring. I did my best to ignore his expression of heartbreak, even as I flashed back to feeding him saxophone bits and waking up to his tiny blue tongue licking my face. I looked away as the agent sealed the lid. He didn't belong to me, and I didn't have time for pets. Carla Espinoza was a different matter; she was an investment, not a pet.

I put Reggie out of my mind and my luggage on the belt. Then, humming a little ditty, I walked through security, clearing the arch without a hitch. My carpet bag didn't fare as well. As it passed through the scanner a dozen different alarms started up all around us. The other buffalitos, their crates already loaded on the armored car, began bleating in terror. The surrogate scampered in place with apparent indecision while the woman accompanying it, and the few couriers that hadn't already exited through the main terminal, all showed good sense and dropped to the ground. I spent several seconds standing there in confusion. That's about how long it took for six security guards and two customs agents to surround me with their weapons drawn.

"Put your hands on your head and lie flat on the ground."

A boot in the middle of my back gave me further encouragement, and I was cheek to floor in less time than it takes to tell. Overhead I heard bits of a whispered exchange between one of the guards and the customs agent.

" . . . you think it's a bomb?"

" . . . too small for that . . . "

" . . . ever it is, it's blocking all the scans . . . "

" . . . don't touch it . . . "

"Excuse me," I said, trying my best to sound helpful. "Can I explain?"

Hands yanked me by my collar and pulled me to my feet. I stood face to face with a guard wearing the Wada Consortium insignia on his uniform. A mirrored helmet hid his face, but when I looked toward the customs agents I could see real fear.

"No," said the guard as he shifted his hand to my upper arm with a grip that left no doubt who was in charge. "Just tell me what's in the bag?"

I started to reach for the inner pocket of my coat. The muzzles of two other guards' weapons pressed against my head. Right. I smiled and managed to say "Papers. In the pocket."

A different guard yanked my hands behind my back, and then she slapped a polymer band around my wrists. The first guard kept one hand on my arm and used his other to reach into my coat. As he glanced at the papers I'd forged for Carla, I could see yet another guard walking towards us from the terminal building. He pushed past the other couriers and the Wada surrogate that was just now getting to its feet. When he was close enough to get a good look at my face he stopped in his tracks, swore, laughed out loud, and then swore again. Something about the voice sounded familiar.

"I saw your name on the list, but I didn't think it could be the same man. The Conroy I knew could never handle a job as dull and honest as courier work."

My jaw dropped and despite a lifetime of glib repartee, I was completely nonplussed. Before I could think of anything to say the guard with Carla's papers waved them and said, "Chief, you're going to want to see this."

He read through them, and turned back to me, whipping off his mirrored helmet and giving me a good look at a tanned face complete with a high forehead, bright green eyes, a nose that had been broken and reset poorly, and a sandy red van dyke. I knew that face. Several years back, during a series of performances in eastern Pennsylvania, we'd briefly been drinking buddies, both of us tossing back our preferred nonalcoholic beverages while sitting at the bar. "Mandelbrot," I said, refreshing my professional smile, "how about taking these cuffs off me?"

He grinned back at me in a predatory rather than a pleasant way. It was the same expression he'd worn the time he'd thrown me into the county lock-up over a misunderstanding involving a nightclub, the drunken friend of a volunteer, and a small amount of property damage. "Now *this* is more what I expected from you," he said, gesturing with the papers. He waved for the guard to bring me along, and then walked to one of the customs agents and handed over the papers.

"What are you doing riding herd on a security detail," I said. "Last time I saw you, you were a county sheriff."

He snorted but didn't look back. "The last time I saw you, you were trying to convince a judge that you'd nearly destroyed a nightclub as a form of self defense."

"I didn't start that fight. And besides, the club owner dropped all charges."

He laughed. "Before or after you blackmailed him?"

"I didn't—"

"His mistress said otherwise."

"Oh. It wasn't blackmail," I said. "It was more . . . an exchange of favors."

"Yeah? Well, don't do me any favors." Mandelbrot cut the bands on my wrists and turned back around to speak to the customs agents. "Mr. Conroy has documentation for another buffalo dog," he said.

As I rubbed my wrists, from the corner of my eye I was encouraged to see the surrogate's pectoral display brighten.

"A second dog?" said the first customs agent. "That *would* explain the alarms. A buffalo dog is impenetrable to scan."

"Impenetrable?" I said, even as I mentally kicked myself. I should have read up on just such details during the trip.

Mandelbrot's hand replaced the guard's on my arm. He hauled me forward, and along with both customs agents we all stepped to where my carpet bag had emerged from the scanner housing. The bag sat, stinking of alien booze, and began to quiver and shake. A muffled bark came from within. The alarms had clearly awakened Carla Espinoza. With his free hand, Mandelbrot reached to look inside.

"Don't!" I shouted. "She bites."

Mandelbrot's hand pulled back just in time. The small brass latch, and a good portion of the surrounding leather and fabric vanished in Carla Espinoza's suddenly visible, rapidly snapping mouth. All around us I heard gasps as the annoyed buffalo dog thrust her head up, stuck out her tongue, and loudly barked her protest.

"Mr. Conroy . . . " said the first customs agent.

" . . .you have a second buffalo dog?" finished the second customs agent.

Mandelbrot shook his head, and muttered my name several times, sounding almost as disappointed in me as my own parents had.

The Wada surrogate trundled towards us, ignoring the guards. "Mandelbrot, you fool," it said, "let go of the man. He's our courier."

Mandelbrot didn't relax his grip. Without taking his eyes off Carla he sighed and said, "I can't do that, Mr. Andrews. Arcon law prohibits the possession of more than one buffalo dog by a courier at any given time."

"You're hired to provide security, not legal opinions," said the face on the surrogate's chest. "Now let him go."

"Sir, I know this man, and much as it pains me, I have no choice but to consider both him, and his second buffalo dog as a security risk."

"I'm not a security risk, Mr. Andrews," I said, putting on my best innocent expression and facing the Wada surrogate. The man looking back at me looked to be in his late 30's, and generally about as nondescript as you'd expect an industry executive to be. And I hoped, just as greedy.

Mandelbrot sighed. "I know you, Conroy. You're a rogue. I don't know how you did it, but I know a scam when I see one being run."

"This is highly irregular," said the second customs agent.

"The Arconi are supposed to resolve any potential problems before any vessels leave Gibrahl," said the first customs agent.

They looked at one another and seemed to come to a decision. "The consulate," they both said.

"What consulate?!" said Andrews.

"The Arcon consulate," said the first customs agent as she reached for her phone. "Let them sort this out."

The Wada surrogate turned to his associate, the young woman with the clipboard. "Penrose, solve this. Now!"

She stepped up and addressed the customs agents. "Mr. Andrews is a duly licensed representative of the Wada Consortium. The Commonwealth of Pennsylvania recognizes and upholds the sovereign rights of such individuals when represented by real-time surrogate or similar communication hardware. This other gentleman," she barely paused as she consulted her clipboard, "Mr. Conroy, is likewise an employee of the Wada Consortium. If his documentation for the second animal is in order, then there is no cause to involve the Arconi. His bona fides are already established by the delivery of his first buffalo dog." She turned her head and acknowledged Mandelbrot with a nod. "Nor can he be considered a security risk."

Mandelbrot shook his head. "The Arconi don't permit anyone to transport two buffalitos. Ever. I don't know how he managed it, but it can't be legal. Your company hired me to provide security, and that includes ensuring it isn't implicated as the recipient of stolen goods. I'm sorry, Mr. Andrews, this is my jurisdiction, and I have to insist."

"Well, that's easily fixed," said Andrews, turning the surrogate to face Mandelbrot. "I'll just fire you."

"What?"

"I'm Glenn Andrews Andrews, vice president in charge of resource acquisitions, and I'm not going to let a an incompetent security chief rob me of an extra buffalo dog. You're five seconds from being unemployed, Mr. Mandelbrot. Now, would you like to reconsider and keep your position with the consortium? There are no stolen goods here."

Five seconds passed, and then another five. Mandelbrot's grip on my arm didn't relax. Andrews scowled.

"Have it your way," Andrews said. "You're history." The surrogate pointed to one of the other guards. "You, you're in charge. Show your former boss where the exit is."

Mandelbrot let go of me. He looked deflated, and in other circumstances I'd have felt sorry for him, but I still had my own problems. I nodded to the customs agents. "Are the papers in order?" I asked.

The first agent sorted through them. "Yes, she appears to be fully documented . . . " Her voice trailed off as she studied the paperwork.

The surrogate stood with its delicate arms akimbo, surveying the situation like a lord of creation. "Excellent, you've done a fine job, Mr. Conroy, a fine job."

Mandelbrot looked over the custom agent's shoulder at some portion of the document that had caught her eye, and he brightened. He turned back to me, a question on his lips. I nodded slowly and watched as his wicked smile broke out again, but this time it wasn't for me.

"Clear out, Mr. Mandelbrot. You've been fired," said Andrews through the surrogate. "Penrose! Pay Mr. Conroy, and then take possession of his animals. We're leaving,"

I didn't want to appear too eager, but the truth is I probably snatched that plastic credit chit with the same zeal with which Reggie lunged for handfed treats. The chit, emblazoned with the Wada Consortium logo, had a balance of five hundred thousand credits. I put it in my pocket.

The other customs agent wheeled the crate with Reggie over to Andrews. Penrose took possession, rolled it to the armored car, and loaded it onboard. The nearer customs agent lifted Carla out of the remains of my carpet bag, ignored her squirming and complaining, and placed her into a second crate and brought it to me.

"What are you doing?" said Andrews. "That second buffalo dog belongs to the Wada Consortium as well."

"Oh?" said Mandelbrot. "Mr. Conroy, did the amount of your payment cover two buffalo dogs?"

"No," I said. "The payment was for just a single buffalito."

"I'll swear out a voucher for another payment," said Andrews. "It's completely legal with you as witnesses. I can take possession of the additional buffalo dog and Mr. Conroy can come with me to redeem the voucher."

"I'm no lawyer," said Mandelbrot, "but I know theft when I see it."

"Theft? You've already acknowledged that Mr. Conroy is a courier for the Wada Consortium. His cargo is our property."

"No, sir," said the first customs agent. "Only the paperwork for the first buffalito specifies Wada as final owner. The second batch identifies Mr. Conroy as both courier and recipient."

Mandelbrot's smirk expanded toward infinity. "Well, Mr. Andrews, I've lost my job, but you've just lost a buffalo dog worth ten million credits to your consortium."

Andrews began to sputter. Penrose stared at Mandelbrot, stunned. The customs agents were conspicuously *not* looking at the former security chief, and the remaining guards didn't seem to know where to look. I took hold of the crate containing Carla Espinoza and began walking toward the main terminal building. Mandelbrot fell into step alongside me.

"You've cost me my job, Conroy."

I bit my lip. Even if he was right, so what? This was the same guy who had tossed me into a jail cell a few years earlier. I didn't owe him anything. He'd only complicated the situation. And yet . . . He'd been doing his job, then and now, and when he wasn't arresting me, I remembered him as a better than decent guy.

"It occurs to me that I could use a security expert."

"I won't be party to theft," he said.

"What if I gave you my word that the Arconi saw me take both doggies onboard ship, that I presented myself to their customs authority and satisfied all their concerns, for both animals."

Mandelbrot grimaced. "Can you prove that?"

"I'll repeat everything I've just said in front of the Arconi consul if need be. Will that satisfy you?"

He looked over his shoulder then, though whether at the customs agents, Andrews, or his assistant I couldn't tell. Then he offered me his hand to shake. "Well, Conroy, as it happens, I'm available at the moment. But you're going to need to acquire a vehicle for us. I think my access to Wada transportation is at an end."

At a little before one o'clock I sat in the passenger seat of a aerosled rental at the far edge of the remote parking lot of ChocoWorld, about twenty minutes west of the Hershey Extrasolar Landing Field. It seemed an odd place for a spaceport to me, but alien demand for milk chocolate had re-energized the location and the population of the greater Hershey area had surpassed both

Pittsburgh and Philadelphia. Mandelbrot sat up front with me while Carla Espinoza glared at us from inside her crate on the backseat. A mild electric current ran through the crate's bars, providing enough incentive to keep the buffalo dog from eating her way out from mere spite.

While waiting at the rental counter, Mandelbrot had worked out an arrangement based on our assessments of one another. I knew he was basically a cop, regardless of what job title he held, meaning that for him it all came down to structure. That kind of personality needs the universe to exist according to an ordered plan with a finite system of rules. Which went a long way to explaining why he had only contempt for lawyers like Andrews who bent the rules with technicalities, and then bent them back as it suited their purposes. I, on the other hand, was just a fellow who'd maneuvered himself between the cracks in the system, thereby revealing a whole new level of rules that Mandelbrot had never seen. That was enough to pique his curiosity and cause him to side with me. I could trust him, which is more than he probably thought of me.

"What's the plan, Conroy?"

"First, I need to get to some place secure."

"You're worried that the suits at Wada are going to try and put in a claim on this buffalo dog? You shouldn't. You've got the paperwork showing she's yours."

I shook my head. "No, that's not it." I stopped, looked away, and then looked at Carla chewing on a double handful of rocks I'd tossed into her crate. "What do you know about dream trackers?"

"The telepaths? They're nuts, mostly. All that time mucking around in people's dreams unhinges them. But they get the job done. The Feds brought one in once on a kidnapping case back when I was sheriff. Why?"

"I've got one after me," I said. "Gregor's not just crazy, he's a psychotic killer, and he thinks I owe him over two million credits."

"You've only been back on Earth a few hours; how does he know you're here?"

"My name popped up on a passenger list. He showed up in my dreams this morning. He's coming for his money at noon tomorrow, and if I don't have it, he's going to rip my arms off."

"Literally?"

"Oh yeah."

"So get him his money." Mandelbrot glanced to the backseat. "You could sell that buffalito to Wada for ten million."

I sighed, gave Mandelbrot a long look and prayed that I hadn't misjudged him. "This isn't your typical buffalo dog. She's special."

"Special?" Mandelbrot's face lit up. It was like he was already wondering what new rules might apply. "Special in what way?"

"She's pregnant."

He gasped at that and stared at little Carla Espinoza with a whole world of respect on his face. Carla must have felt that look because she lifted her head, let a chunk of rock slip from her jaws, and barked at him.

"Conroy, the Arconi don't permit fertile buffalo dogs to leave Gibrahl."

"Yeah, well, they don't normally allow couriers to leave with more than one buffalito either. I figured if I was going to be accused of smuggling, I might as well do it right."

"So you stole a pregnant buffalito?"

"She wasn't pregnant at the time. Reggie took care of that en route."

"Reggie?"

"The other buffalo dog. The one I was hired to bring for the Wada Consortium. But you see why I can't just sell her. She represents a lot more than ten million credits. I need to stall Gregor, keep him from ripping my arms off until Carla has her pups and I can sell one."

Mandelbrot frowned. "You've got another problem. Wada could claim ownership of some of the pups on the basis of paternity."

I nodded. "Great. More people tracking me down."

"I can help you with Wada," he said. "You just need to hole up some place secure. As for your dream tracker, he can't directly find you while you're awake, that's not how it works. He'll be forced to track you by finding reference to you in other people's recent unconscious. Probably other couriers that you met onboard ship."

"So, he's likely to locate me because he'll see me in *your* dreams?"

Mandelbrot nodded, "Me, my former security force, the people from Wada, and the customs agents. Any of us can give you up.

Which is why we need to get physically away from here, and why neither of us is going to sleep any time soon."

"That will only buy me a little time; we can't stay awake forever. I need to give Gregor some false trails."

"False trails? How are you going to do that?" Mandelbrot glared at me like I was either insane or just plain stupid. "You can't parade around with your buffalo dog, Conroy, that will just be more people telling him where you are."

"I've got something a bit subtler in mind. We need to get to Philadelphia, the sooner the better."

"What's in Philly?" said Mandelbrot.

"An old friend who should be able to help me; he owes me a favor."

"I'm not your friend, Conroy," said Leo Baskins. "And I don't owe you any favors."

It started out well. The balding man in his overpriced suit had greeted me with a hearty two-handed shake and a smile on his poreless face. Thirty seconds later and he was steering me to the exit.

"I'm not asking for a favor, Leo, just the opposite. I'm offering to do one for you. A quick show in your platinum members' lounge at the shuttleport, a bit of 'memory improvement' for business travelers."

"You've been black-listed by your own guild, Conroy. I couldn't hire you to do a show even if I wanted to, and I don't want to."

"Leo, Leo, please, this is me you're talking to. I never said anything about you hiring me to do a show. This is a freebie. I just want to try out a new routine. You're right, I can't do my old act until the entertainment guild reinstates me, so I'm trying out a bit of hypnotic self-improvement for white-collar commuters. I need a captive audience, one where if I bomb it won't get out. I'm not asking you to put me in as a headliner at one of your nightclubs, Leo, we're talking about one gig, half an hour before any of the evening commuter shuttles to Asia start to board. Help me out, for old times' sake."

I watched his eyes. In my business you learn how to tell a lot about what a person is thinking by their eyes. And I knew Leo. I knew he knew I wasn't telling him everything. And I knew he was trying to find a way to make a buck off of me along the way.

"Suppose I let you do your bit in my lounge. Is it just a practice run, or is it a tease and you're hoping to hook some fish?"

I put on my best hang-dog expression. It wasn't hard, I was tired from driving across eastern Pennsylvania. Mandelbrot had taken Carla Espinoza and gone off in the rental in search of what he called a 'safe house'. That left me to solve my dream tracker problem, and for that I needed Leo. "Okay, you got me. I'm serious about the act, but my plan is to sell some of these guys on a series of 'private training sessions' and work them for some snowballs into other clients."

"I want a cut," he said.

Same old Leo. "How much? Remember, you're just providing the venue, Leo, I'm doing all the work."

"The venue, *and* the marks. I want fifty percent of anything you get from 'clients' you sign from the lounge, and twenty percent from the next generation of marks they lead you to."

"Leo, you're killing me. I just got back Earthside and I've got debts to pay. I need cash in hand now. Take thirty off the lounge, and I'll give you twenty for the first two generations they give. Do we have a deal?"

He smiled and checked his watch. "It's four o'clock now. I'll call the site manager at the lounge and tell him to expect you within the hour."

"Ladies and Gentlemen, I realize you weren't expecting any entertainment while waiting for your flights, certainly not more than a little piano music, but Excelsior Shuttles knows you have a choice when it comes to business travel, and is going the extra distance to help you do the same. I'm the Amazing Conroy and I'm going to show you how you can improve your ability to remember names and faces, dates and data, immediately and effortlessly through the power of hypnosis. And I promise to do that for each and every one of you before they announce boarding for any of your respective flights. Now, can I have some volunteers . . . "

Two hours later Mandelbrot picked me up and took me to a nondescript row house on an anonymous street in northeast

Philadelphia. I was pleased to see that he'd been busy; the house's living room looked ordinary, but the bedroom beyond it was something altogether different. Mandelbrot had turned it into a command center with video surveillance monitors, motion sensors, and booby traps on the doors and windows. He'd also set up a pile of scrap metal alongside Carla's crate. Unlike the buffalo dog, neither of us had eaten all day. We hit a drive-through on the way back to the safe house and prepared a feast of Philadelphia's finest. Carla consumed a lead pipe and then hunkered down for a nap. Mandelbrot and I sat across from the security monitors and ate hoagies and cheese fries.

"Mission accomplished," I said. "There are thirty people on their way to ten different cities in Japan, Taiwan, China, and Korea. In addition to having some handy mnemonic aids to boost their business skills, they're all going to dream of me standing in front of them and telling them about my epic experience as a buffalo dog courier."

Mandelbrot gawked around a mouthful of sandwich. "You can do that?"

I laughed. "It wasn't all that different from what I'd do during one of my shows. But that should throw off Gregor, at least until Carla here starts popping out pups. So, what's next?"

Before he could answer, several different alarms began pinging and beeping. Mandelbrot was on his feet, a hefty stun baton in hand.

The monitors showed a view of the front door and the walkway leading to it. A young Asian woman in a burgundy jumpsuit had just rung our doorbell. I recognized her as the woman who had handed me my payment chit, though she'd changed clothes and her hairstyle.

"Scan says she's clean," said Mandelbrot. "No weapons, no electronics, no gear of any sort." He fiddled with a few more controls. "There's a single vehicle outside, still warm from use but otherwise empty. Sensors aren't picking up anyone else. She's all alone."

"Let's see what she wants."

He scowled. "Let's see how she found you," he said, and left the bedroom to go open the door. I watched him come into view on the monitor. He opened the door, his baton at the ready.

"Can I help you?"

"I'm here to see Mr. Conroy," she said. "I'm from the Wada Consortium. Or rather, I was with Wada. But that's over. Please, you have to let me speak to him, I have information he needs."

"Inside," he said, gesturing with the baton, and gripping her upper arm as she stepped inside. I left the bedroom and met them just as Mandelbrot closed the front door.

"Do you have a name, miss?" I asked.

"I'm Dr. Lisa Penrose, and I'm here to help you with your pregnant buffalo dog."

Mandelbrot impressed me by not showing any surprise, and I made a mental note not to play poker with him any time soon. As for me, years of hypnotizing people into believing outrageous things had long since taught me to keep my face from giving anything away. If Lisa Penrose had been hoping for a reaction she didn't get one. "Wherever did you get the idea that I have a pregnant buffalo dog?"

"From my sister. She's a resource acquisitions attorney for the Wada Consortium. I believe you may have seen her this morning when you cleared customs? She was on site to assist with paperwork."

"Twin sister?" said Mandelbrot, eyeing her suspiciously.

"Triplets, actually. But that's not important."

"And you work for Wada as well?"

"That's part of what why I'm here," she said. "Did you know the Arconi had alerted Earth authorities about a possible undocumented buffalo dog that was unaccounted for? They sent out complete parameters on her."

"And the point of this is . . . "

"Your second buffalito was fully documented, Mr. Conroy, and both heavier and larger than the one the Arconi *misplaced*, which meant either it was a different animal all together, or that she was pregnant. And given that she was your second buffalo dog, and not the one you turned over to the Wada Consortium, my sister came to the logical conclusion and called me. I came here at once."

"Do you always talk that rapidly?" I asked. She'd managed it all on one breath. "Never mind. Uh, look, Miss Penrose—"

"Dr. Penrose."

"Sorry, *Doctor* Penrose, I think you're making a big deal out of nothing. Carla isn't pregnant. She's just fat. There wasn't much else for her to do on the trip to Earth other than eat. She put on some weight; that doesn't make her pregnant."

"Mr. Conroy, I'm a psychologist. And by that I want you to understand that I'm not a clinician, I'm a behavioral scientist. I specialize in the behavior of certain alien animals, among them Arconi buffalo dogs. Believe me when I tell you that while some buffalo dogs have been known to get plump or pudgy, it is physiologically impossible for them to get fat. Your buffalo dog is the only one unaccounted for by the Arconi, and she's very much pregnant. You know it, and I know it. The Wada Consortium doesn't know it yet, but they'll figure it out soon."

Mandelbrot broke his silence. "So you've come to stake some kind of claim on Carla's pups for them?"

She shook her head. "They don't know I'm here. Neither my sister nor I shared our conclusions, but someone will work it out, eventually, and pass word up the chain of command. I can help you, Mr. Conroy, with things that haven't even occurred to you."

I glanced up at Mandelbrot but the look on his face showed he didn't have a clue what she was talking about either.

"And what things are these?" I said.

She began ticking items off on her fingers as she spoke. "What do you know about buffalo dogs, Mr. Conroy? Particularly pregnant ones? Do you have any idea how soon her labor begins? How many pups she's likely to have? The kind of facilities you need to deliver them, let alone keep them safe? What to do when it all happens? Do you know anything about buffalo dogs other than what they told you so you could transport one—pardon me, two—from Gibrahl? I'm a buffalo dog expert. You need me to help you through this."

She took two breaths that time.

"Why?" I said.

"Why?"

"You've painted a good picture, but what's in it for you? It can't be money, you haven't mentioned it yet. So, why?"

She fell silent, which given her staccato style of speech made for a greater void than normal. She shrugged her shoulders, glared at

Mandelbrot's hand on her arm as if noticing it for the first time, and looked me square in the face.

"Because you have what no one else has, Mr. Conroy. You've got a pregnant buffalo dog. And soon, you'll have newborn pups. And once they're grown the females will be fertile, and in time you'll have still more pregnant buffalo dogs. That's never happened before in Human Space. No one on Earth has ever studied it first hand; it's all been theoretical, textbooks and conference papers, till now. I want to be in on it from the beginning. I have to be."

"That's all fine, I'm sure, but even if I had a pregnant buffalo dog, and if all the rest you said was true, it wouldn't be very smart of me to take in someone out of the blue and trust her with such a precious creature, would it?"

"Dr. Penrose," said Mandelbrot, "how did you know to come here?"

"Customs puts transponders on the crates. Wada has all the codes. I tracked you, and when you stopped moving, I came here. But don't worry, my sister erased your code from the log. Even if they think of it, they won't be able to find you; at least not right away. I had to make sure I had time to convince you to hire me."

"Why is that so important to you?"

"The Wada Consortium looks at buffalo dogs as commodities, Mr. Conroy. They see them as things to buy and sell and lease. Their clients view them as expensive tools, means to achieve various ends. But none of them value the creatures just for themselves."

Mandelbrot smirked. "And you do?"

She turned on him. "I'm the closest thing they have to an advocate in all of Human Space. I understand their commercial value, probably better than either of you, but that doesn't preclude appreciating them in other ways."

"Do you want me to donate one to a zoo?" I asked.

"I want you to let me study them," she said. "You're going to need someone to help you through the birth process. It's not like anything you're imagining. Let me do that for you. Afterwards, you can decide if you want to keep me on. I'm just asking for the chance to be present when this one gives birth."

I nodded. "You make a good case, and I'll consider it. When do you estimate Carla is going to give birth?"

"That's the other reason I needed to find you," she said. "I altered the records in Wada's database; they'll believe she won't start labor for several days. But based on the weight reported by the Arconi, and the weight obtained at customs, you've actually less than twenty-four hours. Please believe me, Mr. Conroy, she can't have her pups here."

"This site is secure, Doctor," said Mandelbrot. "The buffalito is not going anywhere. Especially if Wada is looking for her."

"Not to mention Gregor's more pressing deadline," I said.

"Who's Gregor?" said Dr. Penrose.

"A very large Russian who believes I owe him two and a half million creds that I don't currently have."

"And if he doesn't get it?"

"He'll rip my arms off."

Mandelbrot checked the time. "In about sixteen hours," he said.

"You're exaggerating, aren't you?" said Dr. Penrose. "I thought loan sharks just broke your legs."

"He's a butcher, not a loan shark. And I'm not exaggerating. You ever hear of Dimitri Konstant, possibly the greatest sculptor to come out of Eastern Europe?"

Dr. Penrose shook her head.

"Right, and you won't, because Gregor ripped his damn arms off six years ago. This is not a guy who likes colorful metaphors. When he says he'll rip your arms off, he means it."

"Yeah," said Mandelbrot, "that's another reason we're not going anywhere."

She started to reply to him, but turned to me instead. "Mr. Conroy, despite their outward appearance, Arconi buffalo dogs are nothing like any creature on Earth. For one thing, they're extremely thermogenetic."

I shook my head. "Sorry, I don't know that term. What's it mean?"

"They generate a great deal of heat when they're being born."

"What are we talking about here?" I said. "Are we going to need oven mitts to deliver the pups?"

"Conventional oven mitts would combust, Mr. Conroy. We're talking about bursts of energy of more than two thousand degrees."

I looked around at the safe house's living room, a very flammable living room, not all that different from the flammable bedroom where Carla Espinoza slept inside her crate. Somehow she'd gone from being my ticket to wealth and luxury and become a firebomb waiting to happen.

"Are you insane?" I said. "This is Philadelphia; it's not like we can drive out to the desert and have Carla turn the place into a glassy plane when she has her pups. And even if we could, those pups won't do me much good if I've had my arms ripped off."

To my surprise, Mandelbrot jumped in. "I think I have a solution. Let me make a call. I know a realtor who keeps odd hours. There's an old building that she represents that's not far from here. It used to be a mental health facility. It's been vacant for several years now; it's partially gutted because of a fire on the upper floors, but the structure itself is still sound."

"A mental health facility that's already burned down once? How is that better than where we are now?"

Mandelbrot grinned. "It was originally built as a bank. The vault's still there, and it's intact. The door is solid steel and the walls are almost a meter of concrete reinforced with more steel. It's built to withstand a lot more than just extremes of heat. And best of all, it's secure. You'll need that, for your business, after the initial birthing."

"A bank vault," I said, and Mandelbrot's grin must have been contagious because it had spread to my face. "Make the call. Offer to pay whatever it takes, so long as we get immediate access."

It was Dr. Penrose's turn to look surprised. "You're going to rent a bank? At night? What are you going to tell the realtor?"

I shrugged. "We'll tell her we want to open a bank."

Mandelbrot made his call and an hour later we had packed up my pregnant buffalo dog, my newest employee, and all his security gear. We drove off to meet the realtor and do battle with a stack of paperwork. By midnight the realtor had come and gone, and I had a shiny new lease on a dilapidated building that would soon become the Earth's first buffalo dog nursery. The corner building had an odd, wedge-shaped design, a consequence of the acute angle formed by the two streets that defined it. Most of it had been blackened by fire, and what hadn't burned had succumbed to water damage from the efforts to extinguish the flames. But the basement was sound and its vault still functional.

Mandelbrot went right to work, inspecting the upper floors, installing his security systems and other deterrents. Carla Espinoza hadn't bothered to wake up at any point in the moving process but did look plumper. Dr. Penrose and I carried the buffalito and her crate into the basement's foyer and the vault beyond.

Anything that had survived the fire, or been brought in to refurbish the building, had been abandoned in the foyer. The walls were lined with stacks of chairs, desks, file cabinets, drop cloths, buckets of spackle, buckets of paint, assorted brushes, rollers, and sprayers, broken furniture, and boxes of outdated office equipment. A layer of dust coated all of it. Dr. Penrose sneezed a few times, and went off in search of other supplies. I left Carla to snooze, carefully closing the vault only after I'd convinced myself I could open it again without mishap. I spent the next few hours clearing away debris and setting up a desk and some chairs. Mandelbrot popped in now and then, just to make sure I hadn't fallen asleep.

Dr. Penrose returned with two large cardboard boxes. The first contained an assortment of readymade deli sandwiches, several liters of bottled water, a large can of ground coffee, a battery-powered coffeemaker, and a collection of disposable plates and cups. The second box held a dozen large spray bottles and had been marked with interstellar customs stickers. She piled everything on the desk, and while I brewed the coffee she opened up the vault and checked in on Carla Espinoza. The aroma of fresh coffee had no effect on Carla, who seemed determined to sleep through everything, but the wafting fumes lured Mandelbrot down long enough to grab a cup, scoop up a sandwich, and vanish again up the stairs.

Somewhere, Gregor Ivanovich was tracking through dreams in search of me, and being led astray. I fully intended to pay my debt, buying back whatever insult he felt I'd done his sister, but I couldn't do it in the less than ten hours of his original time table. I couldn't do anything until Carla had her pups, including sleep. Mandelbrot, Dr. Penrose, and I had dosed ourselves with stims before leaving the safe house, and I'd given each of us a quick post-hypnotic trigger which could jerk any of us awake. If we could just keep it up a while longer, I'd get to keep my arms.

Dr. Penrose emerged from the vault and began spritzing orange mist from one of her aerosol bottles, all over the inner seal of the door. The mist foamed, congealed, and left what looked like a candy coating on the metal. It smelled like the water left over after boiling up hot dogs.

"It's a Glamorkan transducing polymer," she said before I could ask. "It will keep the door from fusing." She gestured to the box she had brought in, and I went over and found several more bottles of the gunk. Together we spent the next couple of hours squirting and spraying every part of the vault where the door joined the circular jamb, applying coat after coat until all of it gleamed pumpkin bright and dry to the touch. Then we closed the vault up tight, sat at the table, and helped ourselves to coffee and sandwiches.

"I can't believe Carla slept through all of that. I thought the smell would have brought her around if nothing else."

Dr. Penrose shook her head. "No, that's a good sign, really. What time is it?"

I checked my watch. "Nearly four thirty. She's been sleeping a good ten hours. How long until she goes all thermogenetic on us?"

"Buffalo dogs sleep between eight and fourteen hours before actually entering labor. It could happen any time."

"How will we know?"

She smirked. "Oh, believe me, you'll know. And Mr. Conroy, I meant what I said about the intensity of the heat. Common theory is they evolved it as a defense mechanism to protect the vulnerable mothers from potential predators."

"And Carla won't be hurt by the heat? Not even singed?" I said.

"There's a reason why all those alarms went off when you tried to slip her through the customs' scanners. Buffalo dogs may look like adorable miniature versions of American Bison, but they're complex alien creatures. The curly hide that you think might get singed has a higher melting point than industrial steel. The vault would liquefy before it got hot enough to harm an adult buffalo dog."

"Well," I said, "I'm glad to have someone here who knows what's going to happen. You make it sound like everything I know is wrong."

She froze at that, and just stared at me. I didn't like what I read in her eyes. I saw nervousness, raw fear ready to escalate to terror. A tremor went through her whole body and poof, everything changed. The fear was gone. She sighed, but it sounded more like disgust than tiredness.

"I'm sorry, Mr. Conroy, my sister's expertise with buffalo dogs is genuine, but it's mostly theoretical. Simulations are more her style, not actual hands-dirty fieldwork, so she had a little panic attack. Believe me, it's a one time thing."

Something profound had happened to Lisa Penrose. Her voice was different; the rhythms of her speech had changed. She was looking right at me but avoiding any eye contact. And why was she talking about herself in the third person once removed?

"Your . . . sister?" I said?

"Yes, pretty strange, isn't it. I'm Bess, by the way. I get to handle all the high stress jobs. Say, do you have any gum?"

"Gum? Uh, no. Stop. Back up. What just happened? What do you mean you're 'Bess'? Earlier you told me your name was 'Lisa.'"

"No, earlier Lisa told you that. This is the first time we've met, which is why I'm introducing myself. I'm the practical one. Lisa's the smart one. And Betsy,—you saw her at the port when you cleared customs—she's the sneaky one. There are others, but I don't want to confuse you any more just now."

Carla Espinoza chose that moment to wake up and go into labor. Through nearly a meter of steel came a shrieking ululation that I swear must have sobered every alcoholic within a hundred city blocks. We both clutched our hands to our ears for what felt like minutes. Mandelbrot came scrambling down the stairs into the basement's foyer, wincing in pain.

"What *is* that?" he mouthed, the actual sound of his words drowned out.

I began to feel heat on my back and turned, facing the massive circle of the vault's door. The air in front of it shimmered and the door seemed to pulse in time to the sound, once, twice, and then the shimmer faded. The shriek died away too, or at least its volume dropped below the insulation level of the vault.

"What just happened?" I asked.

Mandelbrot's pocket beeped, a surprisingly loud sound in the quiet after the shriek. He pulled out his commpadd and studied its display. "Fire suppression system in the vault activated, but it's already shut down. The plumbing looks fused or some such. Too much heat too fast from the look of this data."

I turned to 'Bess' and asked, "Was that the thermogenesis you talked about? And what was that horrible sound? We've got to get in there and find out if Carla's all right."

"I told you, I'm not Lisa. I don't have the answers you're looking for. Hold on, let me see what I can do."

It was Mandelbrot's turn to stare, first at the woman who claimed not to be Lisa, and then at me. I stepped closer to the vault, careful not to touch. The metal looked ordinary. I darted one hand forward, barely tapped it with a finger and pulled back. It was warm, very warm.

"All that heat and noise came out of that little animal?" said Mandelbrot.

"If I understand it right, that heat was part of the birthing process. Carla's in labor right now."

Bess stood and a shudder rippled through her again. She lowered her face into her hands for a moment, and when she looked up there were tears in her eyes.

"I'm sorry, Mr. Conroy. I'm back. I didn't mean for you to meet Bess, not like that. But it's not important. Right now you need to open the vault door and get in there, or you're going to lose the pups."

"Lose them? How? Why?"

"Newborn pups aren't as durable as full grown adults. They're born with a protective coating to see them through their own entry into the world, but they can't handle more than a couple bursts of heat like that."

"There's going to be more?" said Mandelbrot.

She nodded, rubbing at her eyes with the back of her right hand. "The first is the hottest, but one burst marks the arrival of each pup in the litter," she said. "Normally, the male parent picks up each newborn and shields it and its sibs from the brunt of the heat with its own body."

The whole concept of birth involving blast furnace special effects still had me dazed. "The male parent? You mean Reggie? We don't have him, the Wada Consortium does." And then I had one of the few moments of insight and clarity that I've ever experienced. In that instance, I knew what to do. I turned back to Mandelbrot. "Give me a hand with the door. Now."

"How do you know it won't heat up again?" he said.

"If what she's saying is true, it will. But that shrieking started first, it's Carla's early warning system. We've got to get in there, find her pup, and get it out before Carla begins wailing like a banshee in labor."

Mandelbrot and I wrestled the door open, and hot moist air rushed out of the vault as our cooler dryer air flowed in. The inner rim of the door radiated a dazzling orange glow where Lisa's spray had absorbed heat and now released it as light. The floor and walls were bone dry, and I could see the melted and mangled remains of the ceiling sprinklers. In the middle of the floor lay Carla Espinoza, still very much in labor and panting like a bellows. Nestled against the short coarse hair of her belly was a golf ball-sized lump of wooly fur that wobbled this way and that.

As Mandelbrot and I gaped at the sight, Lisa rushed to the door, aerosol sprayer in hand, and began inspecting the door seal for spots that needed retouching. I stepped in and knelt next to Carla, murmuring reassuring nonsense syllables in my best soothing tone. I swooped up the little furball with both hands, just as Carla barked once, twice, and then began a low sustained bleat that built in pitch and volume into the soul curdling shriek of new life that we'd heard before.

"Move, move," I shouted, and pushed the others back out into the foyer. I was right behind them, almost physically propelled by a wall of sound that threatened to liquefy my internal organs. The three of us threw our weight against the vault door and shoved it closed. Another pup was on the way.

Carla delivered eight more pups, spacing them out every twenty minutes or so. And each time, once the pyrotechnics and screeching died down, we'd undog the door, dash in, refresh the door seal with more of the Glamorkan polymer, and liberate another newborn ball of fuzz. Dr. Penrose lined a box with a painter's cloth, and the pups snuggled within, jostling one another for the comfiest spot.

Mandelbrot stared down at them. "Shouldn't we take them to their mother? Won't they want to suckle or something when they get hungry?"

"As I told Mr. Conroy, despite appearances they're not mammals. Nor are they particularly maternal. If she feels anything, I would guess that Carla's relieved that the whole process is over and she won't have to do it again."

"What's that mean?"

"Female buffalo dogs can only be impregnated once. That's actually how the Arconi sterilize them before letting them off Gibrahl. They inject them with a retro-virus that convinces the buffalo dog that she's already been pregnant, and it burns out the reproductive system. To make up for the one shot pregnancy, a litter is typically about eighty percent female."

"Typically? How many did we get?" I started doing reproductive math in my head.

"It's too soon to tell. I've never sexed newborn pups before. Let them start eating though, and they'll quickly get big enough for us to tell."

"If they don't suckle, what is it they're going to need to eat? And how much?"

She laughed and reached a hand into the box, lightly stroking the pups. "They're buffalo dogs, Mr. Conroy, they'll eat anything. Probably the easiest thing would be to feed them the refuse here in the foyer. It would save you the trouble of hauling it away. They're going to be ravenous in a short while, I think it's likely they'll devour all of it."

"And what do we do then?" I asked.

She shrugged. "A few hours after they've eaten their fill, they'll be indistinguishable from any other buffalo dogs, at least using any equipment we have on Earth. And you know what that means?"

I passed her a fresh cup of coffee and another stim. "That means I can sell one, and we can finally go to sleep."

Although they hadn't managed to open their eyes yet, the buffalitos soon mastered the art of opening and closing their tiny mouths. Less than two hours out of the womb, the oldest of them began eating in earnest, and the others did not lag far behind. It was all the three of us could do to keep them fed fast enough. For hours we shoveled bits of old furniture, waterlogged case files, chunks of metal cabinets, and moldy linoleum at them. The tiny critters consumed all of it. As fast as we could deliver everything, they gobbled it down. The pups showed no discrimination, devouring everything we dangled into their box. And when we weren't swift enough in finding some new bit of detritus for them to eat they had a tendency to chomp down on the box they were in.

And they grew, lord how they grew! From tiny, round fur balls with slit mouths they expanded in all directions, becoming plump, little footballs with the front defined by the mouth and the back by a stub of protruding tail. Tiny limbs descended from their undersides, unfolding like the landing gear of airplanes, each ending in a delicate and shiny hoof. The front ends with the mouths bulged outward, and a pinch forming behind the bulge became their necks, even as the bulges became clearly differentiated heads. All of them started making cute little whuffling noses as their nostrils flared. And as they opened their eyes, pup by pup, the first thing they saw was me.

"They're getting too big to all stay in the box," I said, offering a stack of waterlogged file folders to three of the buffalitos, making them jump for it.

Dr. Penrose shook her head. "We can't handle them yet. They're still too hungry. If you reach in to pick one up you're likely to lose a couple fingers if not a whole hand."

"What do you suggest then?"

"We need to move the whole box, carry it into the vault and let them loose in there. We can shove their food inside, and seal them in until they're sated if necessary."

"That won't work; it's a three man job," I said. As the noon hour had approached, Mandelbrot had left us to patrol our security perimeter, on the off-chance that Gregor had somehow found me. "We can't carry the box and keep feeding them. They'll chew it up before we can get to the vault."

"Not if we give them something extra chewy first," she said.

I looked around. Other than the paint supplies, the only thing the pups hadn't devoured was more piles and piles of file folders, and that was only a matter of time. I'd saved the supplies, partly because I thought they might actually be useful, and partly to avoid the mess, but I rushed to them now. Among the cans and rollers was a large bucket of spackle! I hauled it over, popped the lid, and started scooping out large dollops into the gaping maws of the pups. They chewed and chewed and chewed some more, amidst tiny smacking sounds as they worked their jaws. I kept scooping; I had enough time to empty the bucket and leave glops of spackle in the box for when they finished their current mouthfuls. Then we picked up the box, carried it into the vault, and set it on the floor alongside a much smaller Carla Espinoza who was happily gnawing on some metal shelving.

"How much longer are they going to eat?" I said.

"Probably another hour or two, but they're not sightless anymore and they're big enough to move on their own now. We can pile up more junk for them to eat, just make piles of it in the vault where they can make their way to it. Once they've had their fill and completed this initial growth spurt, their metabolisms will slow down. They'll fall into a digestive torpor for eight hours or so, and awake as normal buffalitos."

I nodded and began pulling down more shelving and other treats for the pups. They'd almost finished the spackle and several had already started chewing on their box.

I lay sprawled comfortably on a tropical beach. A redheaded masseuse was working me over with scented oils while I sipped from a bottle of Uncle Waldo's™ raspberry rootbeer. Carla Espinoza slept in the sand nearby, soaking in the hot sun and looking as contented as she'd ever been. Gregor must have materialized barely a meter away. I felt his shadow on me, and with equal parts fear and annoyance I opened my eyes and rolled over. My island paradise wavered and was replaced by a grimy hospital morgue. Instead of a beach blanket, I was laying on an autopsy table. Swell.

Wordlessly Gregor glanced at Carla who had remained in the scenario, transferred now to the basin of a stainless steel sink.

"You are pinning much hope on this one, Conroy."

"I'm sorry," I said, "this was a private beach."

He laughed at that, and the fluorescent lights overhead flickered in time. "You lead me on merry chase, but I am thinking you are, closer to hospital than beach." His eyes glazed over a moment, and then he smirked. "I have you now, in Philadelphia at intersection of North Broad Street and Old York Road."

"That's a neat trick," I said. "But actually, I think it was St. Bart's."

"And below ground," he added. "Always being amazing, but not amazing enough. I will join you there in less than hour. But do not worry, I will let you sleep until I am there to wake you personally."

His eyes glazed again and a wave of drowsiness engulfed me. Yawning against it, I sat up and swung my legs off the table. "Sorry, I don't think that's going to work."

Gregor stepped closer and gripped my chin in one meaty hand. "What you think does not matter here," he said. "In dreamscape, I am master."

I tried to push his hand away but my arm seemed paralyzed. I bit back a sudden surge of panic and stared the dream tracker in the eye. "Maybe, but dreams are just another state of consciousness, and I know all about consciousness. If you don't believe me, come see my show some time."

"No more shows for you," he said, laughing.

"Quetzalcoatl persimmon," I said, activating the wakefulness trigger I'd installed using the bathroom mirror back at the safe house. The words worked as intended and I surged to complete wakefulness as an adrenaline rush hit. My dream shattered in an instant, but not before I caught a glimpse Gregor clutching his head in pain. Hah!

I opened my eyes. I was still in the basement foyer in front of the vault, sacked out on the floor, with my coat as a makeshift blanket. Dr. Penrose snored softly in a nearby chair. I stumbled to my feet and shook her shoulder, repeating the trigger phrase. She came around with a jolt and a shiver, staring blankly ahead of her.

"Wha? I . . . There was . . . "

"I know. Gregor's found me."

"What time is it?" she said, and her voice sounded different, firmer somehow. "How long have I been asleep?"

I checked my watch. "About five o'clock in the afternoon. Not bad, we managed a good four hours of rest. And better still, he'll be fighting rush hour traffic to get here, so that might give us a bit more time."

"More time for what? He's coming to rip your arms off."

"Not if I have the money he wants."

"You don't, and you can't give him one of the pups, we haven't sexed them yet."

I reached for my phone and buzzed Mandelbrot.

He answered back almost instantly. "I'm awake," he said. "I've been walking the perimeter. We're secure."

"I never doubted it," I said. "Doesn't matter, Gregor's on his way. I need you to phone Andrews at Wada. Tell him you know where I am, and sell him the address. Think of it as a bonus to what I'm paying you."

"You do realize he'll show up here with enough firepower to overrun the building, right? "

"Someone's got to save me," I said. "I thought it might be fun to let him play the hero. Make the call, and then get down here. I need you in the vault safeguarding the pups." I hung up and found Dr. Penrose facing me.

"Before you begin revealing your master plan, Mr. Conroy, there's something you should know."

"You're Bess, aren't you?" I said.

"Right the first time. I can bring Lisa back, if you need her, that's one of the perks of being eldest. But if things are going to get dicey you're better off with me here. So what exactly do you think we have time to do?"

My new ally was truly strange, but I didn't have the luxury of freaking out. Besides, I'd spent years making people believe they were someone else up on stage, Lisa/Bess/Betsy just managed the trick without hypnosis. I'd ask her about it later, for now I had to go with it.

"How old are you?" I said.

She grinned, but still didn't make eye contact. "More than twice your age," she said. "Don't let biology fool you. Now, tell me, why are you contacting Andrews?"

"According to what Lisa told me earlier, Carla's pups should look fully mature. So, as far as Wada or anyone else can tell, they're just nine undocumented buffalo dogs. And Carla herself looked like she was back or close to her pre-pregnancy weight and shape. Moreover, she should be infertile now, just like her tag says."

Bess nodded. "I think I see where you're going. You're going to take the position that Carla was never pregnant, and thus the Wada Consortium has no claim on the other nine buffalo dogs that just happen to be here."

"They don't know how I managed to sneak Carla in. Why should I tell them my secret method of acquiring nine other buffalitos."

"But they *know* Carla was pregnant. They have vid of her girth and her weight from customs. At a minimum, they'll attempt to tie you up in court for years, and their claim will block your use of your new buffalitos. We've got to get them out of here before Wada sees them or even learns how many there are. It's the only way."

"If Wada was the only one I was hiding from, I'd consider it. But Gregor's on his way, and he's not going to fight his battles with lawyers. I need Andrews to run interference, or losing the pups is going to be the least of my worries."

"You think Andrews will help you?"

"He's not going to have a choice. Wada doesn't want a long court battle. This started because a free buffalo dog smelled like too much profit for them to let go easily. The allure of a claim to a whole litter has to be what's making them nuts."

"It's not just the litter, Mr. Conroy. If they've figured out Carla was pregnant, then they're envisioning a possible breeding program. With that kind of motivation, there's no way you can beat them."

I shook my head. "I've got something in mind, but I need a shrewd corporate lawyer to go over it, plug the loopholes, and put it into legalese. I need to talk to your other sister."

"Oh," said Bess. Then she closed her eyes and bit her lip as a tremor raced through her body. Her posture changed, she ran a hand through her hair as she opened her eyes.

"Okay, Mr. Conroy," said Betsy, "tell me how I can help."

The rush hour traffic bought us a little extra time. Mandelbrot's surveillance cameras dutifully reported the arrival of a small fleet of armored vehicles on both sides of the building, blocking traffic without regard as they disgorged nearly a hundred men and women in matte black riot gear. Their matching helmets bore full-face anonymity shields complete with Wada Consortium logo holograms gleaming above the forehead. Andrews clearly liked things splashy.

We'd emptied the basement's foyer of everything except a desk and a couple of chairs before Dr. Penrose and I had gone to sleep, and the pups had already eaten most of it. I had Mandelbrot's compadd, and as soon as the cams announced Wada's arrival, I'd sealed the vault up tight with him and the pups inside. Betsy sat at the desk, furiously editing a document on a compadd. I stood in the middle of the room with Carla Espinoza tucked under one arm, waiting for Andrews to walk down the stairs.

He didn't. Gregor Ivanovich Skazhitski did, dressed in a white linen suit that I hoped he wanted to keep free of any bloodstains. He carried a butcher's cleaver in each hand.

"Conroy, Conroy, Conroy," he whacked his cleavers against one another to mark the second syllable of my name each time he said it. "Why are you such bothersome person, can you tell me this?"

I glanced over at Betsy. She had looked up as Gregor spoke, but returned her attention to the compadd, trying to finish up. Where was Andrews?

"Gregor, I'm glad you're here. I have a business proposition I want to discuss with you."

"How sad to be you then. It is past noon, past time for talk. Now you have only two things that you can give me to restore my sister's honor: my money or your arms. I see that you have your arms, Conroy. Do you have my money?"

Damn. Where was Andrews?

"That's what I wanted to discuss, Gregor."

"So, you do *not* have my money!" He threw both cleavers to the ground and advanced towards me, flexing his fingers.

I took a step back, and then another. Where was Andrews?

Eight men in black burst through the door from the ground floor. They rushed down the stairs wielding stun batons and smoke-grey polymer shields. All eight of them rushed Gregor and quickly pinned him against the wall.

By some pre-arranged signal a ninth figure in black entered. He had a buffalo dog with him, muzzled and carried somewhat gingerly away from his body. Glenn Andrews Andrews, vice president in charge of resource acquisitions for the Wada Consortium.

"Mr. Conroy, how very nice to see you again. We have much to talk over." He smiled as he made his way down the steps, stopping when he was still halfway across the foyer. He nodded toward Gregor. "I'm sorry, am I interrupting?"

"Not at all," I said. "In fact, I've been looking forward to introducing you. Glenn Andrews Andrews, Vice President of the Wada Consortium, may I present Gregor Ivanovich Skazhitski, dream tracker and professional enforcer of black market Russian beef. I'm sure you have much in common."

Andrews's smile faded. He signaled to his men and one of them drove the end of baton into Gregor's solar plexus causing the man to double over in pain. He fell to his knees and a moment later had his shoulder slammed back against the wall.

"Don't be droll, Mr. Conroy. This isn't a social call. I'm here for your other buffalo dog, and I have all the resources of the Wada Consortium to make sure I leave with it. You can simply hand her over, or I can take her."

"But you don't have the authority," I said and nodded to Betsy. Andrews's gaze took her in and I had the pleasure of watching his smug expression slip to pure confusion when he recognized her.

"Miss Penrose? What are you doing here? I've had people searching for you."

"I'm serving as a witness," she said, pushing back from the desk. She held up a phone, aiming its camera at Andrews. "Wada contracted with Mr. Conroy for the delivery of a single buffalo dog, which he delivered. You have no legal basis for demanding another."

"But I do. The animal he delivered was defective."

"Defective?" I said. "How can a buffalo dog be defective?"

Andrews squatted and set his buffalo dog onto the floor. He removed the muzzle and I recognized him at once.

"Reggie?"

Hearing his name, the buffalito's ears perked up. He galloped over to me and I knelt to scoop him up under my free arm. Reggie squirmed and writhed in an eager and partially successful attempt to lick at my face. Carla began squirming too, apparently also pleased to see the father of her pups.

"He won't eat," said Andrews. "Not a bite. And by definition, a buffalo dog that won't eat is defective. Moreover, he intimidates the other buffalitos, disrupting them from their training and schedules. He's a 'bad seed'. The Wada Consortium paid you handsomely for the delivery, and the creature you delivered does not measure up."

"So you think that justifies you taking this other one?"

"I do, and I believe the courts will uphold such an action."

"And that's it. That's all you want? A trade?"

"As simple as that, Mr. Conroy. You arrived with two buffalo dogs yesterday. I simply want the other one instead. Hand her over and we're done."

I shot a glance over to Betsy. "You get all that?"

"Every word," she said. "Witnessed and recorded as a binding contract."

"Give me the other buffalo dog, Mr. Conroy. Now."

I shrugged, did my best to ignore the eight armed thugs, not to mention Gregor's seething rage as he remained pinned to the wall. I walked forward and placed Carla Espinoza into Andrews's arms. "There you go. You know the way out. Be careful not to trip on your goons."

Andrews took Carla and inspected her. "Wait. This isn't the same animal."

"Same as what?" I said.

"The same as you had at the port. That buffalo dog was bigger."

"Bigger?"

"Pregnant. Stop playing games, Mr. Conroy. Give me the pregnant buffalo dog you carried off the *Bucephalous*."

"That's her," I said, pointing to the tag hanging from her ear. "Carla Espinoza. But she's not pregnant, not any more."

"But that's not possible, she wasn't due . . . This is unacceptable. The trade is off. Where are the pups?"

"What, you think you're going to take them too?" I turned to look at Gregor, then back to Andrews. "Is money the only thing that motivates you people? Tell me, Andrews, is it you that's so greedy, or your company? Because if it's just you, then we have a problem, but if it's your company, I think I can offer you a solution."

Gregor snorted. "I will take great pleasure in hurting you Conroy. Slow pleasure."

Andrews ignored him. "What kind of solution?"

"The Wada Consortium makes money using the voracious appetites of buffalo dogs for terraforming and other projects. You pay the Arconi ten million credits for each buffalito, and because Wada can't acquire them from anywhere else and can't breed them either, you're stuck paying that much.

"But I'm going to help your consortium, Andrews. My attorney, Ms. Penrose here, has drawn up an agreement. In consideration of

Wada dropping any claims on me and mine, my company will give Wada right of first purchase on every third buffalo dog we make available, and at half the price you've been paying."

"Half. . . ?"

"Five million instead of ten million. Think of it as one free buffalo dog for every one you buy."

Betsy tossed the compadd to him. "You're an authorized representative, Mr. Andrews. Look over the agreement and sign it."

"Why should I? You obviously have other fertile buffalo dogs that you plan to breed. Why not just take my chances in court? The Wada Consortium has the resources to wait out any legal battle."

"That's true," I said, "Except, if you walk out without signing, I'll phone the Arconi consulate on Earth. When they find out that you're attempting to set up your own breeding operation do you really think they'll continue to sell you buffalo dogs while you wait to win in court? *If* you even win? That's not going to be good for business."

Gregor snorted. "Amazing Conroy," he said. "Hypnotist, courier, and now blackmailer."

"No one's being blackmailed," I said. "I'm offering Mr. Andrews a risk free deal, one where he comes out ahead, and saves his consortium millions upon millions of credits. We can both win here, Andrews."

He studied the compadd. "What is this 'signing bonus' at the bottom here? Why should I give you five million credits, and why right now?"

He was hooked. I can read people. Andrews just needed a little handling to close the deal. I put on my best 'aw shucks' look, sighed loudly, and gave a guilty glance over toward Gregor. "I have a few debts of my own that I need to clear up before I can begin supplying Wada with its half price buffalitos."

This time it was Andrews who snorted. "I don't care about your problems, Mr. Conroy, why should I help you solve them?"

"Your stated purpose in coming here was to make a trade. We've done that, and more. It's not quite as lucrative as what you were hoping, but it still gives you a tremendous edge over your competition."

Andrews just stood there, silent for several more moments, then pressed his thumbprint onto the compadd and signed it. When he looked up, he met my eyes for just an instant and tossed me the compadd. Then he turned and climbed the stairs, leaving without another word, and taking Carla Espinoza with him. His thugs quickly followed. I held the compadd lovingly in one hand. Somewhere, five million credits had just transferred from a Wada bank account to mine. For a moment.

Gregor rose to his feet and staggered toward me with murder in his eye. Reggie, still tucked under my arm, began to growl.

"Okay, here's the deal," I said. "I'm going to transfer this five million to you, here and now. That's more than twice the price you put on the insult to your sister, and it settles any debt, real or imagined between us."

Gregor shook his head. "Is only money, Conroy. I can always get money, but where else can I get pleasure of hurting you?"

I took a step back and felt the vault door against my back. "I thought this was supposed to be about your sister's honor? If you maim me for your own satisfaction, you do her a greater insult than anything you claim I did."

He stopped. And the murderous gleam faded from his eyes. Then he smiled. "Tell me, Conroy, are you afraid of me? Afraid of consequences of insulting my sister?"

I nodded. "More than I've ever been afraid of anything in my life."

He reached out one thick hand and lightly slapped my cheek. "That will do then. That, and your money. Now."

Betsy hurried over with another compadd. "Your thumb here, Mr. Conroy," she said and held it for me to mark before offering it to Gregor.

He took it, confirmed the transfer of five million credits, and slipped it into the pocket of his immaculate suit. He turned to stare at the exit for a long moment. "This Andrews man," he said, "he needs to be afraid too. I think maybe I am visiting his dreams soon. Several times." Without another word he walked up the stairs, leaving his cleavers on the floor, and the basement foyer empty again except for Betsy Penrose and Reggie and me.

I waited until Mandelbrot's security screens assured me they'd cleared the building. Then I turned to Betsy to thank her again. She had sat down and closed her eyes. A tremor ran through her. When she opened her eyes and looked up at me I asked the only question that made any sense.

"So, who are you now?"

"I'm Lisa," she said. "Can I see your buffalo dog, Mr. Conroy? Betsy told me what Andrews said, and I think I know what the problem is."

I handed Reggie over, though he whined pitifully as she took him from my arms.

"Is he sick? I've never heard of a buffalo dog that wouldn't eat? He's going to be all right, isn't he?"

She poked and prodded him a few times, checked his eyes and squeezed his nose in such a way that made him bleat and stick out his tongue for her inspection.

"Well? Is he okay?"

She set Reggie on the ground and he immediately trotted over to me, hooves clicking delicately on the linoleum. I scooped him up and was rewarded with several licks from his raspy tongue.

"He's fine, Mr. Conroy. Perfectly healthy."

"Then why did Andrews say he was defective?"

"I suspect he was comparing him to the many other buffalo dogs at the Wada Consortium. But yours is very different."

"Different? Carla was the one that was different. I picked Reggie more or less at random out of one of the pens on Gibrahl."

"It wasn't what happened on Gibrahl that made him different. It's what happened while you were en route to Earth," she said.

"Oh . . . You mean he's different because he impregnated Carla?"

"Not quite. That's a necessary but not sufficient piece. I told you before, that impregnation for the female is a one-time event. For the male, it's an opportunity to create a community for the protection of all newborn pups. Male buffalo dogs bond socially with all other males in their pack when they impregnate a female. They become leaders and protectors at that time, responsible for the well being of the pack."

I shook my head, "I still don't understand."

"None of the buffalo dogs that the Arconi sell have been through that experience. None of them are protectors. Yours is."

"So when Reggie mixed with the other buffalitos at the Wada Consortium, they deferred to him?"

72

"In all things. But there's another piece. He didn't have any other buffalo dogs around to bond with after he impregnated Carla. And in pack culture that's just unknown. So, my guess is, he bonded with you. For lack of a better term, he 'imprinted' on you. And he wouldn't eat for Wada because—"

"Because I wasn't there to feed him by hand like I'd done every day on the trip here." I shifted Reggie around until I was holding him with both hands and lifted him up so I could look him in the face at eye level. "So I'm stuck with you, is that it?"

Reggie replied with a short bark and a flatulent toot from the other end. Which reminded me; buffalo dogs fart oxygen, lots of it.

"First thing we need to do is hire an engineer," I said.

Dr. Penrose cocked her head and then nodded. "We're going to need to vent the extra oxygen, or risk explosions. I think Bess knows someone who can do the job discretely."

"Good. One question though."

"Yes?"

"When I hired you, did I hire your 'sisters' too?"

"We sort of go together. Package deal."

"Did the Wada Consortium know that?"

She smiled. "They're large enough, with a big enough bureaucracy, that no one ever worked it out. Don't worry, I'm sure you'll come up with a fair salary and benefits package for all of us. You strike me as that kind of boss."

I winced. Boss. That was going to take some getting used to. But then, so would being the only supplier of buffalo dogs in Human Space, to say nothing of being filthy rich. I had a room just a few steps away containing millions of credits in breeding stock, with plenty more soon enough.

I walked to the vault, pounded out the code that Mandelbrot and I had agreed on, and then unlocked the door. Dr. Penrose helped me pull it open.

"C'mon, Reggie," I said, "time for you to meet your kids."

A BUFFALITO OF MARS

This is the first story I sold to Eric T. Reynolds, the publisher behind Hadley Rille Books. It was for one of his first anthologies, *Visual Journeys*, and the premise required authors to write a story inspired by a brilliant piece of space art. I was working from a painting by Michael Carroll that evoked Martian terraforming. It seemed like a natural avenue for Conroy's buffalo dogs, and I wanted to throw in a small homage to Burroughs' Barsoom (something that I do more blatantly in "Barry's Tale" elsewhere in this collection, as well as in my novel *Buffalito Contingency*). Except, I was coming up short. I had all the pieces, but they just wouldn't fit together for me. I happened to be visiting my mother in Arizona the weekend the story was due, and I phoned Eric to tell him I wasn't going to meet the deadline, something I'd never had to tell an editor before. In response, he asked if another week would make a difference, because he was already waiting on stories from a few other people. At that moment I didn't know if I could finish the story in a week or a month or a year, but naturally I said "yes!" The next morning, after a lovely breakfast with my mother, my wife and I drove away on a side trip to Sedona, a little touristy area that in addition to restaurants and shops featured lots of empty desert and red, red rock. Walking around that barren landscape put me in the mind of Mars, and all the pieces fell into place. Late that night, after we'd returned to my mother's home, I finished the first draft of this story. It's still one of my favorites.

It turns out, we weren't the first on Mars. Six months ago while Seroni was extending the borders of its city-state to include a fifty kilometer canyon of prime Martian real estate, a construction crew stumbled over the remains of an alien artifact at least several million years old.

The Seroni governing board brought in Faith Sands, a renowned archeologist, to establish and supervise the dig site, but they didn't stop their expansion. The population of Mars was booming, and the slow work of rendering its atmosphere habitable had begun. Eight leased buffalo dogs were already chewing enormous tunnels into the Martian rock, faster and cheaper than conventional equipment could manage. As they ate their way through tons of red stone they filled the resulting spaces with vast amounts of freshly farted oxygen. Buffalitos are good for things like that; they look like adorable, miniature bison, but they're natural terraformers.

With the proper schooling, they're also good for delicate bits of excavation. That same talent for eating any solid matter can be combined with discrimination training to allow them to eat away rock or muck or whatever other substance is covering up precious artifacts, leaving the good stuff behind and untouched, save for a glistening bit of buffalo dog saliva.

My company, Buffalogic, Inc., had leased four of our specially trained buffalitos to Dr. Sands for her excavation. The eight animals eating shafts into the canyon's walls had come from the Wada Consortium, our chief rivals. That's how the problems started; that's what brought me to Mars.

Dr. Sands stood across the table from me, both palms flat upon its glossy ceramo surface which projected an aerial view of the dig site. A white circle stood out amidst the surrounding red rock. Even at this resolution I could see complex patterns of squiggles and lines and arcs etched in the white, except where tiny spots of fluorescent yellow ran back and forth, like trails of glowing breadcrumbs. And every bit of yellow indicated a spot where the markings had been scraped clean.

"Hoof prints, Mr. Conroy, buffalito hoof prints. Buffalo dogs have been trampling through my site and causing irreparable damage to the sole artifact that's here. They've crippled this project, eradicated nearly ten percent of the glyphs on the capstone." She spoke Traveler, the adopted language of Mars, but with a Caribbean accent that had first shaped words in Papiamento, a very different creole. That accent, despite the crisp fury behind her words, made me think of cool, clear waters and warm Aruban nights. Her fist banged down on the table and shook me from my reverie. She tossed a sealed bag at me, full of white chips and flakes of an unknown compound that been waiting to tell us a story for millions of years. "Damn it, Conroy, for all I know they've rendered the rest of it untranslatable! What are you going to do about it?"

"There's some mistake, Dr. Sands," I said. "My buffalo dogs' handlers would never allow their charges to run through your dig like this." I looked down at Reggie, my personal buffalito, the sire who had allowed me to start my company in the first place. He lay curled up on my lap, blissfully asleep.

Keeping my eyes on Reggie was safer than looking at the archeologist. She was attractive, sure, but that wasn't what distracted me. Despite her anger, she radiated a kind of purposeful harmony I'd only experienced in the presence of a handful of nuns. And she possessed an intensity of curiosity I'd never seen outside of a group of kindergarteners on a field trip. The combination smote me; I'd do anything I could to help her, over and above what I'd do for an ordinary customer. It wouldn't do for me to reveal that though. Far better to pretend a deep fascination with Reggie's ears.

"No, of course not, the prints aren't from your animals," she said, oblivious to my infatuation. "Yours are perfectly behaved, and besides they're all wearing booties. No, it's the other buffalo dogs that are causing the trouble, the ones being used by the government's construction crews."

I spread my hands wide, careful not to come near any of the dotted yellow trails. "Then why bring the problem to me? Seroni didn't lease those buffalitos from me."

"They're from Wada, and before you tell me to talk to them, I already have. They say it's *your* fault."

"How is it my company's fault?"

"Not your company, just you. Mr. Ahonen, the Wada representative specifically named you. He insists you've tainted your animals, pheromones or something, which cause his animals to escape their pens and come here, trampling my dig in the process. What do you have to say about that?"

I shrugged. "Only that this Ahonen person needs to get better pens, or better handlers."

"So you don't deny this talk about pheromones? Are the buffalo dogs you've leased me in heat or something? Is that what's going on?"

I looked up and met her gaze. It was like sunlight on my face. "Dr. Sands, I honestly don't know what's going on. Buffalitos don't go into heat, not in the common sense. Further, the females in the team you leased have already had their single litter of pups and are now completely sterile."

"Then what—"

I cut her off. "Give me a few hours. Let me talk to my experts back on Earth. Meantime, set up a meeting for me with that fellow handling the Wada buffalitos. One way or another, I promise I'll resolve this and there'll be no more interference from their buffalo dogs."

"You're going to have ongoing interference," said Lisa Penrose. Despite being back on Earth in our corporate office, she was only an ansible call away. Mind you, the ansible was in my shuttle, and it took me two hours to climb my way out of the canyon and reach the ledge where I'd parked. The lesser Martian gravity made the climb easier, but the cumbersome environment suit required by the low pressure and unbreathable atmosphere made it something of a wash.

Lisa knew more about buffalo dogs than any other person in human space. She was the real brains behind Buffalogic, Inc., and I'd learned never to doubt her assessments. That didn't mean I understood them. Before I could find a way around the facts, I needed to know what they were.

"Why?" I said.

"Mr. Conroy, there's a reason I always advise against taking on work near another company's buffalo dogs. And you showing up likely made things worse."

"Me? I didn't do anything."

"You brought Reggie with you."

"Of course I did. I wasn't going to leave him behind."

She sighed at me over the ansible. "He's a pack leader. You've seen the effect he has on our own buffalitos; when he's around they stop whatever they're doing to defer to him and mimic his behaviors. That's part of why we can train ours to perform more demanding tasks. But Wada's animals have never been exposed to a pack leader, or even another buffalo dog who's seen a pack leader. That information is being communicated between their animals and ours."

"Because buffalo dogs are herd animals?" I asked.

"Hierarchical herd animals. And because ours have direct experience of Reggie, they're higher up in the hierarchy. The Wada buffalitos want to know what ours know, and they probably want to join up."

"Oh yeah, that'll go over well," I said, imagining explaining to an industrial magistrate how the most valuable assets of a rival company just happened to follow me home one day. "Is there any way to turn this off? They're threatening the very existence of the archaeological site.

Back on Earth, Lisa Penrose shook her head. "Nope. Nothing short of locking them up. And since they can eat through physical constraints even that won't work."

"Huh. Well, maybe if I talk to this Ahonen fellow I can work out a compromise."

"There's nothing to work out, Mr. Conroy," said the representative from Wada when I went to see him the next day. We met in his pressurized command bungalow less than a kilometer from the archeological site. "I don't know what you've done to your buffalo dogs, but you can't blame mine for being curious about them."

Ahonen was a tall man, blonde and blue eyed, and I recognized him at once. We'd met a year before when Dr. Penrose and I had visited his native Turku to do a favor for the King of Finland. Ahonen had approached us for a job, but he'd washed out of the training program after kicking a buffalito.

"Can you at least corral them with sonic fencing?"

"I didn't bring any. Why would I? I've got tracking chips in their collars, it's not like they're going to get lost. If they stray too far, I send one of the boys to bring them back."

"They're straying into the dig site!"

"Like I said, that's not my problem."

And that's your final word?" I asked.

"Have a good day, Mr. Conroy," said Ahonen.

We both stood, and he walked me to the airlock of the bungalow. I put on my environment suit and stepped outside. Buffalo dogs could tolerate the pressure and atmosphere of Mars, even if humans couldn't yet. Reggie waited for me, sitting right where I'd told him to 'stay'. I'd said it in front of one of Ahonen's unpenned buffalitos, just before I'd gone inside. Three of them sat there now, right alongside Reggie. I scooped him up and climbed into the little buggy I'd borrowed from Dr. Sands.

*   *   *

Bouncing along the canyon floor on my way back to the dig site I wondered if I'd done the right thing. This was my first trip to Mars, and none of it matched the fiction I'd read in my teens. I hadn't yet seen any canals, visited any ancient cities, or saved any alien princesses. Was that my motivation? Had I substituted Dr. Sands for my alien princess? Maybe her artifact contained some piece of an ancient city. I shook my head and tried to clear away the allegories, but I kept my eyes peeled for signs of canals, just in case.

The rest of the day went smoothly. Amidst much oxygenated flatulence, the four buffalo dogs working on the dig ate their way down two meters all the way around the eight meter cylinder that lay under the alien capstone. If there was part of an ancient city in there, its inhabitants had been mighty tiny.

Ahonen showed up in the middle of supper time in the dig site's little mess hut. I'd brought some special supplies in my shuttle, and we were enjoying a delicate mushroom soup with parsnip and macklebee when the big Fin stormed in. He removed the helmet of his environment suit and began shouting.

"What did you do, Conroy? What did you do to my buffalo dogs?"

The archaeologists, Faith Sands included, looked up in confusion. The buffalito handlers kept eating their soup.

"Mr. Ahonen, how nice to see you again," I said. "Can I offer you some soup? I promise you, it'll be the best thing you've had for weeks. The foie gras that's coming next is exquisite, lightly seared amidst a vanilla bean bing cherry sauce. And the main course to follow is a salmon bergeron with fingerling nickels and a caper and lime emulsion that survives interplanetary travel incredibly well. It will make you think you've never eaten fish before in your life."

"I won't ask you again, Conroy. What did you do to my buffalo dogs?"

"Absolutely nothing. I came to see you this morning. We talked. I left. I'm sure you have it all on security vids from several angles."

"I do. But that's not all that happened. You must have done something else."

"Why do you say that?"

"My buffalo dogs have all lined up outside my office, and they just sit there. They refuse to go into the tunnels. They won't dig. They won't eat. Hell, they won't even fart. They're worthless. What did you do?"

"Nothing more than you've already seen," I said. "Reggie and I came straight back here." At the mention of his name, my buffalo dog lifted his shaggy head from the tureen of soup on the ground near my chair and barked twice.

"That's it! You brought that animal into my camp!"

"It only seemed fair," I said. "Yours kept coming here. Curiosity, you said. Reggie was curious too. He wanted to meet them. It's no one's fault that he's a more compelling trainer than you are."

Ahonen stomped closer, hovering over me but glaring at Reggie. "You bastard. I don't know how you've done it, but you've incapacitated eight buffalo dogs. They're worth more than ten million each. That's over a quarter billion Marsbucks to the Wada Consortium that I'm responsible for, not to mention the fines we'll incur for delaying the Seroni construction project. You've ruined me!"

I felt Dr. Sands's eyes on me, an Aruban princess, if not an alien one. I'd saved her, and I knew she knew it. "Maybe you should have thought of that, before you let your charges damage an archaeological site of untold potential."

Ahonen spat at me, he actually spat! "This isn't over. You'll pay for this, Conroy. You and your precious archaeologist." He looked like he wanted to kick something, probably me, possibly Reggie. Instead he shoved his helmet back into place and stormed out of the mess hut. Reggie returned his attention to his tureen. The four handlers all smiled at one another. The archaeological crew sat looking at the airlock, all except for Dr. Sands who stared at me.

I wiped off Ahonen's spittle. "I guess he doesn't like soup."

It wasn't over. The next morning, when the archaeologists and the handlers and the buffalitos all converged on the site to resume their work, they found an empty hole, eight meters across and six meters deep. The alien cylinder with its partially erased capstone had vanished.

I found Dr. Sands staring into the gaping opening, only the rigidity of her environment suit keeping her on her feet. The other members of her crew weren't faring much better.

"How did he . . . Why would he . . . Conroy?"

"The why is easy," I said. "Revenge. As to the how, I'd guess some kind of portable presser/tractor field projector. He probably has several of them on his construction site."

She shook her head, still staring at the spot where her artifact should have been. "No, that wouldn't work. It was too deeply embedded in the rock. He'd have damaged the cylinder."

"I doubt he was worried about damaging it."

She lifted her head and her eyes met mine. "What can we do?"

"Get me the chips," I said.

"What?"

"The chips and flakes that the Wada buffalitos scuffed off, get them. Please."

She turned away, hopeless, but at least with something to do. When she came back moments later, I had gathered the buffalo dog handlers around me and sat in a huddle with Reggie and the other buffalitos. I took the packet from Dr. Sands, unsealed it, and poured the contents into my gloved hand. The pieces gleamed like the polished and shattered bones of tiny creatures. I pushed them under Reggie's nose.

"Don't eat," I said. "Taste, but don't eat."

Reggie lowered his muzzle and the chips vanished from my hand. A moment later he spit them back. The other four buffalitos pressed forward, eager to do the same. When they finished I returned the fragments to Dr. Sands and got to my feet.

"What was all that?" she said.

"We're going to get your artifact back," I said. "Or, at the very least, your capstone."

"How?"

I nodded at my buffalo dog. "Reggie, find!"

He surged into action, racing off like a furry, four-legged cannonball. The other buffalitos followed at top speed, part miniature stampede, part search party. They spread out, bounding across the canyon in the opposite direction from the construction site. I waved the handlers over. "Follow them as best as you can. Reggie will keep them from getting lost, but they'll welcome the sight of you on their way back."

"Are you going with them?" asked Dr. Sands.

"No," I said. "I'm going to find Mr. Ahonen."

*   *   *

I found him in his bungalow. That was my first clue. When I removed my helmet and he saw it was me, his face reddened with renewed anger. That was my second clue. He stood up from behind his desk.

"I didn't think you'd be stupid enough to set foot in my camp," he said. "This is a construction site. Accidents can happen here."

"Why'd you do it? Is your pride so big that it's worth more than an alien artifact millions of years old?"

"What are you going on about? "

"Cut the crap," I said. "The cylinder. Where is it?"

He laughed. I expected him to laugh, but it was the wrong kind of laughter. It wasn't the resonating maniacal laughter of a criminal mastermind as he reveals his diabolical plan. Ahonen laughed the self-satisfied sound a man makes when he's beaten, but it turns out the other guy hasn't won either. Third clue.

"How did you misplace a multi-ton artifact half buried in ancient rock?" And he kept laughing.

Three clues is enough, even for me. I thought about punching him, but I didn't deserve the satisfaction, not until I found the artifact. I slammed my helmet into place and pushed back into the airlock. Ahonen's laughter echoed in my head all the way back to the dig site.

The buffalo dogs hadn't returned. Their handlers were still out there too, checking in via radio with the archaeological crew who had gathered in the mess hut. The buffalitos had left the canyon and were moving away from Seroni.

"It wasn't Ahonen," I said.

"Then . . . who?" said Dr. Sands.

I could only shrug. "We'll know that when we find your artifact. I'm going to climb up to my shuttle. I'll be able to do a wide area search from the air."

"I'm coming with you," said Dr. Sands, which I guess is the kind of thing a Martian princess is supposed to say. I nodded to her, and together we began the ascent to my waiting shuttle.

A buffalito following an olfactory trace at full speed in light gravity can cover a lot of ground. Reggie and the others had been out there for several hours, and I didn't expect to find them right away. I implemented a simple search pattern, extending outward from beyond the canyon. An hour into the search we sighted several of the handlers, adjusted our course, and flew on.

We found the buffalitos half an hour later, more than twenty kilometers from the canyon edge. They'd climbed the slope of an ancient ridge and sat at the opening of a cave, yapping in the thin atmosphere at whatever was inside. I brought the shuttle down as close as I could, and Dr. Sands and I hurried out in our environment suits. We climbed down to the cave mouth and found the four buffalo dogs.

"Where's Reggie?" said Dr. Sands.

I gestured at the cave. "Inside. Why don't you wait here while I go see what he's found."

For the second time in just a few hours someone laughed at me. "I don't think so." She didn't wait for an argument, striding right into the cave. I followed; what else could I do?

What had looked like a shallow dimple of a cave from outside, took a turn into greater depth which the outside light couldn't reach. It didn't matter. A soft glow illuminated the arc of the cave wall. We followed that light another quarter turn and found two buffalo dogs sitting at the back of the cave. One of them was Reggie. At our arrival he yipped and jumped into my arms. The other buffalo dog could have been his exact twin, except that it was pure white and pulsing with light.

"Greetings, Dr. Sands. Greetings, Mr. Conroy."

The white buffalito had spoken, and called us by name, and it hadn't used any sound. Its voice had originated inside my head.

Dr. Sands stared at it, speechless. I managed a droll reply. "You have the advantage of us," I said. "Who might you be?"

"I don't have a name," said the white buffalito telepathically. "But for the purpose of conversation, call me Archive."

"Archive?" Dr. Sands had found her voice. "Archive of what?"

"A distant civilization. Hundreds of billions of beings."

"They must be pretty damn tiny," I said.

The white buffalito barked. "Not the people, Mr. Conroy. I am the archive of their thoughts, their knowledge. I am their art, their literature, their history, and their plans for the future."

"All that in something your size?"

"My creators possessed the knowledge of encoding information within patterns of the subatomic particles of ordinary matter. I contain multitudes of data."

"You're an emergency back-up," said Dr. Sands.

"Yes, Doctor. The galaxy is an unpredictable place; my creators knew that. Stars go nova, planets collide, well-intentioned experiments go awry. So periodically they compiled the content of their civilization and put it some place far away for safe keeping. Just in case. The Seroni expansion project woke me up."

"But why do you look like my buffalito? And where's the cylinder and capstone from the site?"

"My storage vessel. I collapsed and absorbed it to achieve full activation. I removed myself to this cave for just that purpose. That, and to process the information I'd been absorbing from your people on this planet. That's what I was doing when your creature found me. I needed a shape appropriate to this environment. His skill in tracking me made him a viable template."

"Now what will you do?" asked Dr. Sands.

"Nothing."

"Nothing?"

"I've failed in my purpose," it said. "The beings who created me misjudged their own longevity. My scans reveal they no longer exist. They cannot reclaim their knowledge. And I cannot sustain transport off this planet to find others who might be able to. I am done, and wasted."

"But we can," said Dr. Sands, her eyes wide with an excitement beyond anything I'd seen in them. "You can tell us, all about your people, everything. You can share their civilization, keep them alive by passing on their art and history and philosophy to us."

"That would be ideal, Doctor, but I cannot."

"Why not?" I said.

"I mean no disrespect, Mr. Conroy, but your species can't contain it."

"Well, no, of course not," I said. "Not all of it, not all at once, but you can dole it out in manageable bits, right?"

"I cannot. I'm an archive of subatomically encoded engrams, but I store them randomly and without any organization."

"But could we copy and absorb them?" I said.

"Yes, much like the buffalo dogs copy the behavior of your

Reggie," said the white buffalito. "I could easily expose you to an atom bearing an engram, and an atom in your own body that has not experienced subatomic repatterning would automatically make a copy. If you had copies of all the right engrams that combined into a coherent thought, you would suddenly know a piece of knowledge from my creators' civilization."

"Then do that. Pop your engrams onto something we can absorb and we'll grab onto them one by one."

"It would take too long. Any of my creators could have absorbed all of the patterns at once. But a single engram at a time would take millennia, and your people don't live that long."

Dr. Sands nodded. "Because they're not organized relative to one another. Each engram would be like a pixel from a photograph. And even if you had enough pixels to assemble the full photo, you'd have to have all the right pixels from the same photo, and there are billions of photos."

"An apt analogy, though the order of magnitude is severely lacking," said the white buffalito.

I laughed and shook my head. "You're going about this from the wrong direction. Reverse your perspective."

Dr. Sands looked at me like I'd lost my mind. "What are you saying?"

"Think Shakespeare. Monkeys and typewriters. Or in this case, buffalo dogs and typewriters."

"Excuse me?" said the voice in my head.

"When you encode the engram onto an atom, is that atom used up when it's absorbed and its pattern copied?"

"Of course not. There is no 'using up' of matter. If the atom does not combine with other atoms of the body, it can be absorbed by another being."

"Then encode your engrams onto oxygen atoms."

Dr. Sands gasped, and in the next instant was throwing her arms around me and all but kissing me through our respective helmets. "Yes!"

"Clarify."

"You said it yourself," she said, letting go of me far too soon. "There's no using up of matter. The same oxygen that I breathe today will be inhaled by someone else, again and again. Encode your civilization's legacy onto oxygen and release it into the new atmosphere that's being built here on Mars. Given enough time and people, related engrams will combine in the same person, people will get the full picture, one at a time."

The white buffalito sat silent. Minutes passed. And then, "that might work," it said, its voice in my head sounding hopeful. "But it will take a long long time."

"It's going to take a long time to build an breathable atmosphere on Mars," I said. "Not to mention build up the population here that's going to breathe it. But it's nothing compared to how long you've already been waiting."

"I agree. And while I lack the typewriters you spoke of, I have apparently chosen an excellent shape. I shall begin at once."

The white buffalito farted. Reggie barked with approval. The atmosphere of Mars grew by a tiny percentage, and the release of an alien archive into the human realm had begun.

REQUIEM

Every character needs an origin story, and one day I decided to write Conroy's. To make it more interesting, and to stretch myself as a writer, I wanted to try a technique known as "bookending" in which the author actually tells two stories, a main, standalone story which, in this case, was actually all flashback, surrounded front and back by another story. Basically, a story in which someone tells someone else a second story.

Early drafts of this went through a grueling critique process by the small group of fellow writers who vet all my stuff and make me look good. My main problem with this was in the beginning of the flashback: in order to tell the story I had to first maroon a young Conroy on a planet. In the initial version I did this by blowing up a spaceship carrying Conroy, his fiancée, and a hundred or so other college students all off on a semester-in-space. The explosion kills everyone onboard (except for Conroy). Problem solved, right? My critique group shouted me down for this, reminding me that all the Conroy stories were light and happy, and that off-handedly killing the love of his life and a few dozen innocents was not something the story could recover from (this was 2001, two years before the film *Finding Nemo* would insist that you can kill off a nearly entire family of fish, sparing only one parent and one child, and still tell a funny, heart-warming story, but I digress). So I rewrote it. Characters changed and expanded. I ditched the fiancée and added Conroy's already-dead/great aunt. Then I blew up a much smaller ship, killing off only a dozen or so passengers to maroon Conroy. Again my helpful colleagues shouted me down.

In the end, Conroy's ship still blew up, but it's the act of a not-really-alive vat-grown husk who would rather destroy itself than be used as a vessel for another persona, and Conroy ends up marooned as a result and we finally get to move on into the main story. Some of the later events of this story figure prominently in my first novel, *Buffalito Destiny*, and damned if that vat-grown husk—or its ideological cousin—doesn't come back to be a main character in the second novel, *Buffalito Contingency*. I had no idea either of these things would happen at the time I wrote this story. You just never know.

The three men on stage snapped to attention, and began belting out the planetary anthem of the Ice Lords of Sneth, those benevolent purveyors of frozen foodstuffs to the denizens of the Crab Nebula. The audience howled with laughter. I stood next to the trio and wished I was a bit deaf. Each man sang an entirely different tune using completely unrelated nonsense words. There is no Sneth. No planetary anthem, and no aristocracy. I'd made it all up just a few moments before. I invented the whole thing, even down to the bit about frozen food. It's what I do. I'm the Amazing Conroy, Hypnotist Extraordinaire.

As the men finished singing I leaned in and spoke to each, reinforcing their respective trigger phrases. Then I awakened them from the trance, waved them offstage to the applause of the audience, and took my final bow. Ten minutes later I was sitting comfortably in my dressing room, sipping a chilled bottle of Uncle Waldo's™ Raspberry Rootbeer. I heard a knock at my door.

"It's open," I called, and removed my feet from where I'd crossed them on the edge of a table. I sat up.

One of the former 'Ice Lords of Sneth' stepped into the room. In his right hand he gestured expansively, waving a meerschaum pipe intricately carved in the likeness of a majestic swan. A cloud of sweet smelling tobacco smoke entered with him, which caused the room's exhaust fan to kick in. "That was amazing, Conroy, simply amazing."

I laughed. "It goes with the name, Donny. Have a seat."

The fellow with the pipe was Donald Swanseye, a mega-billionaire from the outer colonies. We'd met at a corporate fundraiser two nights before, and afterwards over poker and cigars I'd invited him to see my show.

"I still can't believe it," he said. "All the way through I kept thinking I was fooling you, just going along with the gag."

"That's a common response to being hypnotized," I said. "It's easy to deny what's really happening to you, but trust me, you were well under."

He settled into the only other chair and looked at me, really studied my face, for the better part of a minute. "I don't understand, Conroy. What are you doing here? This . . . show. You're a wealthy man, why are you performing at all?"

I bought a little time by turning and opening the tiny refrigerator under my makeup table. I tossed Donny a frosted Uncle Waldo's™ which he looked at with an expression of bemusement before opening. He smiled at the first sip, and his grin broadened as he drank more. As I said, I liked Donny, and he deserved an honest answer. "Immortality," I said.

Donny chuckled and lifted his bottle in salute. "Trust me, Conroy, you'll go down in history for breaking the buffalo dog monopoly. You're one of the wealthiest men on Earth, but hypnotism? I doubt that talent will be your legacy."

I clinked my bottle to his. "I didn't say it was my own immortality."

"Then whose?"

I chuckled. "An alien criminal who re-introduced me to my great aunt Fiona."

He shook his head. "I don't understand."

I set my rootbeer down and asked, "Do you remember the destruction of a starship, the *Kubla Khan*, about fifteen years ago?"

Donny frowned. "The smartship disaster? Didn't the vessel's captain go mad? He imploded the engines, or some such, killing himself and his crew."

"There wasn't much of a crew. Other than the ship's automatons, it was just Captain Coelacanth and me."

Donny lowered his bottle and gaped at me. "You?"

I nodded. "I wasn't a hypnotist back then, just a college sophomore majoring in xeno-religious studies, with a minor in psychology. I'd grown up hearing stories of my great Aunt Fiona. She'd been among the first Terran missionaries, back when space travel first opened up. But Fiona gave up the religious work after just a few encounters with cultures and recorded histories far richer and older than anything on Earth. She never stopped traveling. Before she died she had probably stood on more alien worlds, spoke more alien languages, than any other Terran. Her exploits shaped my life."

"It sounds like she made quite an impression on you," said Donny.

"She did," I said. "Her adventures were the talk of my family. They generally disapproved of her, particularly her parting with the church. I grew up on tales of exotic alien cultures, and every snippet of her escapades just made me hunger for more. Small wonder then, that between my own devout upbringing and the stories of distant peoples, my studies took me into the study of alien belief systems.

"One of my professors recommended me for a job as alter-shift crew on a smartship. Captain Coelacanth was a vat-grown husk close to ripening, and the ship expected to transfer its own personality into him by the end of the voyage. Other than the ship's automatons, there was just the captain and me, with literally no work to do. Sometimes the captain finished his downtime early and came in during my shift, usually carrying a bowl of pudding. We'd chat a bit while he ate.

The pay was almost nonexistent, but we were scheduled to stop at a dozen different worlds and I had days to explore on each of them. Coelacanth never took a shuttle downworld with me. He just stayed in his cabin, brooding and eating pudding. Sometimes he'd have these weird little panic attacks and back away from some cable or other and scream something about worms. When that happened the ship would medicate him, and moments later the captain'd be fine. I probably should have been more compassionate, but I was overwhelmed by the incredible things I was experiencing at each new port.

"On Krackleburr I witnessed birthing ceremonies from ten alien species. During my time on Venton I was invited to participate in an adulthood rite of Bluie triplets on the rim of an active volcano. And on Kelspar, I actually received payment for serving as an usher at an Arcturan wedding, and tasted twenty-six hour vanilla eel cake served to me by a Taosian bride. The wonders and richness of the galaxy had been laid before me, courtesy of the smartship and crazy Captain Coelacanth.

"The port of call I most longed to see was Hesnarj, oldest of the known mausoleum worlds. Thousands of civilizations perform their rituals and services for death and departure on Hesnarj, and my aunt had herself buried there. Our ship, the *Kubla Khan*, had only just been granted clearance by the orbiting station. I climbed aboard the first or our shuttles taking cargo downworld. It had just disengaged from the *Khan* when I heard Coelacanth shouting about giant worms over the com. That's when the ship blew up . . . "

I awoke in the hospital with little more than a scratch. My shuttle had caught the edge of the explosion and tumbled into the atmosphere amidst thousands of tons of debris from the *Khan*. That's how quickly your world can change. The doctors all told me how lucky I was to be have survived, and left me to rest. The next day I removed the monitoring patches, changed into my own clothes, and checked myself out of the hospital. I had a chit in my pocket to present to the Terran Consul General which would get me passage back to Earth, but Hesnarj wasn't a human world. The Consul covered forty planets in this region of space and his next visit was five months away.

Beggars and panhandlers don't do well on a mausoleum world; the bereaved rarely notice them, and the zealots have no time for them. I needed to find a job if I expected to keep body and soul together until the next Earth-bound ship arrived. That would have been the mature, responsible course. Instead, I set off to get stinking drunk.

I found a bar without difficulty. It looked like it had stood there for centuries. Almost everything in the world's mourning cities was bland, so as to avoid offending any particular culture's taste. Most buildings had been constructed by stacking slabs of flat gray basalt, one atop the other. It was actually more of a lounge than a bar. The polyglot sign out front indicated it served double duty as an eatery during the mornings and early afternoons. Not that I cared; a quick meal wasn't among my plans.

I wandered in and settled onto a bench gracing one side of a stone counter. It was second afternoon of the Hesnarj fifty-seven hour day and the place was packed with mourners, the soon-to-be-interred, thanosists, and a few of the local residents who had decided to draw out lunch and start their drinking early. The air held the faintest of traces of morbidity blossoms, a pleasant mix of vanilla and jasmine that most found restful. The room buzzed with dozens of conversations, which was comforting as well. It looked like an excellent place to get quietly soused and wallow for a while in anonymous self-pity. Anonymity was never an option. My face had been all over the planetary newsfeed, the *Kubla Khan*'s blessed survivor.

I no sooner sat down than a trio of Clarksons appeared at my elbow. They had raspberry hair and fishbelly complexions, and grinned at me like hillbilly lottery winners.

"We buy drink," one of them said in the Traveler pidgin. "Drink for lucky man."

I shrugged and let them. My limited cash would last that much longer if someone else was willing to pay to get me drunk. Others came up to me. Some just wanted to touch me, rub off some luck; most seemed to feel that buying me a drink ensured them a share of my good fortune. It wasn't until my third drink that I started telling them about the smartship, Captain Coelacanth, the explosion, and being marooned. I poured out my heart, pausing only to sob and drink, then wailed some more. It being a mourning city, almost everyone around me had his own story of sorrow to tell.

At some point I excused myself and managed to stand. It was well past local midnight and except for my personal group of co-mourners the place had emptied out. I staggered off in search of the establishment's facilities, following the floor arrows to a clearly marked door. I relieved myself and turned to retrace my steps, passing someone else who had just entered. Before I could open the door to leave, a sack had been pulled over my head. Hands spun me violently around and it was all I could do not to puke. My assailant shoved me. I toppled backwards, struck my head against the wall, and the world went away.

I regained consciousness, courtesy of a bucket of water the lounge's owner threw into my face. He was my first sight as I sputtered awake, a gangly, bright yellow humanoid wearing a bartender's apron. I sat up and immediately wished I hadn't. The bathroom spun. The cloth sack that had blinded me was gone. So were my shoes, my identification, my travel chit, and all my money.

"I've been robbed," I said, voicing the obvious.

My awakener made a noncommittal grunt and helped me to my feet. I followed him out into the main room and back to the bar. The lights had been brightened and only three other customers remained. The ceiling chron showed early first morning. I'd been out for hours. I sat on the bench and rubbed my head, wondering if I had a concussion or just a viscious hangover. The lounge owner puttered behind the counter and set a mug of fizzing blue gel in front of me.

"Drink," he said. "For head. Drink."

I complied, and with the first sip I felt better.

"Thanks, um . . . "

"Rarst," he said, slapping one lemony hand against his chest and nodding. "No charge." Then he turned away, ladled something into a bowl and popped it into a waver.

The drunken fog began to clear from my brain, chased by throbs of pain. I was in even worse straits than before, having gone from little to nothing in the course of a mugging. And I still needed a job.

"Thanks, Rarst," I said, and straightened up on the bench. "I appreciate your kindness. I, uh, don't suppose you're hiring?"

He turned back around.

"What can do?" Rarst appraised me from the other side of the counter. His jaundiced expression reminded me of my paternal grandfather who used to bounce me on his knee; except my granddad didn't have slit pupils like a cat. Maybe Rarst felt a twinge of compassion because I'd been mugged in his bar. It didn't make him charitable, just open-minded. "Can sing?" he asked. "Make music?"

I had no marketable skills. I did my best to look pathetic. It wasn't hard.

Rarst scowled and any resemblance to a long-dead relative vanished. "I need entertainment. You figure talent by first evening, I give meals and room in back. You entertain, we got deal, okay?" He took a bowl of paella out of the waver and shoved it in front of me, and then waddled off to tend his real customers, leaving me to 'figure' my talent.

I began reviewing things I'd learned in my two years of college. The lounge served a dozen alien races, with nary a human among them. I needed something with broad appeal. It seemed very unlikely that leading a discussion comparing and contrasting various religious practices would qualify as entertainment in the current venue. My college major just didn't lend itself to performance.

Then I remembered a psych course from the Fall semester and the week we'd spent discussing hypnosis. I'd been fascinated, even written my final paper on the subject of multimodal induction techniques. During finals' week I had hypnotized my roommate, and planted suggestions that improved his study habits and test scores. Encouraged for the first time since waking up in the hospital, I picked up my spoon and amid mouthfuls of paella began formulating my act.

" . . .and when I snap my fingers you'll awaken, with no conscious memory of anything I've said. But what I've told you remains true; the number eight no longer exists in any form."

I snapped my fingers and the half-ton saurian opened its eyes and straightened up on its reinforced stool. We were alone on the lounge's makeshift stage and the attention of the entire audience, all thirty-seven of them, throbbed with a heartbeat of its own. Time hung suspended in the silence. None of them had ever seen a hypnotist before. I smiled and winked at them. Then I returned my attention to the saurian.

"Your people are responsible for the design and construction of most of the cenotaphs here on Hesnarj; I'm sure that requires tremendous engineering knowledge and mathematical acumen. I wonder if you'd mind giving us a demonstration. What's one plus one?"

The saurian glared at me. "Two," it snorted.

"Two plus two?"

"Four."

"Four plus four?"

It froze, tiny eyes squinching in calculation. "Whah?"

"Four plus four," I repeated.

The saurian squirmed; its spinal plates quivered. It whuffed out acrid air from a trio of nostrils. It rumbled deep counterpoint in two of its stomachs. Finally, with a look of total stupefaction it muttered, "Can't be done!"

The audience howled with laughter and pounded the tables in approval. I'd found my talent.

By the end of the week I was doing two shows a night. I spent the mornings developing new material for my routines, and the rest of the day trying to figure out what to do with my life. Comparative religion had lost its allure, and more than anything else I found myself wishing I could talk with great aunt Fiona about it. I needed someone to discuss my future with, to find some perspective and direction, maybe even real purpose. I couldn't even visit my aunt's tomb; it was half a world away on another continent. I didn't have the funds to travel there, not yet.

News of my act spread and the lounge filled with the motley visitors and bored residents of a world dedicated to housing the dead. Rarst raised his prices, put in a real stage, and even began paying me. The success was a welcome distraction and I threw myself into the work. My technique improved, as did my fluency in

Traveler. My patter grew polished and I began mastering an assortment of gestures and body language from other worlds. More importantly, I quickly learned that some alien races could not be readily hypnotized, and that others were almost criminally suggestible. I started saving money toward a ticket to visit the southern continent and my aunt's final resting place.

Some two months into my run, during the second show of the night, I met Kwarum. He was 'pebbly,' that's the only way I can describe him. Imagine dipping someone in glue and then rolling him around in a gravel bed, with each and every grain polished river smooth. I'd never seen his kind before, but that night there'd been two of them in the audience. One had volunteered, along with a rare human and a Clarkson.

The show proceeded smoothly; the audience laughed and applauded in all the right spots. Along with my usual induced forgetfulness, invisible objects, and dog-barking, I had decided to end that night with something new. A minor scandal had circulated through the city in the last few days; a prominent embalmer had mixed up two clients of vastly different biologies and the resulting stench had necessitated the temporary evacuation of several city blocks. My three volunteers sat entranced upon the stage, calmly discussing the event. When I was convinced that each was familiar with the details I instructed them to believe they were actually the individuals in question. In an instant I had two offended corpses loudly complaining with a pompous and ineffectively defensive embalmer, none of whom was actually the correct race for the part he played. The audience ate it up, and even somber Rarst cracked a smile.

After the show the lounge emptied quickly. I left the stage and headed toward my back room to plan the next day's shows. The other pebbly alien, the one from the audience, stopped me along the way.

"At the end of your performance," she said, "would you explain what you did to my kinsman, please?" She spoke crisply, clipping each word.

I looked her over. She hadn't done anything overtly threatening, but I had an uncomfortable feeling. People routinely approached me with questions after a show, curious and delighted. This woman didn't look happy.

"I told him he was Karsten of Belscape, the former plenipotentiary of the far Arcturan colony."

"This individual you named, he is deceased?" asked the alien.

"That's safe to assume, or they wouldn't have embalmed him." I said it with a smile, hoping she'd catch the joke. She was far too serious.

"You admit it," she said. "You named the deceased and made my kinsman invoke him. There is no higher blasphemy."

"Blasphemy? Hold on, I think there's been a misunderstanding. All I'm guilty of is a little harmless entertainment."

Her hands closed around my arm then, with a grip as unyielding as stone. She leaned in and I could smell her breath, all garlic and shellfish. The pebbly skin of her forehead gleamed with perspiration.

"No misunderstanding. You instructed my kin to invoke another being, one not of our kind. You named the being. You knew him to be dead. You told my kinsman to become a deceased alien. Do you deny any of this?"

"No, but . . . it was all just a hypnotic suggestion. A bit of pretend . . ."

The pebbly nodded to herself. "You admit to blasphemy. There can be no question of your guilt. When I am through, none will find your remains nor speak your name."

Just like that, she lifted me off my feet and carried me out of the lounge. It happened so swiftly, I was through the door before I thought to shout. Outside, the street was deserted. The alien hustled me in the direction of a parked groundcar. A second pebbly stepped around it as we came closer. I recognized him, my volunteer from the show. He raised a hand, pointed at me with his little finger, and said "Let him go."

"Step aside," said my captor. "Your own blasphemy is only slightly less egregious than his. Were we not the only Svenkali on Hesnarj, I would convene a tribunal to denounce you as well."

"Perhaps," replied the new arrival, "but as there are only we two, a tribunal resulting in my early death is unlikely. Now, let him go!"

I winced as her grip tightened instead.

"You may have forsaken our laws and ways, Kwarum, but I have not. The blasphemer must die." The pebbly brought her free

96

hand to my throat. I caught a glimpse of something faceted and shiny clutched between her fingers.

"I can't allow you to kill him," said Kwarum. "Remember and bring forth Hallovesht Funedap Swlekti."

My captor froze. A shudder rippled through her. I felt her fingers loosen and then fall away. She swept a hand across her forehead and then down the left side of her face. Her posture shifted, and when she spoke her voice had changed.

"Kwarum?"

"Hello, Hallo. I'm pleased to see you again. Thank you for coming."

The pebbly snorted with laughter. "As if any of us never arrived once invoked. But why invoke me in another host? Why not simply name me yourself? This is hardly a formal ceremony"

"My apologies; I needed to suppress Shastma from her own zeal." Kwarum gestured to me, and continued. "Yours was the first name that came to mind."

"I'm honored and flattered. It's been many years since I've walked and not just watched. And this is a world I've never seen before."

Kwarum smiled. "Then I encourage you to explore, while you remain. All I ask is that you take your host far from here, before Shastma can reassert herself."

My abductor looked at me and then nodded back at Kwarum. "You have always been fastidious about loose ends. I respected that in all our conversations."

She turned abruptly, and walked away. I watched her, mouth agape, until she rounded a street corner and was lost to view. I turned back to the remaining pebbly.

"What just happened? Did she really intend to kill me?"

"Oh yes, which is why I intervened."

"And now you're just going to let her walk away?"

"No, the one walking away is Hallo. It was Shastma who sat in the audience earlier, but Hallo never saw your show, and so her assessment is based on her host's episodic memory rather than an emotional reaction."

"Reaction?" I said. "Reaction to what?"

"Your inducement that I invoke a non-Svenkali."

"What are you talking about?"

"Plenipotentiary Karsten. You told me to become him, and you spoke his name. A full name and title, with sufficient additional detail to identify him as unique in the universe. That was all I needed to pull him back."

"What, are you saying just because I said his name that you somehow channeled the real Karsten? That's impossible."

He smiled again. "Impossible? Perhaps. But that is the way of the Svenkali. When Shastma held the peeler to your throat, it was my use of Hallo's full name that pushed her away and spared you."

"And this Hallo person you keep talking about?"

"A teacher from my youth," he said, and gazed off in the direction the other pebbly had gone. "And an old friend. I hadn't realized how long it's been since we spoke."

"Why so long?" I said, "and why did you finally meet her on this world of all places?"

"Hallo came at the invocation of her name, as she always has, since her death more than thirty thousand years ago."

I must have looked as stupefied as a saurian engineer who can't recall the numeral eight. Kwarum chuckled and put an arm around my shoulders, guiding me into the groundcar.

"Come," he said, "let us find a conversation house with refreshment and long hours. I have an idea I wish to discuss with you . . ."

"All sentience survives beyond physical death, forming a vast energy field of memory and personality." Kwarum's fingers danced in the air as he spoke, tracing patterns I couldn't follow. "Some races, such as the Svenkali, can tap that field, and enflesh individuals who have long since left corporeal life behind. My people are so in tune with this field that we need only hear the unique name of a forebear to automatically bring her forth. Do you understand?"

We sat around a basalt table in a curved alcove of a local conversation house. The bereaved need places where they can sit and talk, recounting their experiences of the deceased. Imagine a coffeeshop that specializes in wakes and you're pretty close.

A pig-sized robot scuttled up to our table. It deposited cups of the house specialty, a protein broth with a wicked kick to it, a cross between chicken soup and vodka. I swallowed half my cup at a single toss; I had the feeling I'd need it.

"You're talking about ghosts," I said. "Spirits. Like that?"

"No, merely what has gone before. We coexist with our ancestors, learning from them, benefiting from their insights."

I laughed; blame it on the chicken soup. "We've got people who claim to channel the dead. They surrender their own bodies as vessels to them. Most are frauds, preying on the emotions of grieving relatives." I finished the rest of my drink. "You're saying you can channel any member of your race who ever existed?"

He nodded. "We are a long lived people, and we have kept meticulous genealogies from our earliest recorded history. I know the complete and unique names of several million Svenkali, and I could call upon any of them from memory in an instant."

I set my cup down. It didn't seem possible, the ability to conjure up any ancestor at will.

"What does this have to do with my act? Why did Shastma accuse me of blasphemy?"

"The invocation of another is an integral part of our belief system. It assures us immortality. So long as some other can speak our names, we know we will continue to live on in the universe. But my people believe this is reserved for the Svenkali. From infancy we are taught to ignore the rhythms of alien names. No other race shares our facility to blend so readily with those who have gone before us. Thus, to invoke one who is not of our kind constitutes an abomination."

"So when I told you you were Karsten of Belscape . . . "

"I became Karsten of Belscape, or I would have if the fellow's personality had been stronger. He found the invocation so disorienting and confusing that he receded into the blending. Normally both share the body, or when a third person forces the invocation, as I did with Shastma, the host gives way."

"I'm terribly sorry," I said. "If I had known I would never have taken my act in that direction."

"You have no need to apologize; few Terrans have met Svenkali or know of our gifts. Besides, the experience inspired me. Perhaps I required such a radical event to jar me free of traditional patterns of thought."

"I'm afraid I don't quite follow . . . "

"I have a proposal for you," he said. "You see, I am dying,

dying the absolute death."

"Absolute death? But you just said that your people were immortal, after a fashion. Won't other Svenkali invoke you as you have done for your own predecessors?"

The corners of his mouth curled in a faint grin, though his eyes burned with a more somber emotion than I could label. "Alas, no. Among my own kind I am a criminal. My name has been struck from the genealogies, and any of my kin foolish enough to speak it after my death would likewise be outcast."

"What was your crime?"

He dropped his gaze and studied his cup of broth before replying. "Talking," he said, "to people like you. Telling them of the Svenkali gift. That was offensive enough for disapproval, but I didn't stop there. Those conversations fueled another desire, even more debased, and I gave into it. I invoked other races. I enfleshed the surviving sentience of alien beings."

He sighed and lifted his head. His eyes glistened with milky white tears. "I was near the end of a long life, but before I left the physical world I wanted to know the feel of a non-Svenkali mind, to host a consciousness that had never been host itself. It should have been the high point of my life, but my people did not regard it as such. Instead, they have decreed it to be the end of my existence."

I couldn't think what to say. How do you respond to being told an immortal alien is being denied immortality? I stared down into my cup, and waited.

"You are still young, even for your kind, and so you might not understand me. I feel cheated, Mr. Conroy, as simple as that. Every previous generation has lived on through others, and I shall not. Once my flesh has failed, no Svenkali will invoke me. All my life I have participated in the immortality of others, and now it is to be denied me. I thought I had reconciled myself to it, accepted it, until your show."

"My show?" I said.

He nodded. "The inspiration I spoke of, a revolutionary idea. What if members of other races invoked me? Think of the adventure! Not only would I achieve my promised immortality, I would blend again with beings who share experiences none of my kind has ever known."

"But who besides the Svenkali have the ability to invoke you?"

He paused and sighed. "Alas, none really, not to full mutual awareness. But I believe that if an alien were to speak my name, knew who I was distinct from any other being who had ever lived, that would be enough to gather my energies. It would pull my essence from the field of sentience, and for a time let me live again. I would again perceive the physical world, existing for a time in the thoughts and senses of other beings, though they might be utterly unaware of me."

I stared at him. "Are you asking me to do this? To say your name some time after you're dead?"

"Not quite," he said, and the smile was back. "It would hardly be immortality if it lasted only till the end of your own days. But you could tell others, just a few, here and there, when you have them hypnotized. And you could instruct them to do likewise. You could tell them this tale. Along with my name, that would be sufficient to single me out among all who have been. And you could slip in a small suggestion, encourage them to pass the tale along to other generations. Do you see? I would continue to live, long beyond just your span."

"How can you even know this will work?" I asked.

He shrugged. "Faith, perhaps? I admit, this possibility of surviving occurred to me only hours ago. It might fail, but I have nothing to lose if it does, and immortality if it succeeds. Will you do this for me?"

"Why me? I don't know anyone. I'm not really even a hypnotist. In a few months I'll be back on Earth, back in school. I'm not the man you want."

"I believe otherwise. You are the individual best suited to my needs because you are someone who can use the only coin with which I have to pay. I know I am asking much, but I offer you what none but the Svenkali can."

"Coin?" I said. "What do you mean?"

He put his palms together, laced his fingers, and leaned forward. His expression was serious, even somber, but his eyes twinkled with inner merriment. "The facility exists within you. I can sense it, though it is weak. Your people could manage to do this, albeit only infrequently. All you lack is guidance. I could help you to invoke someone, only once and briefly. After some years you might be able to manage it again on your own. But one time at least, I can promise. A few minutes, blended with someone who has died. Is that sufficient payment for what I ask?"

I found it hard to speak, a lump rose in my throat. "You could do that? Anyone at all?"

He nodded, eyes still smiling. "Anyone you can name as a unique individual. Payment in full and in advance, in exchange for your word to share this tale and have others do likewise and invoke me. This is the sole chance at immortality which remains to me. I only wish I could offer you more."

"You have a deal," I said. "How soon can you, um, provide payment?"

His pebbly face relaxed and he sat back. "Immediately, if you wish. You need only place your hands in mine, and speak the name of your intended, distinguishing this individual from all others."

I reached across the table and grasped both of his hands. You might think I had a difficult time making my choice. With all of Earth history, all those famous personalities to choose from. I never gave a thought to any of that; my selection came to me without effort. I closed my eyes. Then I whispered her name, the woman whose adventures had shaped my childhood and brought me to this point. "Fiona Katherine St. Vincent Wyndmoor."

His fingers tightened on mine and a shudder ran up my spine. The idea of her filled my thoughts. I felt awash in memories, catching glimpses of a life that wasn't mine. I saw her laughing as she held an infant upside down by one foot, dipping him—dipping me!—in a lake like a young Achilles. There she was as a young woman, respectful, all in black at a family funeral. Then again, aged as I had last seen her, irreverent and proud as she recounted her tales of travel in my father's study a dozen years ago. Images from her life played out across my mind as a silken current coursed in my brain. I could almost feel neurons firing in patterns and streams that the human brain never experiences. I discovered a new kind of pain and realized I had done something suicidally foolish. An alien was manipulating my mind, poking around in my consciousness. What had I been thinking?

And then the memories fell away and she surrounded me, enveloped me. My great Aunt Fiona was there, in my head. I could sense her surprise, her wonderment, and then her joy. It was like she had never died; she was with me now, the adventure of her life not yet ended. I tried to recall all the things I'd always wanted to say to her, but came up blank.

"I'm sorry," I said at last.

"Hush, boy, you've nothing to feel sorry for."

"But you're dead."

I heard her laugh, the sound echoing softly in my mind. "I've had more of a life than any seven people I ever met put together." She paused and smiled. "Excepting maybe yourself."

"I don't understand."

"Nephew, look where you are. Recognize what you're doing. Books and lectures are fine things, wonderful things, but they're not the same as the people who inspired them. Your family never understood, but I always hoped you might, that of all of them, you just might make the leap.

"The leap? I said. "The leap where?"

"Off Earth," she said, laughing, and I could have sworn I felt her hand ruffling my hair. "Away from home and safety, removed from the comfortable and familiar. And now you have. I can see it in you, you've left that parochial world and that provincial boy behind you. You've dared, deliberately or not, to embrace all that lies beyond."

"I hadn't thought of it that way."

She laughed again. "Says the young man talking to his dead aunt! But enough, tell me while we've time, tell me of the people you've been meeting and the things you've been doing."

And I did. I recounted all the shows I'd done in Rarst's lounge, all the aliens I'd met, from Coelacanth up through Kwarum.

We shared an eternity that lasted only minutes. I felt her start to fade, and I opened my eyes. Aunt Fiona gazed with me at the Svenkali sitting across the table. My mouth moved and we said "thank you, Kwarum," and then she was gone.

"Thank you, Kwarum," I repeated, unable to stop the flow of tears down my cheeks. "Thank you for doing this thing."

He released my hands, patted them gently. "There is no need," he said. "You did it yourself, I merely guided the way. If anything, I thank you, for immortality."

*   *   *

"And that's why I'm still a hypnotist," I said, sitting back in my chair and draining the last of my raspberry rootbeer.

Donny cleared his throat. "That's quite a story, Conroy. So, did this Kwarum fellow die yet?"

"Twelve years ago," I said.

"And you've invoked him as he asked. Has it worked?"

I shrugged. "The human mind doesn't easily go where the Svenkali wandered at will. But I like to think he's here, that telling you his story like this has brought him back. He might be peering out of my eyes, this very moment, looking right at you."

Donny nodded and moved to relight his pipe. "You astound me, Conroy. Keeping faith with a telepathic criminal member of an alien race. I doubt I would have done the same."

"I disagree. I think you'd have liked him, Donny, and he you. I'm certain you'd have told his story if our positions had been reversed."

"Nice of you to say so," Donny replied. "It's a flattering speculation." He puffed on his pipe and put the lighter away.

"Ganesha hazelnut," I said, and smiled to myself as Donald Swanseye slumped into a deep trance in response to the trigger phrase I'd implanted earlier in the evening.

"Trust your judgment, Donny, and in the years to come when you meet someone of character and caring, someone whom you know in your gut will believe or at least want to believe, tell them the story I have just told you. And when you have done so, charge them to do the same, on and on. Do you understand?

"I understand," Donny murmured.

"Very good. Now I'm going to count to three, and when I reach three you'll awaken with no memory of what just occurred, though the compulsion will remain. But before I do, I want you to do one thing for me now. Repeat this name with me; you'll need to know it so you can pass it along when you tell this story. Repeat it and invite him in, Kwarum Sivtinzi Lapalla, the only Svenkali ever to be hypnotized."

"Kwarum Sivtinzi Lapalla," said Donny, "only Svenkali ever hypnotized. Come forth" A shiver rippled through him.

I thought of Fiona for an instant, as I always did when I passed Kwarum along. I felt an echo of her, warm and comforting in my memory. I smiled and searched Donny's eyes for signs of someone looking back. Was there an answering twinkle there? "Hello Kwarum," I said, and counted to three.

Donny took a deep draw on his pipe. He frowned down at it and reached again for his lighter.

"Well," he said, "either way, it's a hell of a story."

BARRY'S TALE

For many years, when attending science fiction conventions, I've wandered around with a cute, plush bison riding on my shoulder. His name is Barry (and involves a truly atrocious pun which my wife has made me promise not to include in this book), and he is so adorable that people always stop me and ask about him. This was the plan all along, as it allows me to talk about buffalo dogs and Reggie, and then make a pitch for my latest story or book about the Amazing Conroy. This little plushie is so popular that he's had his own Facebook page for years, and more recently a Google+ page too. People love to pose for photos with him.

As a result, I've been promising to write a story in which he figures prominently, and I've known that when I finally got around to writing that story it would be called "Barry's Tale." At times it seemed like I could hear that plush buffalo whispering to me, its mouthless muzzle pressing against my ear, nagging me to stop dithering and wasting time, to write its story. This collection became the excuse to do it and silence that inanimate voice once and for all.

However, over the years the story began taking on a lot of extra weight. That plushie has been riding my shoulder since long before the first Conroy novel. As I began to plot out the multi-book arc that I need to tell my protagonist's full story, I realized I had to start slipping in bits and pieces into Conroy's past that I would be able to pick up in later books. The results pushed this tale of a child and her toy from a simple story to a much more complex novella, the longest non-novel length Conroy adventure I've yet told, and I absolutely love it. I love it for the ideas that I got to play with and how it redefines what I think of as the "Conroyverse." I love it for the characters that surround Conroy, human and alien and inbetween. I love it not just for the story it tells, but for the stories hidden within it. And Barry seems to love it too. He still rides on my shoulder at conventions, but he's finally off my back.

What do you do after you've broken an alien monopoly, beaten a multinational consortium at its own game, and set in motion all the pieces to build a billion-dollar company? This question is probably on the final exam at whatever fancy business school most golden boy, industrialist CEOs graduate from. The thing is, I never finished college, never so much as took a business class. A few months ago I'd been earning my living as a stage hypnotist on a circuit of third-rate alien venues. I'd turned all that around by an act of audacity. Now the smart move would have been to sit tight, keep a low profile, and stay out of trouble, but if I was on my way to becoming a plutocrat, I figured I could do a lot worse than follow that line about more audacity, always audacity. After all, it had worked for Georges Jacques Danton, except for that whole guillotine part.

Which is why I'd left my nascent company, Buffalogic, Inc., and its three dozen gravid buffalitos in the capable hands of Dr. Elizabeth Penrose. Then I'd maxed out my recently secured line of credit and traveled to the farthest edge of Human Space to pitch a business deal to Amadeus Colson, the most famous recluse since Howard Hughes. More than sixty years earlier Colson had discovered an unknown planet in an uncharted solar system, claimed it as his own, and lived there with a few hundred humans, ten thousand head of cattle, and a half million bison. "Colson's World" was a watery planet with only a single sizeable land mass that could easily be mistaken for Kansas's big brother. Immigration didn't exist, visitors weren't welcome, and diplomatic envoys had been met at the planet's lone space port by teenagers sporting old style rifles loaded with buckshot.

Colson also controlled the portals that allowed passage to the solar system, and opened them for only three reasons: to bring in supplies; to ship out the signature meats and cheeses that were the source of his wealth; and for one month every ten years to host the best barbecue competition in the galaxy. I'm a foodie, and I took the opportunity to combine business with pleasure as a good omen.

I traveled first-class most of the way, a massive luxury cruiser full of the kind of beautiful people and professional artistes who make it their life's work to take cruises and be 'seen'. No doubt variations on buckshot awaited any of them that might have tried to go on to Colson's World, but the cruiser didn't stop there. It couldn't. Old Man Colson deliberately limited the size of the ships that could fit through his incoming portal. In the company of a batch of barbecue enthusiasts eager to catch the last days of the Festival, I transferred to a small vessel that was little more than a retrofitted in-system tourist bus. The tiny ship slipped through into his system and eventually made landfall at the tiny port.

A projected hologram of Amadeus Colson spoke to us upon arrival, stating unequivocally that his word was law here and reminding us that our visit was at best brief. The facilities reinforced that impression. Other than the temporary structures of the Festival that had been erected nearby, the port consisted of only two hotels, eight restaurants, and a couple dozen shops. Adjacent to these stood a squat, ugly housing complex that accommodated the port personnel. The whole of the port was contained within a square half-kilometer of high walls with assorted gates, a pair of which opened onto the grounds of the Festival. The staff at the port did not include any humans, just an assortment of Trelniki, Renz, and Dlabble, all hired on single rotation, short term contracts that kept them on planet for less than six months.

Working some pretty seedy lounges had taught me the value of traveling light, and despite my improved circumstances I retained the habit. I stepped onto the surface of Colson's World carrying everything I needed. One hand held a carpet bag with some toiletries and a spare set of clothes. The other supported my new best friend, Reggie, the buffalo dog I'd 'acquired' from the Arconi and the cornerstone of my burgeoning financial empire. Imagine an alien creature that looks like a cartoon version of an American bison, but small enough to cradle under your arm. Colson's World had no shortage of buffalo, but mine was the first buffalito to visit. And unlike the massive herbivores that roamed the plains here, buffalo dogs could eat literally anything.

That was my hook. I wanted to secure an endorsement from Colson himself, the hermit who had founded a planet, told the rest of the galaxy to get stuffed, and then had the nerve to charge obscene amounts for imported buffalo meat that had fed on the sweetest plains grasses anywhere. Yeah, audacity. It was the perfect mash up to my tiny buffalitos that chewed through rock or metal or sludge as easily as Colson's buffalo roamed the planet that bore his name.

The Festival featured professional chefs, self-proclaimed barbecue masters, and talented amateurs. Hundreds of grills and pits and smokers spread out in aisles and rows upon a grassy plain, punctuated over and over by lightweight ceramo picnic benches where gourmands and gourmets alike could sample platters in an ongoing orgy of cooked meat. Walking the grid of the place brought on an olfactory rapture as you passed through clouds of sweet smoke heavy with familiar herbs and exotic spices that changed every few steps. All the Festival attendees wore luminous badges. A bright blue badge revealed each culinary competitor. A vivid purple one indicated a staff member, one of Colson's employees imported to work the event. My own badge showed a rarer green, marking me as someone who'd come to sample but not to serve. Reggie didn't get a badge, but he was more than happy to taste anything I did, trotting along beside me as we moved from contestant to contestant, or perching next to me on a bench when we paused with a platter. We were just settling down with a dish of Montréal-style barbecue that uses a sauce blending Worcestershire with cola syrup, and that had recently become the rage on Titan, when a voice that I hadn't heard in more than a decade called my name.

"Conroy? Is that really you?"

I turned toward the voice, the way you always do when someone you don't expect ever to see again calls your name out of the blue hundreds of light-years from the last place you saw her. The face matched the voice, and after only a couple seconds my memory served up a name that went with both.

"Bethany…" And I trailed off, not because I didn't remember her last name, but because it couldn't be her. Bethany had been the track star roommate of a girl I'd dated back during my freshman year, just a few months before I left on the adventure that caused me to drop out of college and ended with my becoming a hypnotist. She'd been nineteen back then. The woman coming toward me, tugging a little girl by the hand, looked exactly the same, still in her late teens instead of her early thirties. Then my memory added her last name to the mix, and while I still didn't understand how she could look the same, I realized it had to be her. "Bethany Colson!"

She wore a loose-fitting work shirt and faded jeans. A ranch hand's stun baton was strapped to one thigh, a small canvas kit hung from her belt, and a pair of serious work boots climbed halfway up her calves. Swap the work shirt for a tee and the boots for sneakers, lose the baton and kit, and she could have stepped out of the dormitory room where I'd last seen her. Long chestnut hair hung down her back and was kept off her face by a brick-colored felt Stetson. As I continued to stare and stammer, I tried to remember why I'd been dating her roommate and not her.

"Bef'ny, why's his buffalo so little?" The girl half hid behind Bethany as they came closer but kept popping her head around to peek at Reggie. She had a round, cute face, made cuter by the absence of an upper front tooth. Pale blonde hair hung to the waist of a white sundress embroidered with yellow flowers. The tops of a pair of heavily tooled, pink cowboy boots disappeared under the hem of the dress. I don't have a lot of experience with kids, but something about the way she moved looked wrong, a jerky, hesitant gait that put me in mind of zombie urchins. And her voice lagged, as if every word were an effort to string after the one before it.

Bethany paused, the smile on her lips and in her eyes changing to confusion as she looked away from me and noticed my buffalo dog for the first time. "I don't know, Gel. You'll have to ask him."

"Bethany, you look . . . I mean, you're still..."

I'd scrambled up from the picnic table and stepped forward even as Reggie jumped down. He closed the distance between us and the new arrivals with a mad scamper that ended with him bumping his head against the little girl's knees. I wasn't paying attention, though; my focus was all on Bethany.

Her smile came back and without any warning she was hugging me. "I know. Long story. It started when I came back home, the semester after you vanished."

As the embrace came to an end I held her at arm's length. "Back home . . . here, you mean. To Colson's World. Amadeus Colson is your—"

"My great-grandfather. And this is Angela, though she never answers to it. Gel, can you say hello to Mr. Conroy? He's from Earth."

At this point the girl had both hands buried in the dense curls of Reggie's shoulder hump, kneading him like she was a cat or he was a lump of bread dough. She looked up from her task with glazed eyes that had nothing to do with my buffalito. "Earth? Is that why his buffalo's so little?"

"His name's Reggie. He's not from Earth though, just me. And he's not really a buffalo, he's a buffalito. Buffalitos are supposed to be that size."

Bethany crinkled her nose and asked, "What's a buffalito?"

"A business venture I've embarked on. They're gentle creatures, omnivorous like nothing you've ever seen. And they fart oxygen. I'm actually here to talk to your great-grandfather about them, if he'll see me."

Our lunch had had sufficient time to work its way through Reggie's innards, and he demonstrated the second of his species's remarkable abilities by releasing a long toot of fresh flatulence. Gel squealed with delight.

"Gran only talks business with people he invites over, and he never invites anyone during the Festival. He's not the most social person around. Most days, he works in the cheese house from dawn till dusk, and I've known years to go by without him seeing anyone but family. It's how he likes it."

"Is Reggie family, Bef'ny? I bet Pop Pop would wanna meet him."

"He might at that, honey." She winked at me. "And who knows, maybe even Mr. Conroy too."

"Maybe. But Reggie for sure and truly." Some of the torpor had left her voice, but when she looked up at me her head lolled like a broken doll.

"Is your daughter all right?"

The kid frowned at me, and went back to playing with Reggie. I looked to Bethany and her earlier delight had been replaced by a stony expression.

"She's not my daughter. She's . . . you don't know much about what Gran's done here, do you? After the Festival ends and all these people go away, outside of the minimal staff who keep the port operational, everyone else lives in our house back at the ranch. All two hundred and six of us."

"That's a big house."

"It's an orphanage. Angela's one of the children my great-grandfather has taken in."

"Oh."

"And she's fine. She's a bit sluggish because of the medication she's on. But she's fine."

"I didn't mean anything—"

"No, of course you didn't. I'm sorry. It's just . . . she's such a sweet kid. It's . . . a neurological condition, and it's not fair. She's only six."

"She must be very special. Reggie's certainly taken a liking to her."

She watched the pair playing, Gel's fists still tightly gripping Reggie's curls, while my buffalo dog pranced and skipped in place. "I think it's mutual. I haven't seen her so excited about anything since her treatments started." She lifted her gaze to mine, and her eyes smiled again. "If that's not worth an introduction to Gran, I don't know what is."

"Thanks. It's not necessary, but I'd really appreciate it. Though I think Reggie appreciates having a new playmate more."

Bethany took my arm and slipped hers through it. "Have you seen much of the Festival yet?"

"We only just arrived a few hours ago." I gestured back at the wide gate of the space port, its upper half visible above the array of tables and booths that lay between us.

"Oh. You've barely seen anything yet. C'mon, you're about to experience the backstage tour that most people never get. I can even get us in to see the thoats."

"Thoats?"

"Mmmhmm. You've heard of them?"

"Yeah, but I thought . . . they're fictional, aren't they?"

She laughed. "Yes, and no. It's a big galaxy. These things may not be *exactly* what Burroughs described back in the twentieth century, but they're darn close. Gran grew up on books about Martians, back before any aliens showed up on Earth. When he heard that someone had something like thoats he made it his business to get some. They're grazing animals, same as the bison, just a lot bigger. You'll see."

"Thoats!" With her fists still buried in the buffalito's fur, Angela began pushing him forward. Once he realized the game, Reggie scampered ahead, pulling the girl along while being guided left or right by tugs from one hand or the other and cries of "nooooo, that way" and "nooooo, this way."

Bethany bit her lip, "Should I stop her?"

"Not on Reggie's account. He's loving the attention. But does she know where she's going?"

112

"Oh sure, I bring her out to the Festival every day. Since she's been on her meds, it's about the only time she's even remotely her old self. Come on, we shouldn't let them get too far ahead."

Because of the difficulty in reaching Colson's World, let alone receiving permission to land here, the Festival differed in a major way from other barbecue events and cook-offs I'd known. People. This wasn't like a country fair. You couldn't buy tickets to at the last minute, toss the kids into the car, and head out to spend the morning eating deep-fried curiosities and the afternoon puking them back up courtesy of the Tilt-a-Whirl. There were no crowds, no lines, no litter, and no rides. All attendees at the Festival had either a profound respect and appreciation for the art and practice of barbecue, or possessed much more money than sense. The handful of exceptions included people like me who had crept in as foodies but had another agenda, and locals like Bethany and little Gel, who lived here year round and came as much to enjoy the Festival as they did to enjoy the people who came to enjoy the Festival. The rest of these folk had been assigned formal space to set up their wares, their grills, their soapboxes, and even the rare souvenir displays touting the event's cartoon mascots named Thelma Thoat and Barry Bison. In that sense it felt more like a trade show. When the participants weren't actively working at their own booths they wandered about visiting with colleagues, sampling the competition, and generally immersing themselves in obscure areas of their passion. The result was a vast field of enthusiasts that filled the area, but did so without the usual claustrophobic side effect.

Which is why we were able to let Reggie and Gel run ahead of us without ever losing sight of them as they darted and dashed through attendees on their way to the animal pens at the far end of the gauntlet. Like most buffalitos, Reggie was proving to be nigh indestructible, and if Bethany wasn't worried about the little girl it wasn't my place to be. Besides, I had other things on my mind.

Beside me, Bethany continued that trick of smiling with her eyes. "Have you changed that much, Conroy? You used to be so talkative."

"It's that you haven't changed. You said it was a long story, but you must have had plenty of time to edit it down. Give me the quick version, because from where I'm standing it looks like you've stopped the aging process. And not just you. I knew the senior Colson on this planet was still alive, but I didn't think he'd be active and working. Your great-grandfather was well into middle-age when he discovered this system; he'd be over a century old by now."

"He's a hundred and thirteen, but you wouldn't know it to look at him. If he's not running cheese production, he's supervising the meat processing, training the quality control tasters in the packaging house, or instructing the next year's batch of older children on how to ride range. When you come over for dinner you'll swear he's barely middle-aged."

"How is that possible? Even assuming some of the more exotic alien life-extension treatments, no one's been able to add more than twenty years, and none of that is cosmetic. Is that why he doesn't allow immigration? Are you hiding some kind of Fountain of Youth here?"

Bethany shook her head. "It's not that simple. Yes, there's something about this place that retards the aging process, but it only works for Gran and his descendants. It's a fluke of planetary conditions and our DNA, and nothing else is affected. Believe me, it's been tested. But if word got out about it, no one would believe the findings. They'd look at me, at my great-grandfather, and they'd insist the explanation was a lie. We'd be overrun in no time, by the aging and the infirm, by people looking to bottle and sell what doesn't exist. They'd destroy the paradise he's built here for his family, and they'd gain nothing for themselves in the process."

"So why does he allow this Festival then? Isn't he worried about the secret getting out?"

"Why should he? He's not directly involved in any of it. I handle all the arrangements with the people who have secured importing licenses from us, and they're only too eager to take care of the rest of it, within the guidelines that Gran's established. Look back the way we've come, Conroy. You can still see the towers of the port. No one who isn't family ever gets beyond sight of it. Not the Festival attendees, not the personnel from the supply ships, and not any of our distributors. This is a closed world. That's the deal Gran made. That's what keeps us safe here. It comes at a cost, but for the most part it's one we've been happy to—oh no! Gel! What are you doing?"

We'd reached the end of the current aisle. On our left a vendor was doing a reasonable trade in commemorative cookware, recipe flimsies, and assorted sizes of plush versions of Thelma Thoat and Barry Bison. To our right a trio of Jamaicans were fussing with a metal drum the size of a small swimming pool into which they had somehow maneuvered a whole buffalo carcass supported by a series of spits, slathering it from one end to the other with wet jerk spice as they prepared to lower it over enough charcoal to warm a household through winter. Neither of these had caught Bethany's attention. She focused on the scene directly in front of us. Reinforced fencing had turned a broad meadow into a impromptu corral. Angela had slipped through the fence and sat some ten meters in, playing with Reggie in the close cropped grass, where living examples of the same animals that were being served up at the Festival roamed to and fro, nibbling grass and observing social mores apparently common to ruminants from different herds across several worlds.

Dozens of grapefruit-sized, ceramo drones hovered at four-meter height throughout the corral, each armed with a proximity stunner that kept the massive creatures from approaching the perimeter. Whoever had programmed the drones' sensors had included a lower limit well above the mass of either a child or an Arconi buffalo dog.

Both Gel and Reggie lifted their heads to stare back at Bethany. The child looked around and as if realizing where she was for the first time, or at least acknowledging that she wasn't supposed to be there, pointed at the buffalo dog and with the solemnity of a judge insisted, "He did it!"

Reggie objected to the tone, if not the actual words, and responded by farting. This caused Gel to burst out laughing, and she fell over in the grass, hugging the buffalito to her chest as she rolled. The sound of laughter drew attention from the nearer animals in the corral. Neither Bethany nor I were laughing.

At some level I knew how enormous bison were, but abstract facts learned from books or childhood visits to zoos lose some of their force, particularly when you've been spending time with alien creatures that look like cutesy, miniature versions. Reality corrected this misperception by the simple expediency of framing Reggie alongside a living, breathing thousand kilo buffalo. More massive still were the thoats that Colson had found. These weren't the horse-size creatures favored by Burroughs's red Martians, but the much larger sort, towering three meters at the shoulder. In contrast to the bison, the thoats were entirely hairless, a slate gray in color that lightened to a dull yellow at the feet, all eight of them. Feet, not hooves. Also a broad flat tail like a gigantic flyswatter. One thoat stood nearby, its long, sleek body supported by eight powerful legs that would have done Sleipnir proud. Any resemblance to a mythic equine vanished at the head, which bore an almost reptilian mouth that gaped so wide it nearly split the beast's face in half. It stood less than ten meters away from Angela and Reggie, maybe twenty from the fence that lay between them and us. It stared in our direction, either at Bethany and me, or at Angela and Reggie, or maybe just at a couple buffalo that grazed as close to the edge of the fence as the drones would allow. The gleam in the thoat's eyes suggested displeasure, even to me who'd never seen one before. But more, I had the feeling that a decision was working its way through that massive head, a plan of action to resolve its unhappiness. Bethany noticed it too. She stopped dead, flinging one arm back to halt me as well. When she spoke, her voice had a calm, sing-song quality that belied her words.

"Gel, you need to stand up. Right now, honey. Stand up and walk toward me. Look right at me and start moving, easy and slow. Your friend will come too."

"What's going on?" My own voice had dropped to a whisper without my thinking why.

"Thoats can get territorial this time of year. This one was probably transported here with the buffalo, already knows their scents and knows to share the space with them. Your pet and Angela, not so much. It's deciding whether or not to charge. Damn it! Angela knows better! She's been raised around these animals her whole life. It's got to be the meds muddling her."

"We have to get them out of the corral!"

"No! The thoat has seen us too. If we move closer, it will think we're part of the threat and react to the increase in opposing number. And until they get closer, there's no point overriding the drones to stun it; it would charge them before I could bring it down. They'll be fine as long as they start moving and don't make eye contact. They just need to make it to the fence. It's the territoriality thing again." She pulled the baton from her thigh and thumbed a switch that made it hum.

Gel had gotten to her feet, giggles still spilling from her lips, and started walking towards us. She veered slightly, angling her path to intersect one of the buffalo between her and the fence. Reggie crouched in the grass behind her for just a moment before scampering after her. The thoat continued to stare, its body tense and ready to defend against any perceived invasion.

As they approached the buffalo it snorted at Reggie, its confusion apparent as it tried to resolve the image of familiar appearance with his impossible size. Gel giggled and waved at it, already halfway to the fence and safety. Reggie responded to the larger creature with confusion of his own, and plopped his rump down in the grass as he looked back over his shoulder, likely hoping to see whatever had puzzled the buffalo and finding nothing but the patch of green he and his playmate had just left. Then he lifted his head and saw the thoat.

And the thoat saw Reggie seeing it. And charged.

A lot happened in the next few seconds. Bethany lunged toward the fence, waving her baton to direct the drones toward the thoat, desperate to reach Gel before the beast plowed through her. I raced right beside her. The buffalo sped away parallel to the fence. Reggie spun back around, lowered his head to the ground, and barreled into Gel, knocking her legs out from under her and causing the girl to sprawl across his back, her fingers reflexively digging into his wooly fur as he darted for the fence. And the thoat, like a monster out of nightmare, leapt forward far faster than something the size of a small bus should be able to move and landed where they'd stood an instant before.

In that moment I knew we'd never reach her in time. I knew the buffalo would be okay. And I knew that Reggie, despite his best efforts, had only bought them an extra second. And then the impossible happened.

Gel screamed as the thoat loomed over them, an instant away from trampling them beneath its massive feet. She let go of Reggie with one hand, thrusting it out at the thoat, fingers splayed, all but touching the monster the moment before it would destroy her. And then the thoat was gone.

Seconds later Reggie's trajectory had carried them to the edge of the coral and we were clambering over the fence. Bethany whisked Gel up into her arms and tumbled back, hugging her fiercely. I reached out to Reggie and he jumped up into my grasp. The buffalo stopped and looked at us like we were crazy. But of the two-ton behemoth that had set everything in motion, there was no sign.

I helped Bethany back over the fence and stood nearby as she dried the child's tears, stroked her hair, and calmed the hysterics that had gotten through whatever insulation her medications had provided. Reggie looked up at me, looked back out into the coral, and then down at Gel. We were probably thinking the same thing.

"What happened to the thoat?" I said. No one answered.

When the first aliens reached Earth in 2012, they brought along a huge upgrade to our technology. My great aunt Fiona once told me that we already had limited three-dimensional printing machines, the underlying concept behind today's fabricators, and whether or not aliens had showed up on the doorstep, the ability to mass produce the pieces to build almost anything would have forever shattered the economies of every nation, big or small. When a Clarkeson sold us those first desktop-sized fabbers, our leaders glommed on like remoras. In exchange, the Clarkeson asked for and received an exclusive extra-solar export license for a few hundred common Earth food items. Where was the harm? Humans didn't have any markets beyond our atmosphere yet. We must have thought we were gaining everything and paying nothing.

It didn't take long to discover we'd been suckered.

Those other alien races all had bigger and better fabbers. Most anything they wanted could be churned out and assembled at minimal cost. All of them had everything that any of the rest of them had. But none of them had cheeseburgers. Or Belgian chocolate. Or kobe beef. Or New England cider. Things that fabricators can't fabricate because the chemistry that makes them possible is too complicated, reflects too many factors, or requires the invisible hand of an artisan or master. As the newest kid on a very old block, Earth found that demand for its foodstuffs far outstripped supply. For a few years it became impossible to find Earth-grown food in eighty percent of human communities. Eventually new laws were passed, new trade restrictions enacted, and the chaos subsided. Meanwhile, human explorers equipped with extra-solar vessels and the fabber plans to construct portals moved into space and led the effort to identify and colonize new systems with a rapaciousness that hadn't been seen since Europeans stumbled upon the new world.

Amadeus Colson had been one of those. Legend has it his one-man scoutship hit some astronomical anomaly that whisked him deep into the vastness of space where no alien had ever been, to this tiny star system with only a single habitable world. Soon he had an annual export of a couple metric tons of bison steaks. Alien governments, already used to paying obscene prices for commonplace Earth goods, fought one another for a chance to buy the odd protein from exotic animals that had been raised and slaughtered on a new world. As demand grew Colson kept supply low and drove the price higher. Some portions he sent as gifts in exchange for political favors. Some he auctioned off, others went into a wildly popular lottery. When he began adding cheese to his exports the galaxy trembled. Colson became a legend back on Earth—the consummate explorer turned entrepreneur, an iconic name in business schools like Carnegie and Jobs, and as famous a recluse as Hughes or Fischer. He had an entire world to call his own, and he liked it that way.

I followed Bethany to a luxury aerosled that had been parked at the port. At her direction I guided it past the facility and slapped one of two preprogrammed buttons on the console and sat back as the autopilot drove us to her home. We skimmed over endless, open fields while Bethany comforted Angela and fought some internal struggle that involved the answer to my question. What had happened to the thoat? Eventually the child fell asleep. Bethany set her comfortably on the seat, covering her with a blanket. She took a field hypo from the kit at her waist, popped in a slender ampoule, and applied it to the girl's arm.

"Gel's not on medication for a neurological condition. She's got an . . . ability. It started a couple months ago. Things around her started going missing. Small things at first. Odd things. A toy. A lamp. The big rock in the field that the kids use as 'home' for some of their games. Something had taken them, leaving no trace. At first we all thought it was just one of the kids, acting out, going through some weird phase, you know?"

I shrugged. "Sure. Kids. Orphans especially. Lots of issues, I suppose. Inexplicable at times. "

She smiled at that. "You don't know much about children, do you?"

"I've been mostly working lounges and nightclubs as a hypnotist since we last met. Not really the right venue for spending time with kids." Reggie snuffled against my shoe, so I picked him up and put him on my lap, feeding him a couple ball bearings I usually carry around for that purpose. He gulped them down, yawned, and settled in for a nap.

"It wasn't any of the other kids. It was Gel. I saw it happen. She'd been up too late the night before, hadn't gotten enough sleep, and was cranky that morning. I was leading arts and crafts that day. She was trying to sculpt something out of clay. I don't know what, it was just a lump, and giving her difficulty. She went from cranky to sullen to petulant. I don't put up with that from any of the kids. Art is a privilege and she knows that. So I sent her out of the room. She stomped out and as she passed it by, a twenty-kilo slab of river clay disintegrated."

"Excuse me?"

"I know, it doesn't make any sense. I told my great-grandfather, and he fabbed a small spy-eye that followed her and recorded everything she did and everything around her. Nothing happened for days and days, but then, twice more objects just disappeared, and both times it happened when she was upset. Last time it was a doll that one of the older kids had snatched from her in a game of keep-away. Angela's always been a happy child, but when we started checking, going back and talking to the older kids who help out or work at the ranch, we found witnesses who could confirm that she'd been angry or frustrated with something or someone around the time the other things had vanished."

"So you've had her on tranquilizers or something?"

She nodded. "It kills me to see her doped up, walking around like a zombie child. But I didn't know what else to do. I searched through every medical database I could find, and there's nothing even remotely like what she's doing in any of them. It only happens when she's upset. Not every time though, like she needs a couple days to recharge or something, but still. She's six years old, and she's manifesting a mutation that could accidentally kill another child if they argue over some toy. As soon as I realized that possibility I started the meds."

"How long ago was that? And has it worked?"

"She's been fine, other than being stupefied. No further incidents, at least not until today. And you saw her, you saw how groggy she was. Whatever this thing is, it's growing stronger."

"Bethany, if it hadn't, she'd have died. That thoat would have trampled her." Reggie had opened his eyes at some point in the conversation and farted softly.

"I . . . I hadn't thought of it that way."

I shrugged. "I have an outsider's perspective, and I'm only now finding out about the special circumstances. But, from what you've told me, I would think today's events are a good thing."

"How is this a good thing? This power of hers is getting stronger. She's never disintegrated anything even half that big before."

I glanced out the window, and watched the plains roll past us as our aerosled sped onward. I chose my words carefully.

"From what you've told me, it didn't sound like Gel had any control over her ability."

"She doesn't. I told you, it happens when she's upset."

"Maybe. But I don't think that's what we saw today. Maybe it's not simply something that is set off by her emotions reaching some critical point. What if instead it's more like a reflex, something that's controlled at an unconscious level."

Bethany stared at me like someone who hadn't eaten in days and I was a ham sandwich with extra mayo. "You said you're a hypnotist? You know all about the unconscious?"

"I said I've been a stage hypnotist, and I do work with people's unconscious minds, but I'm not a clinician."

"I hadn't looked at it that way before, but if you're right, if it is an unconscious reflex, could you help her?"

I looked down at Gel, as innocent a sleeping child as I could imagine, and then back up at Bethany and her eyes that had gone from smiling at me to pleading. There was only one answer. "I can try."

By late afternoon we came in view of a curved ranch house and surrounding buildings that looked large enough to require their own internal rail system. I'd seen smaller royal palaces and luxury hotels. Granted, some of the effect resulted from a single story sprawl, but even so there had to be room for a couple hundred residents in that main house, more if most of them were children and you didn't mind packing two or three to a room. The arc of the house faced a single tree—the only tree I'd seen since arriving on the planet. Deep furrows in its grey-black bark marked it as a black walnut, as did the plethora of brownish-green husks that littered the ground in a wide ring all around the trunk.

The aerosled aimed itself for a slot in a vehicle port angled off at one side of the main house, and as it slowed to park, a single figure separated itself from the tree's long shadows and stalked our way, arms held rigid to his sides with fists clenched. He was tall, tanned in the way that the first generation of space explorers had always been tanned. He stood wire-thin and fit, and if not for a head of silvery hair I'd have marked him at just over forty.

"Tell me that's not your great-grandfather," I said, but Bethany was already nodding and opening the door. Colson stopped alongside the sled as Bethany stepped out. He took Gel from her, cradling the child in his arms. Relief and concern warred on his face.

"A staffer called from the Festival. Said something about you *stealing* one of the thoats." He peered into the aerosled and frowned at Reggie and me. "Please tell me you had it strapped to the roof and it slipped off on your way back home."

"No, sir. It was—"

"Hush, Bethy. No need to air our problems in front of others. I know what it was."

"Gran, this is Conroy. I know him from when I was at school. He saw the whole thing. He knows about Gel. He thinks he can help."

I'd exited and stepped around the aerosled by this point. I had Reggie tucked under my left arm and put out my hand as I said, "Mr. Colson, it's a great pleasure to meet you."

He ignored my hand and jerked his chin towards Reggie. "That's an Arconi buffalo dog, isn't it?"

"You're familiar with buffalitos?"

"I read a lot. Toyed with the idea of getting a few, for the novelty of mixing them in among the bison herds, but the damn

Arconi only wanted to sell sterilized females, and at a ridiculous price at that. Not the way I like to do business."

"They had the monopoly on them," I said. "It's allowed them to set the terms and conditions."

"Had?"

"I recently broke it. That's partly why I came to your Festival. Maybe we can help each other out."

"What's this have to do with Angela and her . . . situation?"

"Nothing."

Colson frowned. "I'm not following. Talk sense, or get out. I don't have time for strangers and flibbity-gibber."

Bethany interrupted. "Conroy's a hypnotist, Gran. He thinks he can teach Gel how to control her—"

"Hypnotist! What does that have to do with Arconi buffalo dogs?"

"Nothing," I repeated, and hurried on as Colson's frown deepened. "Like I said, that's a recent development. I've been a working hypnotist for the past thirteen years. From what I saw, the little girl's problem isn't random, and it might be an unconscious behavior. Hypnosis can help people acquire deliberate control over previously unconscious processes."

The frown changed to something between longing and distrust. "I'm sorry that Bethany's wasted your time, but this is a family matter. We'll handle it ourselves."

"Gran, please. Angela was on a full dose of her meds when today's incident happened. I know you want to keep things private, but if we're not past that point we're getting very close to it, and whether you want to think of it as luck or fate, we have someone right here who might have the answer. Won't you at least let him try?"

He grunted, looked at Bethany, then back to me. "You've done this before?"

"Not this specifically, no. Like I told Bethany, I'm not a clinician. But I'm familiar with the concepts involved. The trick is to come up with a metaphor that the person can use to understand and justify their control."

He stared at me a moment, the wheels of his mind whirling. He must have come to a decision because he asked, "What do you need?"

"Excuse me?"

"Don't be stupid, son. What do you need to help her? What gear? Equipment? Supplies?"

"Nothing, really. A comfortable place for her to sit, some quiet. And something to focus her attention, but Reggie can help with that."

"That's all?"

I shrugged. "I like to travel light."

"Don't be smart with me, son."

"Gran, he's here to help."

He scowled. "Why aren't you afraid she might zap you while you're trying to help? You or your critter?"

I swallowed, thinking of the thoat. "Bethany said she needs time to recharge. That means we're in some kind of refractory period. But yes, if you want me to make the attempt, it should probably be sooner rather than later."

He gazed down at the child in his arms and all the gruffness melted away. She may have been some orphan he'd taken in, but at that moment all I saw was the unconditional love of a parent for his child. When he looked up at me a moment later, his eyes held the same hunger and plea that I'd seen in Bethany.

"I've had a long life, and I've done more with it than most men ever imagine doing. I've never been afraid of anything, but I'm afraid now. I'm afraid for her, you understand? This thing in her, it's growing stronger. If we can't control it, it's only a matter of time before she accidentally kills someone here."

"Gran, no! It won't come to that."

"You don't know that, Bethy. I have two hundred children here, Conroy. I don't want to sacrifice one to save the rest, but I will if I'm all out of options. Anything I have is yours, if you can give me another choice."

Night had fallen while we'd stood there deciding the fate of a small child. Nearby, the lights of Colson's enormous house beckoned, warm and welcoming. "I'll do my best. If you've got a quiet, private room in there, we can get started."

We entered the main building and stepped into a great room packed with dozens of boys and girls ranging from toddlers to early teens. They had a range of skin tones and body types but all looked healthy. They'd been watching from every window and, judging by the expressions on their faces, they didn't get a lot of visitors. They yelled greetings at us as we passed through, Bethany clearing a path toward a door at the far end. Colson smiled and nodded, tousled a few heads, patted a few cheeks, and basked in the orphans' love and respect. They didn't know him as the veteran explorer, the man who'd defined one edge of Human Space, or a legendary entrepreneur. He was just 'Sir' or 'Gran' or 'Pop Pop,' a father figure who had taken them in, put a roof over their heads, kept them fed, provided clothes and toys, and given them an education and the opportunity to dream.

There were several near doors to the right and left, and hallways opening on either side beyond them. Colson led the way to a single door on the opposite wall. It opened onto his study, a small room with a comfortable leather chair, an end table with a tall reading lamp, a water pitcher, and two empty glasses, and a narrow daybed. Bethany closed the door behind us, hushing and waving away the more curious of the children in the outer room. With the door sealed we might have been the only beings in the house; it was that quiet. Colson placed Gel upon the bed and stepped back, leaning against the door, unwilling to leave but uncertain if his presence might interfere. Ignoring him, I put Reggie alongside Gel and then settled into the chair facing them. I heard Bethany lean against the back of my chair, her arms resting across the top. I turned down the lamp, casting the room in shadows, with the only light falling upon me in the chair.

"Wake her up, boy. Big kisses."

Reggie scampered around on the day bed, closing in on her and then dashing back.

Colson grunted from behind me. "What's that critter doing to her—"

"If you want to stay, that's fine, but if you want me to do this you'll listen to what I tell you. She needs to focus on me and my voice. Which means you need to keep quiet."

"This is my home, Mr. Conroy, my world! I don't take orders from anyone here."

I didn't move. I'd run into old man Colson's type before, rugged individualists with forceful personalities who routinely shaped everything to their own will, rarely if ever encountering resistance from other people. Arguing with him would be a mistake; there would have to be a clear winner and loser, and he wouldn't allow himself to lose. For a moment I wondered how long it had been since he hadn't gotten his way.

"You misunderstood me, sir. I'm not telling you what to do, I'm telling you what has to happen if you want this to have even a chance of working. You don't have to take my word for it, but I think you'll be hard pressed to find another hypnotist for a second opinion on such short notice. Particularly one who's already learned of the problem you're trying to resolve. Now, can you keep silent and not interfere, or do you want me to leave?"

I could practically feel Colson fuming behind me as his need to control every situation warred with his love for the little girl. If nothing else, my years as a hypnotist had made me a good judge of character, and the ensuing silence proved me right. Above me Bethany whispered, "Have a little compassion, would you? This whole thing has him feeling helpless, and he's not used to that."

"You need to be quiet too. She's waking up."

Reggie had finally pounced, pressing his wooly beard against Gel's neck, his quick blue tongue licking her face in the shadows of the day bed. Amidst giggles and ineffectual head-shaking she brought her hands up, but he kept butting them aside with his head to continue his tongue lashing.

"Reggie really likes you, Gel. Do you like him?"

At the sound of his name, Reggie sat back on his rump alongside the girl. She opened her eyes and lowered her hands, wrapping her arms around the buffalito in a fierce hug.

"I wanna buffalito."

"I know just how you feel. I'm happy to share him with you while we visit. I'm kind of busy, so you'd really be helping me out if you'd keep Reggie company and play with him, and be his friend. Could you do that for me?"

"Sure. He's my friend too." As she had earlier in the day, she buried her fingers in the curly fur of his hump, pulling him closer. Reggie gave out a half-hearted bleat and allowed himself to be adored.

"His fur's so soft, isn't it? It's nice to just work your fingers through it. He likes it when you dig in with your fingernails and slowly scratch over and over. Nice and slow."

Gel followed the suggestion, and Reggie obliged with a happy rumbling from deep in his chest. In the dim light I could see Gel smiling as she continued.

Hypnosis is all about inducing a relaxed state in the people you're trying to hypnotize. The classically trite way involves focusing their attention on a swinging pocket watch, but the point of focus isn't what's important. It's just a distraction of your own choosing, separate from all the other distractions around them, as you speak in a calm voice and through a series of indirect suggestions guide them deeper until they've achieved trance and become receptive to whatever you want to tell them. Hypnotizing children is trickier because they haven't learned to filter out half the things that adults do. I'd cheated by dimming the lights so Gel couldn't see anything but me, that and giving her Reggie to play with. He's much better than a pocket watch.

I hadn't ever hypnotized children as part of my lounge act. None of the aliens I'd met allowed kids to frequent the kinds of places that tended to hire me. Nor had things ever gotten so bad that I'd been reduced to performing at kiddie parties or bar mitzvahs. But over the years I'd had an occasion or two to help a friend whose child needed some focus in school, or a hand in getting past some trauma, or a way to sneak up on and accept an unwelcome truth. Each time the key had been to approach the thing as a game, and I used the same technique with Gel. As I eased her into a deeper trance, I explained the rules that she and I and Reggie would play by. I made it fun. I made it entertaining. One rule was that she couldn't hear anyone else. Another was that until I told her otherwise, nothing I said mattered or could even be remembered, unless I said her name. I painted a magical picture for her that included the three of us flying through the sky, gazing down on the vast herds of cattle and bison and thoat, giving names to each animal we saw and introducing every one of them to every other one.

I rose from the chair, stretched, and turned to face Bethany and her grandfather. Behind me Gel slumped forward, completely at ease. She sat with her arms around my buffalo dog, softly murmuring an endless litany of made-up names. "This is phase one," I explained as I turned up the light. "She's in a deeply relaxed state right now, and open to suggestion. Before going any further I need to get a few answers and make sure I understand what's going on."

Bethany raised her eyebrows at me and I nodded to her. "Sorry. You can talk now. She can hear everything we say but none of it matters to her and she's not paying any attention."

"That's the damnedest thing," said Colson, coming away from the door and stopping just short of the day bed. A tiny bit of hope had crept into his face, but he was all business when he turned back to me a moment later. "What do you need to understand?"

"From what Bethany told me on the way here, all of Gel's 'incidents' have occurred during an emotional event."

Colson nodded. "Yeah, best as we can tell. She gets pissed off, the way even a sweet kid can, and then she zaps something."

"Except today," said Bethany. "She wasn't angry today when she zapped that thoat."

I nodded, more to myself than to them. "Not angry, scared. Not to get Freudian on you, but it sounds like whatever she's doing is tied up with her Id. The Id is all about satisfying basic needs, getting what it wants, when it wants it. When her wants are blocked or threatened, along with the basic emotional response you'd get from any kid, she lets lose with whatever it is she does. Does that sound about right?"

"How does that help?"

"It helps us understand the mechanism, which is critical to changing it. What I'm going to do next is build a bridge in her understanding. One that connects her anger and fear with an idea that's more concrete, with the idea of giving her some control over it. I'm going to build her a metaphor using something she already knows."

"What do you need us to do?" said Colson.

"Tell me about the tree out front."

"It's older than this house," said Colson, "descended from a black walnut that grew out behind my parents' home. I planted its seed the day I arrived here and claimed the world, back in '26."

"The children here at your ranch, do they climb it?"

Bethany laughed. "They're not supposed to, but they all do. It's kind of a rite of passage, to climb to the top and gaze out over the plains before any of them leave home. They all claim they can see the space port from up there, though you really can't. More than a few have climbed too high before they were ready and fallen out, breaking an arm or leg. But Gel hasn't climbed it yet. She's still too small. "

"Good. That gives me plenty to work with. Time for phase two."

The others stepped away. I sat forward in my chair and spoke to Gel, pulling her back into our game, reshaping the rules as I went along. In her mind's eye we flew to her home and stood in front of the tree. She wanted to climb it, longed for the day when she could. I fanned the flames of that hunger, built it up greater and greater, and then with Reggie still frolicking at her side, spoke her up its furrowed trunk. Hand over hand we climbed, branch after branch, neither of us worried over how Reggie kept up. I let the seasons spin around us as we ascended. Leaves sprouting, unfurling, expanding, turning color, and falling away. Fruit appeared all around us, tiny nubs on branches which grew as time scurried past into thick green husks that soon hurled themselves to the ground. And still we climbed.

We reached the top, clinging to limbs that barely held our weight. I conjured up a wind, strong enough to make us sway. Gel clung half a head above me, unafraid, smiling down at Reggie perched upon my shoulder. On the daybed her face beamed with joy.

"I see it. I see the port!"

"Of course you do, Gel. You've climbed to the top of the tree. You're a big girl now. Want to try something else that you've never done before?"

"Sure. I'm big."

"Feel the wind, Gel. Feel how it wants to shake all the leaves from the tree and blow them all away, like the wind is mad at them, mad at the leaves, mad at the tree."

Sitting on the daybed, Gel trembled. Her mouth fell open and her eyes widened as she gazed at something only she could see.

"It's not the regular wind at all, Gel. This wind is special. It's a part of you."

"I'm the wind?"

"Anytime you get angry, really really angry, that's the wind that lives inside you. It comes out when you feel bad. It's trying to help you because it thinks you're just a weak little girl. It's there when you get angry, it wants to blow everything away. Can you remember feeling like that?"

"Uh huh."

"When was the last time, Gel. I know you remember. Tell me, please."

"When Kelly took Captain Stacey. She made me so mad."

"That's the doll that went missing," said Bethany from behind my chair. "A few months back the younger kids renamed all the toys and gave them ranks so they could play war games."

"Right," I said. "And what happened to Captain Stacey? What did the wind do to her?"

"It made her go away."

"The wind blew and blew and she was gone, right?"

A single tear ran down her face. "I miss Captain Stacey."

"Of course you do. I bet you wish you could have stopped that wind from blowing her away."

"Yeah."

"And earlier today, when you got scared? When you thought that big thoat was going to trample you, could you feel the wind in you then?"

"Yeah. It blew the thoat away."

"That's right. That's what the wind does, Gel. That wind that's part of you, but it only comes out when it thinks you're weak. That's why it's blowing all around us right now, way up here in the tree. It's swirling and whipping the leaves and branches and me and Reggie too."

"I don't wanna blow you and Reggie away!"

"Of course you don't. That's why I'm going to tell you another secret, Gel. The wind is wrong; you're not weak at all."

"I'm not?"

"Not a bit. Just like that wind is a part of you, so is this tree."

"The tree?"

"That's right, and no matter how hard the wind blows, the tree doesn't care. It's not going to get blown away. It's not going anywhere. It's a big old tree, and it's stronger than the wind."

"And I'm the tree?"

"Absolutely. Feel it. The wind is dying down. Now that you know you're the tree too, that you've got roots going into the ground, as deep down as the branches reach up into the sky, the wind can't do anything. That's the piece you were missing, Gel. But now you know. So when you're mad at someone, or when you're scared, the wind won't go blowing around anymore, because now you know you have all the strength of this tree. You're big and strong."

"I'm strong."

"And the next time you get really angry or scared, you'll also still be strong. And the wind that's been blowing things away, it won't need to do that. It won't even be able to try. Because you know the secret now."

And from the look on her face it was clear that she did. I guided her through it several more times, building up the metaphor from several directions. Over and over the wind whipped at us, throwing leaves in our faces, shaking the branches under us, rocking the very tree itself. Each time I asked Gel if she was weak or strong, and when she said she was strong the wind stopped. She didn't need it any longer. She could have her anger or her fear, but neither would make the wind come back.

"It's okay to get mad sometimes, or to be frightened. It happens to the other kids too. To me. To Reggie. But after a bit we stop being angry or scared, and you will too. You just didn't see that before, because you hadn't climbed to the top of this tree. But now that you have, you'll always remember how you feel now. You'll remember being here at the top of the tree, and stopping the wind, and how strong you are."

"I'll remember."

"Of course you will. You're a big girl. You'll remember. And one more thing: in a moment we're going to climb down from this tree and go back inside, but from now on, whenever you hear me say 'Janus Banana' you'll find yourself right back here. No matter where you are or what you're doing, if I say those words to you, you'll be here at the top of this tree, feeling big and strong, and we'll be able to talk just like we're doing now, understand?"

"I understand."

"I knew you would. Now it's time for us to climb back down. Branch by branch, back to the ground. Climb with me now, Gel, branch by branch..."

We made our way back, effortlessly descending, pausing a couple times to reinforce the idea about her newfound powers of control, until we'd quit the tree and come inside, and she was there, on the bed, waking up with my sleepy buffalito still in her lap.

Before she ran off to put Gel to bed, Bethany offered to show me to a guest room for the night. Her grandfather immediately quashed that idea by suggesting I'd be more comfortable in my room back at the port hotel. The way she nodded was just more proof that things always ran the way her great-grandfather wanted them to. Including me, apparently. It took several minutes to pry Gel's arms from Reggie, and a couple more to pull her away from me as she insisted on giving me a goodnight hug.

"Can Reggie and me play some more, tomorrow?"

Bethany took her hand and gave it a squeeze. "Sure, honey. We'll see them at the Festival soon."

"'kay!"

Colson walked Reggie and me outside toward the aerosled. Despite sending me away, his demeanor was the kindest I'd yet seen from him. Was he going to drive me back himself?

"Don't take me the wrong way, Conroy. You're not a bad sort, I'm just not . . . comfortable around people. You understand?"

"You have a household of two hundred here."

"They're not people, they're family. Bethany comes and goes, but I don't leave the ranch anymore." He opened the aerosled's door. Reggie jumped inside and Colson waved me in after. "You said you didn't come just for the Festival, but to see me. What about?"

I knew I'd only get one chance to make my pitch, and this was it. "A marketing angle. This solar system defines the farthest edge of Human Space. You made that happen. Your name's synonymous with the best of human endeavor. Between that, your buffalo exports, and the gross physical similarity between bison and buffalitos, I wanted to discuss an endorsement arrangement, and to offer my services in exchange."

"I don't need your services, Mr. Conroy."

"With respect, sir, buffalitos are very versatile. You don't know what I can offer."

"Doesn't matter. Anything I want, I can feed plans into a fabber and build from parts. Anything I need done, I can do for myself. I like my things simple."

"But I—"

"Let me be blunt and save us both some time. I understand what you want, and I think I understand why you want it. But I don't care. I don't allow anyone to pair my name to anything. It draws more attention to me and mine, and I don't like attention. So, I respect what you're doing with your little friend there, but you won't be making me any part of it."

"I understand, sir, but . . . It's been a stressful day. Can I ask you to at least sleep on it?"

He actually hrumphed, but nodded. "We'll talk again, by screen, before your ship leaves. I meant what I said about you helping Angela. I'm deep in your debt for that, and I pay my debts. Now though, let's get you back to your hotel."

"I don't want to be a bother."

"No bother at all," said Colson. "The sled's autopilot will get you there straight off, and an attendant will send it back."

"Oh. Autopilot. Is that safe?"

He snorted. "Did you see much traffic on the road on your way here, Mr. Conroy?"

"I didn't even see a road."

"That's the point. You see the two big buttons on the console? One takes you here and the other takes you back. There's nothing to drive to on this planet except this ranch and the port, with just empty plains and the herds between the two. The animals should all be bedded down for the night, and if one wasn't it would still give the sled a wide berth."

The aerosled rumbled along, traversing the darkened plains of a mostly empty world, its search beams cutting the blackness in front of us into tiny pieces that reassembled themselves behind us. When the space port appeared on the horizon it seemed like a jeweled city blazing in the night. Up close it was a pretty standard collection of ceramo towers and walls, not unlike a medieval fort or a themed shopping mall. My heart yearned for it all the same. The evening had been very instructive. Colson enjoyed his isolation and pseudo-frontier existence, but that would never work for me. I needed people around me, preferably in great variety. I wanted to hear voices, both human and not, raised in both irritation and song, swapping tales and telling lies. The night was still young, and I had no doubt I'd have my choice of several venues where I could find people arguing, at the very least, the merits of dry rub versus wet sauces, vinegar versus molasses, obscure Earth-based flavorings for cooking barbecue and exotic alien choices.

My ride rolled to a stop a short distance from one of the tower entrances and the door popped open of its own accord. Reggie didn't need any further encouragement to exit and I followed his example. Two aliens came towards us, their luminous purple badges identifying them as members of Colson's staff long before I could mark them as Trelniki in the darkness. I assumed they wanted to take charge of the vehicle, but as I stepped away from it they altered their course to intercept me.

"Mr. Conroy, may we have a moment of your time?" Her voice was two octaves higher than mine, its words tinkling like glass.

"I'm sorry, do we know each other?"

"Not as such, no," said the other Trelniki, a male who rumbled in contrast to his colleague. "But of necessity we are here."

"Your necessity or mine?" Reggie had run on ahead, past the aliens, and turned to regard me from the threshold of the port's entrance. Just a pace or two beyond him was light and noise, with no shortage of human beings and other fans of barbecue. Out here there was just the darkness, me, and my two new friends, except I had a very strong feeling friendship wasn't part of the equation.

"Let us say rather, the child's necessity," said the female. "We are concerned you don't properly appreciate her power, or the threat she poses."

"You know about Angela?"

They said nothing, but managed to do it with a disturbing intensity that made me want to keep talking.

"Look, it's under control now. She won't disintegrate anything else."

"She hasn't disintegrated anything," said the male, glancing to his partner for confirmation.

"You weren't there. I know what I saw."

"On the contrary, you saw what you saw, and have misunderstood it. The child's power is not destruction, but rather displacement."

"Excuse me?"

"She did not destroy the thoat. She moved it."

"Moved it? Where?"

Both Trelniki sighed and shrugged at that question. The female raised a hand, drawing my attention back to her. "How can you hope to help her when you don't begin to understand her situation."

Light and warmth and fellowship—not to mention my buffalito—lay a short walk beyond. I shook my head and turned to go. "Look, I don't know what your deal is, or what you think you know, but I don't know you, and—"

Both aliens spread their arms wide, palms out toward. One moved in front of me, putting himself once more between the port's entrance and me. The other stepped behind me. Their outstretched arms acted like a boundary, hemming me in, not quite touching me.

Reggie barked once and began running back toward me, toward the aliens, at breakneck speed.

"We will show you our 'deal'."

And all at once I was squeezing my eyes shut at bright sunlight that hadn't existed an instant ago. Both aliens were gone. So was the night, and the space port too. I was somewhere else. Sometime else. The sky above was a pale green, the sun a deep orange and larger than what we have back in Earth's sky or the one Colson's world orbited. There was sand beneath my feet, and I could hear the soft plish-plash of waves on a shore. Reggie was nowhere to be seen. I stood in a circle made of three squat, roughly humanoid statues, hands interlocking as if in some ritual or dance. The stonework was blocky but polished, translucent and honey-colored, with scatterings of tiny dark flecks, like tiny insects embedded in anthropomorphic amber. None of it made any sense. I turned slowly, looking for the Trelniki, for the space port, for anything remotely familiar. Nothing. I saw the edge of a lake or ocean, the water a vivid blue. I felt the wind on my face and smelled salt in the moist air, but that was it. Nothing here but me and the ring of bright golden stone figures.

"Welcome, Mr. Conroy. Let me begin by apologizing for the abruptness of your visit."

I spun around. One of the statues had spoken, and all were releasing the hands of one another and dropping their arms. The other two bowed their heads or nodded to the one who'd spoken and walked to the water's edge and then beyond, quickly vanishing beneath the waves.

"What's happening? Who are you? Where am I? And how did I get here?"

"I need to discuss the child Angela with you. My name is Ytpino. You're the first human to stand upon this planet. It is some fifty-three thousand light-years from your home, on the other side of the galactic core."

"You expect me to believe I'm not on Colson's World any longer?"

"Believe your own senses."

He had a point. The nearest shoreline should have been several hours ride from me. Night had become day. The sky was the wrong color. Gravity felt slightly off in a different way than it had felt off when I'd first arrived from Earth. I traveled to a different planet, without benefit of vessel or time, and if my host was to be believed I was further from home than any human being had ever been.

"Okay. How did I get here?"

"You were brought here by my fellow Plenum."

"Is that a social organization of some kind? Do you all raise funds for worthwhile charities, or do you limit your activities to kidnapping hypnotists?"

"The Plenum are one race, Mr. Conroy, though to your perceptions we appear as members of other races. We have a team on Colson's World that would seem to be a perfectly ordinary pair of Trelniki, no different from a dozen others of that race. But along with their other duties at the port, they've also been monitoring the situation with the child. After the event at the Festival today, they sought advice from a few elders, expressing concern over your involvement. And they asked me to intervene."

"So, what, your people mimic the appearance of other races?"

"Not at all. The Trelniki are indistinguishable from other Trelniki, down to the cellular level. Just as I am from other Gris, and others of our kind on other worlds are in no way discernible from the natives of those places. But we are also all Plenum."

"What does any of this have to do with an orphaned human child?"

"She too is Plenum."

"Excuse me?"

"The little girl you spent time with today is Plenum. As are all of the 'orphans' that Amadeus Colson has taken in. All of the children on that planet are Plenum."

"If that's true, why do you have a human being raising your kids?"

"Because they are human too. We grow up believing we are precisely what others perceive us to be. It is our way to blend our people with other races, to spread ourselves throughout the galaxy by living amongst the rest of you. We gave Colson a world and long life, and in exchange he agreed to become the progenitor to our next generation, so that as humanity extends itself out into the galaxy we can go with you."

"Why are you telling me this? If you can whisk me across the galaxy you've obvious got more than enough power to conquer humanity if that was your intention. Why this creepy hiding amongst us?"

"It was the assessment of the team that sent you that you needed a fuller understanding."

"Understanding of what? That Plenum can zap giant animals with a wave of a hand and make them go away?"

"Indeed, gone, but not destroyed."

"That's what the Trelniki said. That she's moved it."

"And to convince you of this, they moved you, Mr. Conroy. The Plenum do not destroy. Rather, any two or more of us can open one end of a vortex which provides passage through to the other end, which is created by another collection of Plenum. That is how you arrived here."

"And Gel?"

"She *moved* the creature. Sent it elsewhere."

"You said you need at least two at either end to create a vortex."

"The child is an anomaly. A dangerous fluke of a kind we have seen before and which is not evolutionarily viable. On the extremely rare occasions that this mutation occurs it causes its own destruction."

"Because she can't control it?"

"You understand completely. It is tragic, but inevitable. Our concern, which we communicated to Amadeus Colson, was for the other Plenum in his care who might be injured or lost as a consequence. We hold no sway over a progenitor, but we know he shares our concern. Though it pains him to, he has prepared himself to act for the greater good."

"You mean he's screwing up his courage to kill her."

"For the greater good."

"But I may have given Gel control. It's too early to tell, but what if she masters her ability? What if she stops being a danger to the others?"

"It has never been achieved before, not in the long history of the Plenum."

"You've probably never encountered hypnosis before, or maybe spread your kind among races that were open to hypnosis. You don't know if it will work or not."

"Also true, but would you have us risk the others? You have made Colson's task all the more difficult by giving him false hope."

"You think he's changed his mind? He's giving her a chance?"

"The Plenum do not destroy, nor may we interfere with a progenitor's offspring on the world of their birth. Only he can take the life he has quickened. We bear the child no malice. But we fear for the others. Our children are precious to us and we do not believe your interference will eliminate the problem. Resolution was close at hand, until you arrived."

"You say they're precious to you, but isn't Angela one of your children too? If there's even a chance that I've helped her, isn't it worth seeing it through, to give her that chance?"

"You would have us delay, knowing that every day we wait is another day that could end in disaster?"

"Are all Plenum so fatalistic? We humans have this thing we call hope. It's something all of the Colson's children have had ingrained into them. If you're raising them to blend in with my kind, then shouldn't their nature be part of the decision? To a human being, there's always hope."

Its mouth grimaced. It turned away from me and gestured at the sea. Two amber figures emerged from the sea, whether the earlier Gris or different I couldn't tell. They took up positions around me, forming a loose circle and only then did Ytpino turn back to face me.

"Take another day to explore hope. If you are successful, you will have our gratitude to the end of your days. But if not, and your meddling is found to cost us even one of our new children, we will bring grief to you wherever you find yourself in the galaxy."

"You guys don't believe in half measures, do you?"

"Your actions have already compromised the progenitor's resolve and we fear and he may not be able to restore it before the child accidentally harms another. If you would save yourself, then save the child."

Ytpino brought his arms up, completing some circuit with the other Gris. The world went away and another took its place. I stood in darkness, encircled by two Trelniki. An aerosled waited nearby on the grass. As I stumbled backward Reggie leapt into my arms.

"Save the child," said the female.

"And you save yourself," added the male.

They nodded to me and without another word climbed into the aerosled and drove off.

"Right. And good night to you too."

Reggie licked my face and farted.

Reggie and I made it to our room in one of the port's hotels and the rest of the night passed without further incident. By mid-morning we had wandered back out to the Festival. I let Reggie lure me over to the section where merchants sold a wide range of Festival souvenirs, everything from colorful 'kiss-the-cook' aprons to data chits with recipes and preparation for thousands of variations on barbecue. I had no doubt he had every intention of devouring some overpriced commemorative paperweights if only I'd let him. Instead, I bought one of the Barry Bison plush toys as a gift for Gel. It wasn't quite as large as a buffalito, but it was almost as cute. Reggie sniffed at it suspiciously, whuffled once, and turned his back on the thing.

With shopping done I decided it was time for us to break our fast. We headed toward one of the cooking areas and settled in at a picnic bench between two competitors' booths. One, run by a family from New Achaemenia, set me up with kabobs of seasoned bison steak as well as still-warm lavash they had grilled over a fire pit that used charcoals formed from trees that had never existed on Earth. The neighboring booth belonged to a tiny Argentine who insisted everyone call him El Tio. At dawn he'd started cooking using a portable adobe oven. He plied me with thoat asado cooked with onions and chili peppers, and fed Reggie several plates of offal. Mornings like this reminded me of why I was a foodie: what we cook and how we cook it tells the story of who we are, human or alien, ancient civilization or first generation colony. Despite its focus on barbecue, the Festival understood that. As I basked in the fellowship of wildly diverse approaches to this cuisine, I wondered if Colson himself appreciated it or simply saw it as a marketing tool. That in turn started me thinking again about ways to use his endorsement to expand my newborn company. Ideas danced like sugarplums in my head, and I had just started trying to wipe away some of the grease Reggie had smeared into his beard, when I saw something I knew Colson and I could agree on. Skipping down the row of competitors' booths was Angela in a slightly different, belted sundress and the same pink boots as the day before.

She looked happy and carefree, but she ratcheted that up a notch and squealed when she saw Reggie, her skip transforming to an arm-waving blur as she changed direction and dashed to hug him.

"Gel! Don't get so far ahead." Bethany came running into view an instant later, and slowed when she saw why the girl had rushed off.

I offered her a kabob and a piece of lavash. She declined the meat but took the bread, smiling when she discovered it was still warm. I looked to be certain that Angela was still distracted with Reggie and then handed Bethany the plush bison. "I got this for Gel, if that's all right."

"You didn't have to do that, you know. It's very sweet of you. She'll love it. Gel, come see what Mr. Conroy got you."

Gel popped back up. "For me? Thank you!" She snatched the toy and immediately showed it to Reggie who was busily eating the last of the lavash.

Bethany laughed and as I finished off my kabob I resumed our conversation. "I had an interesting encounter with a Gris last night," I said, and watched confusion pass over her face.

"What's a Gris?"

"Kind of a squat, honey-colored, translucent alien, living on a planet on the other side of the galactic core."

The look of confusion on her face was too perfect. Back in college she'd run track and been a business major. As far as I knew she'd never tried her hand at acting. Which meant she really had no idea what I was talking about. "Nevermind, I—"

"Bef'ny! He's eating the plate!"

Gel had pulled herself up onto the bench alongside Reggie, and had just finished feeding him one of El Tio's ceramo plates, keeping her fingers out of the way as my buffalito took large bites out of it and dropping the last piece when she had nowhere left to hold it. I gave Reggie a scritch behind his ears and explained, "He likes to eat whatever I'm eating, but he can eat anything, really. Plates and clothes and furniture. Anything."

"Oh. He must have really really sharp teeth!" She chewed on her lower lip and while cradling her plush toy against her chest, inspected her fingertips to make sure they were all still there.

"Well, not so much. It's kind of a trick that all buffalitos have. But don't worry, he won't accidentally eat your fingers. Reggie never ever bites people, not even by accident."

"Never?"

I picked up the remaining fragment that had once been part of a plate and held it in the fist of one hand while I coaxed Reggie to open his mouth wide with the other. Then I shoved as much of the first hand in as I could. Reggie's mouth clamped down on my fist, and I could feel his tongue squirming in between my fingers. When I pulled my hand out, it was empty and my buffalo dog was swallowing the last bit. I waggled my fingers at Gel.

She giggled and hugged him again. "How come the big buffalos don't eat plates?"

Bethany pulled the child to her feet and set her on the ground. "Our buffalo come from Earth, honey. Mr. Conroy's friend comes from . . . well, I'm not really sure, but somewhere else."

"Can I feed him stuff?"

"If it's all right with Bethany."

"You're sure she won't make him sick?"

I shrugged. "I haven't been able to yet, and I've fed him everything from molten lead to industrial acid. If Gel thinks she can put him off his feed, she's welcome to try."

"Can I, Bef'ny?"

Bethany looked at me like I'd grown an extra head, then reached down to take Gel's hand. "Why not? But I'm going to come with you."

"'Kay! C'mon, Reggie, I'm gonna get you rocks and stuff to eat!"

Gel waved at my buffalito and trotted off in search of some small stones, dragging Bethany along. Reggie glanced up at me for approval, yipped once, and careened after her. I finished the last of my asado before pulling a warm, cloth towel from one of the stands that had been erected throughout the Festival for that purpose and cleaned my hands, then turned to follow Bethany and the others.

A Trelniki stood in my way. Picture a tall and slender topiary project, a tiny-leaved bush the color of sand in the shape of a human being.

"She doesn't know about us."

I stared at the alien. Female, with a purple badge, and I made the connection from the night before. But, to be sure, I asked, "Us? Us who?"

"We met last evening, Mr. Conroy. My name is Yeung. My cohort Bedra. We are the Plenum assigned to this world to assist Mr. Colson should he have need of us as he raises our children."

"And his great-granddaughter doesn't know anything about this?"

"She believes the orphans arrive from offworld as infants, and she knows that upon reaching their majority they leave to receive schooling upon some human world. On the rare occasions when one has cause to return, she is diverted away from the ranch or is offworld herself. This is how Mr. Colson prefers things."

"And you just do it that way, because he *prefers* it so?"

Yeung shrugged. "He is the progenitor. Upon this planet, he has final say over all Plenum of his seed."

"His seed? If they're descended from him, why don't they look like him?"

"The process draws upon his entire genetic heritage, not simply the current expression of his genes. He is the representative of your race to our people, and the children resemble *all* of his forebears."

"Yeah, but—"

She cut me off, lifting her chin and waving a hand in the direction Bethany had gone. "As Ytpino explained to you. It is not our way to interfere with the progenitor upon his world, but too it is his wish to keep his great-granddaughter ignorant of the full arrangement. Please do not resume your attempts to query her about the events of last evening. She has no knowledge of them, and moreover it may only cause her to ask questions the progenitor does not wish to answer."

"That's your only purpose here?"

"That, and to observe 'hope,' and to confirm that your treatment is truly efficacious."

I nodded, turned to go after Bethany, then stopped. "And if it's not?"

The Trelniki shrugged again. "Then it falls to my cohort and I to meet with Mr. Colson, and offer our support in his culling of the aberration. Now, please, go after the child, Mr. Conroy. Stay with her, and ensure your efforts are not in vain. We very much want you to succeed, even as we prepare for the alternative."

I left, eager to rejoin the others. I found them by another barbecue booth. Gel had tucked the plush toy into the belt of her sundress. Under Bethany's supervision and wearing quilted oven mitts intended for hands much larger than her own, she was using a pair of metal tongs to feed Reggie red hot coals from a cooking pit. A trio of braai aficionados representing the best meat grilled on the African continent watched with a mix of wonder and horror, all thoughts of barbecue presumably stripped from their heads. Reggie snarfed the coals from the tongs as quickly as the little girl could serve them up, swallowing each in a single bite and without any apparent discomfort from the heat or the composition. Gel was delighted.

"Mr. Conroy! Look! Reggie's eating fire!"

At the mention of my name Bethany turned to smile and wave. Reggie swung his head around too, saw me, and immediately trotted over. Gel had just come around again with the tongs and another glowing coal for him to snack on, only to find he wasn't in position to receive it. She tried to follow him with it, but as she did the tongs slipped from her grip in the over-sized mittens. The coal fell to the ground and bounced toward her. She scrambled away from it, back-peddling her feet while windmilling her arms. Gel put a good *pedaling* distance between herself and the coal, but in doing so she stumbled against the ring of low stones that defined the cook pit and fell over. Her right hand landed in the fire.

The mitts Gel wore had been designed to keep the wearer safe when handling extremely hot objects, but they had never been

143

intended for direct contact with open flame. The one on her right hand caught fire and blazed like a torch.

Reggie barked. Gel screamed. Bethany turned to see what had happened.

And I watched as flame, oven mitt, and the entire fire pit winked out of existence leaving behind a few wisps of smoke and a ring of barren ground to show where it had been.

"Honey, are you okay? Let me see your hand?" Bethany knelt in front of the girl, cradling a tiny pink hand in both of hers. Gel was crying and had her face buried in Bethany's hair, but otherwise didn't appear injured. The remaining mitten slipped from her left hand.

Reggie pressed forward until his own face was against Gel's, whuffling with encouragement or sympathy or just friendly consolation. Gel spared one of the arms she was using to hang onto Bethany to hug Reggie as well.

"Shhh, it's okay, it's okay. You're fine. Everything's fine." Bethany looked up at me, relief on her face. "She's not hurt. She was just scared."

But she wasn't fine. Whatever hope for control I thought I'd provided had come unraveled, and in hindsight it seemed pretty obvious. It wasn't about trees and wind and remaining calm in the face of the storm. Hypnosis or no, I couldn't expect a child to be able to master her fear or anger before some part of her automatically reacted. As had just happened.

Gel wasn't fine, and I was scared.

The confused family from South Africa hovered solicitously as Bethany opened her kit and gave Gel a sedative. She lifted her eyes to meet mine as she finished, and the question there was all too clear. I left Reggie with her and ran back, looking for a port employee. Yeung met me as soon as I was out of Bethany's view.

"I felt it. The child's ability has manifested again."

"My hypnotic block didn't work."

"Obviously. She must be taken to the progenitor. I have already summoned an aerosled."

"She's been sedated. Bethany can keep her drugged until we can come up with a new plan."

"Unlikely, Mr. Conroy. As you saw yesterday, medicating her no longer works. Moreover, the period between manifestations has dwindled and our past experience suggests it will soon cease entirely. A new plan will not be forthcoming. This situation is extremely rare, but the Plenum have endured it before. We have explained to the progenitor what he must do. It is . . . more difficult for mammalian races, but it must be done all the same."

"Colson is *not* going to kill her!"

"Then he condemns one or more of his other children. Is that a better choice?"

"Can't you . . . can't you send her somewhere?"

"In her current state, the child would destabilize any vortex, and likely destroy those attempting to form the conduit for her."

"Well, what about a ship?"

"Her ability is not dependent upon planetary gravity. Here, or in space, she remains a danger to everyone around her. There is only one solution."

"But—"

"Return to the child. Inform Ms. Colson that a vehicle is coming. You may accompany them if you desire. It will be best for all concerned if we can conclude this business without delay."

Reggie chose that moment to come trotting up to me, having made a distinction between being left to wait and being told to stay. He sat on my foot and stared up at Yeung who stared back and scowled. "Your creature is an unaccounted factor in all of this."

"He's just my companion animal."

"Perhaps. It may simply be that the child's ability had reached a natural growth spurt in its maturation. And yet, the ineffectiveness of her medication as well as her last two manifestations coincide with her encounters with it."

"With *him*," I said.

"My apologies."

"And I thought the Trelniki were all far too rational to mistake correlation with causality, or does your dual nature spare you that tradition?"

She blushed at that, the leaves of her cheeks and forehead going almost as purple as her employee badge. "All Plenum partake of the best and worst of their generation. I would be grateful were you to allow me to study him and explicitly test my hypotheses. There are

145

no Plenum among the Arconi, and their buffalo dogs are more rare even than Plenum. The sacrifice of a pet is a small thing compared to the potential knowledge to be gained."

An aerosled appeared at the far end of our aisle, gingerly moving forward as Festival-goers noticed it and got out of its way. I stooped and picked up my buffalito. "I told you, Reggie's my companion; he's not a pet. And even if he were, the answer would be the same. You want a lab specimen, you can get one yourself. But you won't be acquiring it from me or my company."

Yeung did not reply, but stepped aside as the aerosled closed. I turned my back on her and followed after the vehicle. When I caught up with it, Bethany had already climbed in and was securing Gel to the rear couch. The driver, Bedra, Yeung's cohort, stood outside.

"We're coming with you," I said, putting Reggie next to Gel. He settled in against her, looking as protective and loyal as any Earthborn mutt ever had.

"I'm taking her back to the ranch. Gran needs to know what's happened."

"I suspect he already does," I said, earning me a look of confusion from Bethany and one of annoyance from Bedra.

"Do not interfere, Mr. Conroy," said the Trelniki.

Bethany moved to the far end of the forward couch and waved me in next to her. She hit a switch and the door sealed behind me. An instant later she began guiding the vehicle back through the narrow lanes of the Festival. "It's what I promised I would do. She could hurt someone."

"Bethany, he doesn't think he has a choice. He's going to do a lot more than hurt her."

"Don't you think I know that? She can't live around other people anymore. He's going to have to send her away."

"What?"

She wiped at her eyes as her tears began, nodding to me. "I told him I would go too, to take care of her. There's a hydrosled waiting, when he decides it's time, to take us to an island far enough away that we'll be safe. It's a risk, but what else can I do?"

I wanted to believe her, but last night's chat with Ytpino hadn't include an isolation option, and Yeung had been very clear. Bethany didn't know it, but the only choice Colson had left was to kill Angela.

Bethany didn't bother with the autopilot buttons. Once we cleared the Festival grounds she did something to the controls that overcame the governor, raised us significantly higher above the ground than before, pushed the aerosled to its maximum speed and aimed for ranch house.

We'd sped onward, Gel asleep in back, and Bethany and I lost in our own thoughts. After several minutes and more than a few kilometers the vehicle's comm broke the silence. It was Amadeus Colson.

"Bethany, stop wherever you are and activate your emergency beacon."

"What? Why? We'll be home soon, Gran."

"Which is the last place I want you to be. Do what I tell you. I'm on my way to you now. Colson out."

We spun in a wide arc as Bethany slowed and eventually stopped us. Her hands shook on the controls and her face had paled.

"What's wrong? You didn't react this strongly when Gel—"

"He's left the house!"

"So?"

"He doesn't . . . He never . . . If he leaves the ranch, he'll die!"

"What are you talking about?"

"There's something there, something at the ranch that keeps him young. Both of us. I can go offworld and my clock just starts again, and when I return I get young until I hit the age I was when I first came here. For him though, maybe because he's so old, it just keeps him in middle age. But the price of it is he can't leave. Ever."

"Then why would he—"

"Because he's going to do it!" She spun on the couch and looked back at Gel, still asleep with Reggie at her side. "Don't you see? He's going to kill her, but he doesn't want any of the children to see or know until it's too late. He's taking it all on himself to spare them any part of it."

We waited there for half an hour before a speck appeared on the horizon and rapidly grew into another aerosled. If I thought Bethany had been driving fast, it was nothing compared to the speed of Colson. He rumbled past us, doubled back, overshot us again, and eventually dumped enough velocity to manage a jarring stop alongside our vehicle. When he got out he wasn't alone; a squat, oddly translucent, honey-colored figure stumbled from the vehicle after him.

We climbed out of our aerosled to meet them. I nodded to them both. "Mr. Colson, Ytpino."

Bethany whirled to stare at me. "You know that being? Gran? What's going on? What, who is that?"

"I am Amadeus's oldest living friend," said Ytpino. "Sixty-three years ago I found his scoutship floating dead in space. He was near death but I revived him. We struck a bargain and I brought him here. Everything he has built here goes back to that day."

Colson took her hands in his. His voice rasped as he said, "I never knew your grandfather, Bethy. Your great-grandmother never told me I'd fathered a child on her. I was the last of my line when I went into space and I expected the family name to end with me. Then Ytpino saved me."

"What are you saying?"

Colson gestured toward the alien. "By all measurable means he's a member of a race known as the Gris. But he's also a Plenum. They claim to be as old as space, and integrally tied to it. They spread their genetics around to other sapient forms so they can live among most of the people of the galaxy."

"Your people are new to space," said Ytpino. "The bargain I made with Amadeus was for him to father a new branch of my people. Plenum, who are also human. They used my genes to quicken untold numbers of eggs hidden in vaults beneath the house."

Bethany's jaw dropped as she put it together. She stared at her great-grandfather. "So all the orphans here..."

"My children. Your great uncles and great aunts. Thousands of them. I raised them to be people of good character, saw to it that they attended the best schools in Human Space, and sent them out to find their destinies. Who could ask for a greater legacy?"

"Gran, why are you telling me this now after all this time? Why are we here? Why is he here?"

Ytpino motioned to me and I stepped away, giving the other two at least the illusion of privacy. Colson looked older than he had the night before, but that could have been from the pain on his face.

"Because it ends today. I told Ytpino I couldn't continue our bargain after today."

"But…"

"You know why, Bethy."

"But the hydrosled . . . the plans we made for the island…"

"I was just trying to spare you, Bethy. I can no more sacrifice you than I could any of the other children."

"But I'm willing to—"

"No. No one else can do this for me and it has to be done. Give me your cattle baton."

Her hand shook as she began to hand it over, then refused to let go as she realized too late what a device designed to stun a buffalo or thoat would do to a little girl.

Colson wrestled it from her grasp and signaled to Gris. "Ytpino, keep her still." He stared at the baton like he held a serpent in his hand. "I have to kill one of my own children. Today, right now. Angela has to die before she hurts anyone else. And I have to kill her."

The alien grabbed Bethany's arms and held her back. That left only me. I didn't think, I just moved, and the next instant I was tackling a hundred thirteen year old man and wrestling him to the ground.

"I can't let you kill an innocent child!"

As we grappled he must have activated the baton. Even a glancing blow was more enough to scramble my nervous system. He struggled up onto his knees and steadied himself for a direct strike on me as I lay there twitching and helpless.

"I can't let you stop me. She has to die!"

As the baton began to descend I heard my buffalito barking, followed by a child's scream.

"POP POP! NO!!!"

His hand paused at the sound of her words. He turned to look at the child. One moment she was there, clearly visible through the open door of the aerosled, kneeling on the rear couch with her arms wrapped around Reggie. In the next instant she was running toward us, Reggie racing alongside her, and the aerosled, over a ton of fabricated ceramo and metal, was gone.

Colson staggered to his feet and lunged. She dodged easily and he lumbered after. Bethany had broken free of the Gris and pursued her great-grandfather. The chase that followed would have been comical if it hadn't been so tragic. A terrified six year-old girl darted across the grassy plain, followed by the old man she just learned was her father and the young woman who'd always been like a big sister but was really a niece two generations removed. They circled the aerosled that had brought Colson and Ytpino. Gel bobbed and weaved, all the while shouting "No! No! No!" Bethany had a grip on Colson's arm, keeping him from even trying to reach for the girl with the baton. Reggie ran over to me, licked my face once to assure himself I was okay, and then began racing loops around the rest of them as if it were all a great game. Ytpino stood motionless, either because of his earlier explanation that he could not interfere with any of a progenitor's offspring or because he simply wasn't built to run after a human child.

I had just managed to throw off the worst of the stun's paralysis and sit up, when Gel's criss-crossing, madcap dash led her back towards me. She dodged at the last moment, Reggie hot on her heels, and threw herself into the remaining aerosled. The buffalito leapt in just as the door closed and locked. Through the windshield I could see Gel clasping her hands together and slamming them down on one of the autopilot dumbswitches. An instant later the vehicle rose on a cushion of air and left the four of us standing helplessly choking on its dust as it sped off in the direction of the space port.

"I have sent word to the Plenum at the port," said Ytpino. "They will send a new vehicle for us."

Bethany stared at him. "What about Gel? Can they override her sled? Maybe slow it down, keep it going in circles until we can catch her?"

"Alas, they cannot."

"Can't, or won't?" I said as Bethany helped me to my feet. I impressed myself by not falling back over.

Ytpino gave a small bow. "They are the same in this instance. As I told you, we cannot interfere with the child while she is on this world. We can render Amadeus assistance, provide information and advice, but no more. Direct action we must leave to the progenitor."

"She's just a little girl," said Bethany. "She's just learned that the man who's raised her, the person she loves most in the world, is her father and he intends to kill her. She's terrified!"

"And in her terror she zapped an aerosled and everything in it," said Colson. "Sedation no longer works on her, and if she still has a refractory period delaying her, it's no more than an hour now, not a matter of days. She's out of control."

"You're wrong," I said. "This is more control than she's ever shown."

Colson gasped, bent over with his hands on knees as he tried to catch his breath. "What are you talking about, Conroy?"

I gestured where our aerosled had been. Lying in the vehicle-shaped imprint on the grass was the plush bison I'd given Gel. "She didn't zap everything in the sled. She kept Reggie and she kept her toy. That speaks of a selective, if unconscious, control. And this time it wasn't reflexive like when she was about to be trampled by the thoat or when her mitt caught fire."

"But it was," said Ytpino. "This was a fear response like the others."

"Fear yes, but not like the others. She reacted to what she heard. She understood the meaning of the words. She didn't act just out of instinct. Otherwise, why is Colson still here? Why didn't she do him like she did the thoat? Why get rid of a vehicle that wasn't a threat instead of the man who was?"

"You're saying it was a plan? To eliminate one sled and take the other? That she planned this?" Bethany shook her head.

"Not consciously, no. But I think she's learning?"

Colson shook his head. "And what if you're wrong? What if zapping the aerosled is actually a sign of the indiscriminate expansion of her ability? A sign that the next time she'll take out one or more innocent bystanders? Perhaps some of her siblings? No, I may have waited too long as it is. She doesn't know how to override the autopilot; it will take her back to the port. We'll follow her there, and when I find her I'll end this."

We were spared from further debate by the appearance of another aerosled in the distance. It sped towards us and settled to the plain a few meters away. Colson rushed to it even before the doors opened and the two Trelniki, Yeung and Bedra, emerged. I grabbed Bethany's arm. She barely moved, just lifted her head to gaze at me with despair.

"Come on. We have to go with him. We have to stop him!" I dragged her with me to the vehicle and pushed her in before Colson could shut the doors.

"But what if he's right? What if this is the only way?"

I ignored Colson's glare as I climbed in too.

"But what if he's wrong?" And none of us said another word all the way back to the space port.

I thought Bethany had pushed our aerosled to its limits on our aborted trip to the ranch house. Now Colson proved there were piloting tricks he'd never taught her. He burned out the vehicle's engines in returning us to the port. We landed hard and loud, almost flipping the sled completely over before we slewed sideways and finally came to a stop by crashing into Gel's sled where she'd abandoned it at the edge of the Festival grounds.

Colson flung open the door and hobbled from the vehicle while it was still vibrating. He paused and turned back to us, the baton in his hand. He'd aged at least ten years.

"I have to do this. Stay out of my way." Then he was gone.

"Bethany, he's not only going to kill Gel, he's killing himself in the process. You have to go after him, talk to him. You have to stop him."

"You heard him. There isn't any other option. He's out of time."

"Time may be the thing that Gel really needs right now. Maybe she can't get conscious control over her ability like I tried to give her, but her unconscious mind is starting to get a handle on it. We need to help her bridge that gap between conscious and unconscious."

"You're just guessing. She may never be able to do that. And right now she's somewhere in the middle of the Festival where she could be a danger to hundreds of innocent people who know nothing about Gran or the aliens he made a bargain with."

"You're right. I might be completely wrong. But if you have to risk being mistaken, wouldn't you rather do so on the side that gives Gel a chance at life? You need to stall him." I climbed out of the aerosled and started out in a different direction from Colson.

152

"Where are you going?"

"To find Gel before your great-grandfather does."

Colson had headed into the thickest portion of the Festival, the cooking areas where the different competitors vied for one of the dozen trophies that would eventually be awarded for best barbecue in each of the different divisions. The Festival teamed with cooks and judges, staffers and visitors. If I were a little girl looking to hide from a murderous old man, it might seem like as good place to do so as any other, and Colson probably thought so too. But I had something he didn't; I had the plush buffalo that Gel had spared. And I knew something Colson didn't know. I knew about Reggie.

I remembered Gel's tight-fisted grip in Reggie's fur, and the way he had pulled her through the crowds of the Festival the day they'd met. Just as I remembered his preference for the denser offerings at the souvenir booths over the food stands. Likely Gel would have calmed down some during the ride back to the port, but she'd still be scared, and still taking comfort and possibly guidance from my buffalo dog. I trusted to that and plunged deeper into the Festival in search of geegaws and keepsakes of barbecue glory and hidey holes for an alien animal and a little girl.

"Reggie! Where are you, boy?" I called for him as I checked out every vendor, stuck my head into each stall. As I was about to pass the eighth stand I was rewarded by a quickly cut-off bark and a harshly whispered 'shhhh!' I doubled back and began searching through a crate overflowing with commemorative t-shirts in an endless variety of garish colors. Something squirmed at the bottom of the box as I began digging through it and seconds later my buffalito had jumped up and was licking my face. Behind him, one hand still holding on to Reggie, was Gel.

That's when the idea hit me. Like a thoat colliding at full charge. The piece that was missing, the reason why my earlier hypnotic fix hadn't fixed anything. Gel's unconscious mind knew what it needed, had found it, and now held it out to me.

And provided I could avoid getting zapped by the girl, I knew how to take that missing piece and help her build the bridge she needed.

"Hi there, Gel. Do you remember me?" I stepped back from her box she'd been hiding in, holding the plush bison in front of me with both hands.

Tight-lipped and grim, she nodded.

"Thanks for taking such good care of Reggie for me. I bet he was really scared. Thank you for being so brave for him."

Gel kept her eyes locked on me but said nothing, did nothing.

"You left your own buffalito behind by accident. I thought you might miss him so I brought him along. He seems really happy to see you. Does he have a name?"

Her gaze shifted to the plush and comic buffalo in my hands, then back to me, searching my face. Was I serious or was I mocking her. She chewed her lip while she seemed to think it over and a moment later said, "Barry. Barry Buffalito."

I eased forward just far enough to set the toy down and stepped back. Gel took hold of it with her free hand.

"Hello, Barry. I'm very very happy to meet you. I know that you and Gel are going to be the best of friends, just like Reggie and me."

Ever so slightly, Gel wriggled her hand, causing the toy to nod in agreement.

"Good. I'm glad you think so too. Oh, that reminds me. Gel?"

"Yeah?"

"Janus Banana."

Fifteen minutes later, Gel and I came strolling through the Festival together, my left hand in her right. A couple hundred aromas, by turns succulent and sweet, spicy and compelling, savory and mouth-watering, battled for our attention as steamed, roasted, smoked, grilled, baked, basted, boiled, braised, grimped, swerzled, and sun-dried meats of several species and worlds of origin represented the best of all possible manifestations of barbecue. Reggie lay straddled across my right forearm, lolling his head against my chest. Gel had Barry pinned against her, its weighted legs flopping over the side of her arm. We were just two friends taking their buffalitos for a walk on a lovely afternoon, even if we were the ones doing the actual walking. All around us people delighted in the best Festival the planet had ever known. That changed when Colson shouted my name.

"Conroy! Step away from my child."

Everyone recognized the voice and recognized the power behind it. Like characters in a gunfight scene on a dirt main street in a Western historical, the people who had been laughing and sampling, arguing and judging, fled our aisle and sought cover and a safe view, leaving it empty except for me and Gel and—barely ten meters away—Amadeus Colson. Instead of a six-shooter, he held a cattle baton.

"There's no need, sir. Your, uh, problem's been solved."

"I want to believe that. You have no idea how badly I do, but I know better. We both know how this has to end."

Gel's hand tightened in mine. "Is Pop Pop still mad at me? Why does he look so old? Is he sick?"

I knelt down so that I was eye-level with Gel. "He's not mad at you, and he's not sick; he's just very very tired." From her expression I could tell she knew part of what I'd said was a lie, but couldn't puzzle out which part.

Time was catching up with Colson. Twenty-four hours ago he could have been mistaken for forty-two, silvery head notwithstanding. That number had climbed to eighty now. In less than an hour he looked to have lost twenty pounds. Deep wrinkles creased his face. His eyes appeared sunken. His thin frame had acquired a hunch and the hand that gripped the baton shook with an uncontrolled tremor.

"Step away; I won't tell you again."

"Even if I believed that, Mr. Colson, it wouldn't matter. We've both seen that you're in no shape to chase down a little girl and ask her to hold still while you use that baton on her?"

"They're not just for close work." He raised his hand and gestured above our heads with the baton. I followed the direction with my gaze and finally noticed a pair of ceramo drones hovering out of reach, their stunners aimed right at us. I pulled Gel in against me, blocking the drones from a direct shot at her. Colson directed the drones lower. They swirled around us, dipping closer. Having had a taste of Colson's baton I didn't know if I could survive a direct stun capable of subduing a buffalo, but Gel certainly couldn't.

"Gel, do you remember what we talked about a bit ago, when we were back up in the tree?"

"You was telling me all about buffalitos, like Reggie and Barry."

"That's right, and how, as their friends, it's up to us to make sure they eat when they're supposed to."

"I remember."

I pointed above at the drones. "Barry is hungry right now. I bet he'd love to eat those things. Can you help him with that?"

The drones were just out of reach, darting from side to side as I pivoted to keep myself between them and the girl.

"Oh sure. C'mon, Barry. Yummy time." She gripped the plush toy across its back and thrust her arm out in the direction of the drones, bobbing it up and down as if it was chewing. "Nom nom nom!"

The drones went away.

That's when I realized that I'd been shaking.

I looked up to find Colson had halved the distance between us. The baton was still in his hand as he reached out toward us. I pointed it out to Gel.

"Is Barry still hungry? Look, Pop Pop is holding a treat for him."

"Nom nom nom!"

Colson's hand was empty. He stared at it, wriggling his fingers as if counting them. He let the hand fall to his side.

"What did you do, Conroy?"

"I didn't do anything. That was all Gel."

"Nuh uh!" said Gel. "Barry ate it all up."

"Barry?" Colson stared down at the toy in his daughter's hand and then back up at me.

"Barry is her pet buffalito. It's her responsibility to make sure he only eats when he's supposed to. She's responsible for his meals. And she knows that buffalitos can eat anything."

"Nuh uh! They don't eat people or other living things."

I smiled and met Colson's gaze. "A very good point, Gel. Thanks for reminding me. Barry would *never* eat someone. Just things."

"But how…"

"I told you, her unconscious was already working out the control. She just needed a bridge to her conscious mind. A focusing point. That's Barry's job."

"I still don't understand…" His voice trailed off, weak and breathless.

"She's not *zapping* things. It's not disintegration. Ytpino explained that she's sending them somewhere. It took me a while to reframe it this way, but when a buffalito eats something he makes it

156

'go away' too. I had the right idea, just the wrong metaphor. And I needed a tool. Now Gel has both."

Tears were streaming down Colson's wrinkled cheeks. "I don't have to…"

"No, sir. I don't think you do."

"Gran! Gran! There you are! What are you—"

I looked up and saw Bethany running towards us. She'd lost her hat somewhere, and her hair streamed out behind her, reminding me again of how she'd looked back in college running the relay. She could easily be nineteen still. I turned back to her great-grandfather.

"If we get you back to your home—"

"Yes, the aging will reverse. Hurry, please. I'm not in such a rush to end things now."

Five minutes later I had eased him into another aerosled and Bethany was piloting us back to the ranch. He'd aged another ten years and lost consciousness by then, but as I watched his breathing grew stronger and his color improved. When we reached the house, a mob of his children rushed out to tend to him and carry him to their infirmary, but he was already looking a mere septuagenarian.

Two days had passed since I'd introduced Gel to Barry. Amadeus Colson looked and felt middle-aged again. Recent events had taken the edge off his usual arrogance and general crankiness, but it was anyone's guess if the change was permanent or would fade as time resumed passing him by. A collection of teenagers had arrived on individual aerosleds, fresh from riding the range and armed with brass instruments which they used to mark the last day of the Festival with fanfare and tuckets. A delegation of purple-badged Dlabble and Renz awarded trophies and ribbons for various barbecue competitors, and more quietly signed and handed out a number of lucrative contracts for importers of the coveted Colson's World meats and cheeses.

My room at one of the space port's two hotels had been comped and upgraded to a luxury suite, the swankiest accommodations that Colson had allowed to be built there. I'd been assured by the manager—a very pleasant Dlabble whom everyone called 'Dave'—that planetary heads of state had stayed in that same room. Not wanting to be rude, I refrained from asking him if they'd found the thread count on the linens as stingey as I did.

I was sitting in the parlor of my suite in a comfortable lounge chair upholstered in surprisingly soft thoat leather. I had a cold bottle of Uncle Waldo's Raspberry Rootbeer in one hand, and with the other I lazily fed corundum nodules from a paper bag to Reggie sprawled upon my lap. The bag and the soda had been provided by Ytpino, who along with Bethany Colson occupied a matching couch on the other side of a low coffee table from my chair.

"So what happens now?" I said.

Ytpino made a gesture that involved shrugging and unshrugging his shoulders and waggling his hands. No doubt it conveyed great meaning to another Gris, but it did nothing for me. Seeing my non-reaction he added, "Events on this planet resume their normal sequence. Everything is as it was before."

"Not quite everything. I can think of two differences. You're no longer hiding the truth from Bethany."

She nodded in agreement. "Which just means I can take a more active hand in some of the subterfuge required to keep up the story of Gran's orphanage."

I held up one finger. "That's one."

"And the second?" asked Ytpino.

I added a finger. "I now know that the galaxy is full of Plenum. That you have the means to travel anywhere in the galaxy without physical requirement or delay, effectively subverting the system of portals that everyone else believes to be the only means of traveling between the stars at useful speeds. And I know that you're hiding in plain sight among the other races."

"Oh. That."

"It doesn't concern you?"

"Only Plenum can detect other Plenum. To everyone else we are exactly as we appear. Who would you tell, Mr. Conroy? And more importantly, who would believe your paranoid tales? Aliens possessing instantaneous teleportation? Beings capable of blending in among all the races of the galaxy? No, this does not concern me."

"What does?"

Ytpino scowled, the expression looking like it ran all the way through his translucent, amber face. He turned to Bethany who far from sharing his displeasure wore a sunny smile.

"Gran told the Plenum that they're in your debt."

"Does that mean he'll endorse my company? That's what I originally came here for."

She shook her head. "No, he insists anything with his name on it could draw unwanted attention to the generation of Plenum he's raising. He asked me to apologize on his behalf, but he also said you'd understand. That, and he'll try to make it up to you in other ways."

"What other ways?"

Bethany gestured back to the Gris. The scowl hadn't gone away.

"It has been suggested that for ensuring the survival of the child Gel, that you are entitled to transportation."

"Transportation?"

"For life," said Bethany.

"Excuse me?"

"Within certain limits. We cannot provide you the means to identify Plenum on other worlds, but when you have real need there are certain code phrases that can be used to allow them to contact you."

I laughed. "So, what? I post an ad on the local Globalink and someone shows up to provide a trip to the other side of the galaxy?"

"Essentially. Though it would always be two someones."

I let that sink in. It was the ultimate first-class ticket. "What's the catch?"

"It's limited to those worlds where Plenum reside."

Bethany smirked. "And apparently they don't have any on Earth, or most of the other planets in Human Space."

"Not quite accurate," said Ytpino. "There is currently a pair of Plenum on Earth, but they only passing through. They will be gone before you return. But fear not, the lack of Plenum in Human Space is only a temporary situation. One that Amadeus is helping us to resolve."

"Right. But in the meantime, you owe me a debt that I can't collect."

Ytpino stood up. "We will meet again, Mr. Conroy. The progenitor has made it clear that the debt must be honored, and it falls to me personally to keep you apprised. Until then, I bid you and your companion animal safe travels, albeit by more conventional means." He nodded to Bethany, bowed to me, and let himself out of the room.

"I should be going too. Gran wants me to pick some of the older children to become a round-the-clock babysitting squad for Gel."

"She's doing okay?"

"She's spent the last two days introducing Barry to all of the other children, one at a time. Some of the younger ones were jealous of him and I had to defuse a plot to play a prank on Gel by swiping and hiding him. Gran called everyone in—and I mean everyone, including the older teens who work in the fields or on the range—and created a new law: under no circumstances does anyone separate Gel from her toy buffalito. Ever."

"Is that going to work? I mean, I'm no expert, but don't some kids deliberately push and test all sorts of rules?

"They do. That's why before coming here I met with our vendors and bought up all the remaining bison mascot plushies from the Festival. I figured it couldn't hurt to have some backups, just in case.

"Yeah, that's probably a good idea."

She smiled. "I thought so too. Well, goodbye, Conroy. Thank you so much for all you've done. It's been wonderful seeing you again."

"You too. Even if you haven't changed a hair from the girl I knew in school." I dumped Reggie from my lap and stood up so Bethany and I could hug farewell. The hug lasted a long while, but even so ended too soon.

She left, and I followed a few minutes later. Nearly all of the people who had come in for the Festival had moved on and it was time for me to do the same. The last of those retro-fitted tourists buses had arrived earlier in the day and would be lifting off in a few hours to pass through the portal that linked Colson's World to the rest of the galaxy and, most importantly for me, a much nicer cruising vessel that would take me back to Earth and my new company. With my few belongings stowed in my carpet bag and Reggie tucked securely under my arm, I wandered through the few shops of the port searching for an appropriate souvenir of the trip and some small gifts to bring back for Dr. Elizabeth Penrose. I had no idea whether or not she liked barbecue.

"Are you Mr. Conroy?"

The question came from a Renz in the livery of the space port.

"That's me. Can I help you?"

She handed me a disposable padd. "Priority message for you from Earth. Came in on this morning's ship. I've been looking to deliver it. If you want to send a reply, you can compose it at your convenience and give it to the purser when you board. They'll transmit it as soon as they clear the portal. It will beat you to Earth by a few days."

"Thanks." I tipped the messenger, and checked the return address. My blood ran cold when I saw it was from Dr. Penrose. I couldn't imagine any reason why she'd contact me unless the news was truly dire. Had my newborn company met with disaster already? I keyed the display and immediately relaxed. Nothing so dire after all, but the need to return home with a really nice gift had definitely increased.

Apparently *someone* had been thoughtful enough to deliver an assortment of smoked meats and cheeses to my new headquarters, on the order of several thousand kilos of each, and they were filling up the lobby.

TELEPATHIC INTENT

I sold "Buffalo Dogs" to Warren Lapine, who published it in the Summer 2001 issue of *Absolute Magnitude*. I'd been sending him fiction for a couple years, and while I'd come close to making a sale with a few other pieces, that was the first one to break through. This made me very happy, and Warren had seemed pretty pleased with it as well. So naturally, when I had the idea for another Conroy story, I sent it to Warren first. Instead of responding by mail or email, he phoned me.

"It's a great story," he said, "I'm not going to buy it."

I'd heard both of these phrases before (the latter more frequently than the former, alas), but never in the same sentence. I expressed my confusion to Warren with a muttered "Huh?" and he repeated himself. I asked him if there was anything that could be fixed or tightened or changed that would make the story more desirable to him, but he assured me it was wonderful as it was, and again that he wasn't going to buy it. After some more prodding he explained that he was putting out four issues a year, and was looking for the ten best stories he could find. In that grand scheme, my story was number twelve. Sorry, not going to buy it.

I spent a few more days being confused, and then queried Steve Miller, half of the brilliant writing team responsible for that series of stories and novels known as the Liaden Universe. Curiously, there'd been a Liaden story in that same issue of *Absolute Magnitude* as my first Conroy story, and I'd come to know Steve from panels on self-promotion at the Nebula Awards Weekends. To keep Liaden fans happy between novels, he'd started his own small press and had been publishing chapbooks of two or three stories—some reprints, some new work—and I wanted to pick his brain regarding the expense of such an endeavor. My thinking was that if Warren wasn't going to publish my new story, maybe I could bundle it with the first one and publish it myself as a chapbook, and begin to build an audience.

Timing, as has been noted, is everything. Steve told me he was at the point where he wanted to begin experimenting with publishing chapbooks of other authors' works, and perhaps I might like to be the first. All at once I went from spending my own money to self-publish and hope to find an audience to being paid a modest amount to be published by someone who already had an audience eager to read similar stuff. It was the start of a very satisfying business relationship and friendship. SRM Publishing went on to do three Conroy chapbooks in all, but it all began with this next story, my first attempt at a science fiction, romance, murder mystery.

I admit that I'm not the nicest guy in the galaxy, but I never expected to be arrested for murder. It all started on Brunzibar during a lawn party at the estate of a local corporate industrialist. I'd recently reinvented myself as a sort of global mogul, the CEO of the newly formed Buffalogic, Inc. I was the man responsible for breaking the alien monopoly on the rare and obscenely expensive Buffalo Dogs, delightful little creatures that ate anything and farted oxygen. My position required me to rub elbows with the rich and powerful—a tough job, but you know what they say. Brunzibar's a mercantile worldlet, a settled moon in neutral space where deals are made by governments and planetary corporations. The resident population is primarily human, but many alien governments and corporations maintain embassies and offices there. The current party was a typical example of the high level mingling commonplace on Brunzibar.

I had arrived with Calinda, the Baroness Parmaq, one of only three members of Traken nobility on Brunzibar and easily one of the sexiest and most intelligent women I've ever had the pleasure to hypnotize. I was there because she wanted me there; that's the way it is with the Traken. Call it telepathy of intention, call it unconscious mind control, the Traken nobility may act the very definition of conservative decorum, but they're also the most self-assured people in the galaxy. Traken nobles always seem to get what they want without even asking for it. For reasons known only to herself, the Baroness wanted to be with me. I wasn't about to argue.

It was a brilliant spring day and the lawn had been set up early for croquet. A wave of Terran Anglophilia had recently swept over Brunzibar. I didn't mind the tea and crumpets so much, but there's something unsettling about seeing aliens explain the merits of cricket. There was a lovely gazebo with a stringed quartet and elegant tables laden with eclectic English snack food; delicate finger sandwiches lay displayed side by side with bangers and blood pudding. It was a prestigious event, with only the highest social and political types in attendance, a Who's Who among the rich and

163

famous on Brunzibar, both human and alien. We had just started at croquet, playing with a set of mallets, wickets, and balls fabricated from a local wood and painted with painfully bright colors.

"No, Mr. Conroy, you're swinging your mallet much too hard. Let me show you." Baroness Parmaq moved behind me and her arms surrounded my waist as her hands grasped my forearms. I did my best to hold onto my mallet. Trakens are aliens, but they're human looking aliens—third cousins, if you will. In the case of the Baroness, kissing cousins. She was a stunningly athletic woman half a head taller than me, and I'm considered tall. Her hair was blonde and coifed in an elaborate swirl of spiraling locks that cascaded all around her head and made me think of a force of nature, like a hurricane. Her skin had tanned to a golden perfection, and her face would have sparked envy in Helen of Troy. She strolled along the lawn in an airy frock of iridescent pearl that showed a great deal of leg and left her shoulders bare. So, no, I didn't mind in the least getting croquet instruction from her, and didn't care whether that attitude originated in my head or was something she'd slipped into it. I was in the arms of a sophisticated woman who also happened to be fabulously wealthy and powerful. I had nothing to complain about, but not everyone shared my view. Which is how the trouble started.

Reggie, my buffalo dog—and the most likely reason that the Baroness had latched onto me—had been happily nibbling the grass near my feet. He began bleating plaintively and scratching at my shoes. A shiver ran through me, and then I heard a familiar voice.

"Get away from her, you . . . you . . . human!"

I'd been looking down at my croquet ball. I looked up in time to catch a fist to the face. It was a powerful punch but I didn't fall. I couldn't. The Baroness, inadvertently but quite effectively, held me up. As a result, I received a second blow before I could stagger free. I turned to confront the bastard who'd sucker-punched me, Lord Ramilon Nerkt, President of Trakus Industrials. I'd met him the same day I'd met the Baroness; I hadn't much cared for him then either. He glowered now; his eyes radiated hatred and contempt with just enough jealousy to justify their brilliant green. He had enjoyed a relationship of some sort with the Baroness, and it had ended rather badly just days ago. Clearly, he thought I'd replaced him. He came at me again and I raised my guard; he wasn't going to get another freebie.

Only, I couldn't lift my arms up. Part of me just didn't want to, and that part held control. I felt loathsome, despicable, an utter cad. I deserved a good thrashing. His third punch caught me just below my left eye and snapped my head back hard enough to bounce my brain against the inside of my skull. It was only right. I dropped to my knees like a broken thing, sobbing. Lord Nerkt hovered above me. He chortled, and I wanted to wipe the smirk off his face. I could take him, I knew I could, but . . . I couldn't. Nerkt's fist landed in my gut and knocked me onto my back. I watched, paralyzed and helpless, as he raised his boot over my face and prepared to stomp down with his full weight.

And then he fell over. My head cleared instantly and I could move again. Reggie stampeded over to me and began licking my face with his tiny blue tongue. I gathered him into the crook of my arm and scrambled to my feet. The Baroness stood holding a croquet mallet as she frowned down at the unconscious Lord Nerkt.

"Are you all right, Mr. Conroy? I'm terribly sorry," she said. "I had no idea that Ramy would be here, let alone behave so poorly."

I paused a moment and checked to see if the bastard had broken my nose while also trying to figure out what had just happened. "What just happened? I couldn't move . . . couldn't fight back."

"Of course not," said a new voice. "Ramilon Nerkt didn't want you to have a chance of fighting back, he wanted you defeated at his feet."

I turned to see who had spoken and found myself locking eyes with Chancellor Vishto, the ranking Traken on Brunzibar. He reached out, lightly touched my face, and scowled. "You'd better get some ice on that. It looks worse than it is, but it's still going to hurt."

I nodded. He was right. I should get some ice. I turned to do just that when one of the servants appeared at my elbow with an ice bucket and clean towel. Other servants were hauling Lord Nerkt to his feet and applying a cold compress to the back of his head. I gingerly touched a towel-wrapped chunk of ice to my face and regarded Vishto. He was handsome, in the way that an aging matinee idol is handsome. Impeccably dressed in a dark suit of living fibers, he toted an ornate walking stick of some dark wood.

His face was deeply tanned and lined, but you wanted to trust those lines; his age spoke of experience and wisdom. He'd been advisor to three generations of Traken sovereigns. His milky blue eyes radiated calm. I felt much better.

"Calinda," he said, addressing the Baroness, "I thought you assured me Ramilon wouldn't be attending this function."

"That was my understanding, Annaran," she said as she lowered her mallet to a more typical position. "He told me he was returning to Trakus on the next ship."

"He seems to have changed his plans. Perhaps you should return to the embassy. Alone."

"And desert Mr. Conroy? I could never do that. Besides, we'll be playing charades soon and I don't want to miss it."

Two humans hurried over. I recognized one as our host, Spencer Novato, the wealthiest man on Brunzibar. We'd met a few days earlier, a casual conversation over brandy and cigars, while our respective teams of lawyers hammered out the details of a mutually beneficial business arrangement. Novato was a light-haired man with a dark mustache and an easy smile. He was shorter than me and moved with an extra tension of energy, like a sprinter waiting for the starting pistol. He wore a tailored outfit of white linen, expensive and flawless, as always. I didn't know the fellow with him, a bigger man with an inexpressive face and a drab brown suit that looked as if it belonged to someone else. "Are you all right, Conroy?" said Novato.

"I'm feeling much better, thanks," I said.

He glanced at Vishto and then looked more closely at me. "Are you sure?" He laid a hand on my shoulder and everything changed. I didn't feel better, I discovered; although Vishto wanted me to. I could discern his desire somehow, but it wasn't taking hold any longer. I looked at the Baroness and I could feel her unspoken, possibly unconscious, need to be loved and realized that my attraction to her, though not as strong as before, was nonetheless my own. The effect was like the sun coming out from behind a cloud.

I turned back to Novato. "What did you do?"

He shrugged. "Just brought you a moment's clearheadedness." He nodded to the Chancellor. "My apologies. Lord Nerkt had come to see me. We'd recently ended a business negotiation, rather sourly

I'm afraid. That's why I asked Chief Miles to be here." He gestured at the brown-suited man to his side. "I'd feared Nerkt might do something violent, but I assumed the violence would be directed at me."

"Police Chief Matthew Miles," said the chief, bowing his head lightly as he added, "Baroness, Chancellor." He offered me his hand, a firm grip and a brisk handshake. "Do you want to press charges, Mr. Conroy? There are plenty of witnesses."

Novato still had his hand on me, as if doing so kept me free of Traken influence. I looked around our little group, glancing in turn at the two humans and the two Traken, and shook my head. "No, that's all right. I'll let him have that one, but if he tries it again it will be the last time."

Lord Nerkt chose that moment to begin bellowing. The servants let go of him and he stormed over to the knot of us. I could feel his rage, his hatred, beating against me. He wanted me broken, humiliated, or dead. The emotions washed over me but none of them stuck. Novato's hand remained on my shoulder.

"I might have known it," Nerkt shouted at me as he drew closer. "It's a human conspiracy to destroy me. You and Novato are in it together. You want to shatter my financial life as well as my personal life? I won't let you! I'll see you both dead first!"

"Oh, shut up!" Novato removed his hand from my shoulder and sprang forward. He drove his fist into Nerkt's face and the Traken went down a second time. Even aliens can have glass jaws.

Chief Miles frowned at Novato and then began issuing orders to the servants. They hauled Lord Nerkt to the main house, and the police chief went with them. After a moment's silence the rest of us rejoined the party.

Half an hour into a disappointingly subdued game of charades Novato appeared at my elbow and drew me aside.

"Say now, Conroy, I understand you're something of a hypnotist. Maybe you can put on an impromptu show, lighten the mood a bit?"

For more than a decade I'd made my living as a stage hypnotist working spaceport clubs and dives in some out-of-the-way places that were desperate for live entertainment. That was all in the past though. Thanks to breaking the monopoly on buffalo dogs I was now rich as Croesus and trying my best to become a gentleman of leisure. While you couldn't pay me to do the old "watch the pocket watch" game nowadays, I still like getting my ego stroked as much as the next man. At the request of Chancellor Vishto, I'd done a command performance a couple days earlier after dinner at the Traken embassy, even hypnotizing the Baroness—much to Lord Nerkt's displeasure. My dinner companions had all been fascinated, and I'd been invited to stay on at the embassy as a guest. Apparently word of my little show had reached Spencer Novato.

The Baroness appeared instantly alongside me; Traken hearing is annoyingly good. She tugged playfully on my arm and said, "Oh, yes, be a dear. We'd all love for you do it again. And this time I get to watch."

What could I do? My lovely Baroness wanted the thing and I was the only one around who could provide it. The quartet had left so I claimed the gazebo as a makeshift stage and accepted volunteers from among the party guests. The people I was about to hypnotize had wealth on a planetary scale. This was not a crowd to make cluck like chickens or to otherwise embarrass. I selected three volunteers—a Carlysle, and two humans. All went under without difficulty, each with a different trigger phrase. I'm partial to two-word triggers, usually a flavor or food and a mythological reference. That's not the sort of combination you're apt to hear in casual conversation, which is what makes it so effective as a trigger. I implanted a few common suggestions for the audience's amusement: I turned my hypnotic subjects into robots, I convinced them they were madly in love with their shadows, I regressed them to early childhood and asked them about their favorite toys and imaginary friends. The Baroness sat in the front row with Reggie snuggled comfortably in her lap. She laughed at all the right spots, her eyes twinkling with delight. It felt like the best performance I'd ever given.

I left my volunteers with the usual courteous suggestions, rewarding them for their participation by making them feel refreshed and vibrant for the rest of the day. The audience applauded and I stepped down from the gazebo, reclaiming my buffalo dog. Baroness Parmaq slipped her arm through mine and we made the rounds; Reggie dozed, curled under my other arm. We mingled. The other guests all made a point of complimenting my little show. Novato strode up and again clapped me on the shoulder.

"That was astounding, Conroy, utterly astounding," he said, taking a flat gold case from within his coat. He opened it, withdrew a cigar and then offered the case to me. I helped myself. The cigars were a brownish purply hue: Infinity Smokes. Each one cost more money than I used to make in a year. Novato took a small polyblade tool from his pocket and snipped off the end of his cigar. I bit through mine and spat the tip out. We lit up. Novato took a deep draw, held it a moment, and then blew a perfect ring of acrid and slightly minty smoke. He gave me a knowing wink, as if the sharing of cigars marked us as members of some secret tobacco fraternity.

"And it's so very different from the talents of our Traken friends," Novato continued, gesturing in the air with his cigar. "So . . . deliberate. And do I understand you hypnotized the Baroness the other night?"

"He did indeed, Mr. Novato," said the Baroness. "I quite enjoyed the experience."

"Amazing. Just think what a talent like yours would do for my negotiation skills. I'd be able to turn the tables on our friend Lord Nerkt. Why, with just a snap of my fingers I'd have my competition signing away their corporations for a fraction of their worth."

Another voice intruded before I could reply. "Mr. Conroy, I've been doing some reading on the subject. I confess, your expertise is why I invited you to dinner the other night." Chancellor Vishto had come up on the Baroness's other side and joined us. He wrinkled his nose at the smoke and Novato didn't offer him a cigar. "I was of the understanding that hypnosis could not cause one to perform an action he would not normally undertake." He paused and gave our host a cool stare. "It would take a subtler power than hypnosis, Mr. Novato, to effect your desires."

"That's true, Chancellor, but it's far from insurmountable," I said, making an effort to direct my smoke away from Vishto.

He turned to me. "How so?"

"Hypnosis is all about suggestion. Mr. Novato might not be able to hypnotize his competitors to sign a one-sided contract, but that's not to say he couldn't make them sign something else. The trick is to present the individual with a context in which the target action not only makes sense, but is desirable."

"I don't follow," said the Chancellor. I felt a compulsion to explain and alleviate his confusion.

"You're saying it's really about just making them sign a piece of paper," said the Baroness. "They wouldn't sign a contract, so you don't give them a contract. Instead you tell them it's something else."

I nodded. The lady was sharp. "That's right," I said. "You could tell your subject that he's a famous media star and you're his biggest fan. You've seen all his vids, and you've waited hours in line to meet him, and oh, would he be ever so kind and autograph this page you happened to have brought?"

"But, he's not signing an autograph," said the Chancellor.

"But he would, and that's the key," I said. I stared into the Baroness's eyes and continued. "Create a compelling situation, and it's not difficult to elicit the desired response."

Novato laughed smugly, looking right at Chancellor Vishto. "Subtle enough for you, Vishto?"

The Chancellor eyed Novato like a bug. "Thank you, Mr. Conroy. Most illuminating. None of my sources presented it quite that way."

I shrugged, causing Reggie to let loose several farts of oxygen, the trademark of all buffalitos. I worried briefly about the cigars, but Reggie quickly subsided.

"Perhaps," said Calinda, returning my gaze, "it's the difference between theory and application."

"Or knowing and doing," I said.

"Indeed," said Vishto. "I shall endeavor to remember that." He nodded politely and took his leave.

The party was definitely breaking up and the Baroness and I left soon after. We returned to the embassy but not to my guest suite. Instead, Calinda insisted on inspecting and tending to the bruises Lord Nerkt had inflicted. She took me by the hand and led me to her own set of rooms. I ended up spending the night. I'm too much of a gentleman to elaborate, but it's fair to say I've never been a more attentive lover. Blame that telepathic intention of hers; I was in no position to complain.

In the morning, my Baroness was gone. I was surprised by how much I missed her. I found Reggie curled up on her pillow, snoring softly, and now and then licking the air.

I slipped on a robe and walked from the bedroom to the adjacent parlor, hoping to find her there. I didn't, but discovered a sumptuous breakfast of Eggs Montrachet, a rasher of Traken bacon, a pot of coffee, and two kinds of citrus juice. My napkin lay wrapped around a small gift box. I poured myself some coffee and unwrapped the box. It held a flat, two centimeter disk of burnished bluish metal, a medallion of some kind, connected to an intricately wrought platinum chain. There was also a note:

Dearest—

I'm sorry I'm not there with you now. I remembered an early morning appointment that I could not break. I'll see you again tonight and we can pick up where we left off. Till then, a small gift to remember me. Wear it, and it will keep you safe from a repeat of yesterday's misfortune.

She'd signed it with an elaborate glyph of curves and acute angles, her royal mark. The chain was beautiful and expensive. The dangling disc felt cold to the touch and vibrated softly. I slipped the chain over my head and tucked the thing under my shirt. She was sweet to leave a gift, all the more so if she were hurrying to an appointment, but I didn't see how it would keep me safe. I planned to do that myself through the simple expediency of avoiding Lord Nerkt. Given his earlier rage at seeing Calinda and I play croquet, I doubted he'd take the latest development in our relationship at all well.

I ate breakfast and got dressed. Then I scooped up Reggie, fed him the last of the bacon, slipped out of the room and headed for my own suite and a fresh change of clothes. After setting my buffalo dog in his daybed by the door as I walked in, I continued through the anteroom to the bedroom and started to unbutton my shirt. I stopped halfway across the floor. Chancellor Vishto was sitting at the bedroom's dressing table. He didn't look happy.

"Mr. Conroy, you are not of Trakus and so I must excuse your ignorance of our ways. There are certain protocols that apply to the noble born, protocols that have sadly been ignored. Though it pains me to say so, I believe you have worn out your welcome here." His eyes locked with mine and I could feel his desire to have me out of the embassy. More than that, there was a strong suggestion that I pack immediately and never so much as speak to the Baroness again. I recognized the cold, hollow sensation at once; the same thing had happened the day before when Spencer Novato placed his hand on my shoulder.

It all clicked. Whether by some natural ability or technical marvel, Novato was immune to the projective influence of Trakens. He had extended that immunity to me while he touched me. Then, as now, I could feel the desire from Vishto, recognize it, but not give in to its compulsion. I turned my back on the Chancellor and rebuttoned my shirt, fingering the disc hanging from the chain around my neck. I was beginning to appreciate the gift Calinda had left me.

A diffident knock sounded on the door and a servant stepped in pushing a small cart.

"May I help you with your luggage, sir?" he said.

This too was Vishto's doing. His wish to have me out of here radiated from him and influenced the staff accordingly. I shook my head at the servant. "No thanks, I'll manage by myself." I stepped over to Chancellor Vishto, meeting his stare. He still looked every bit the kindly old man and I could feel his devotion and concern for the Baroness. His wants had no power over me. He was just trying to protect her, and it wasn't my place to convince him that the lady didn't need protecting. I'd already managed to piss off one Traken; I didn't need to pick a fight with another.

"My apologies, Chancellor, if I have through some ignorance offended your hospitality. If you will excuse me, I will change my clothes, gather my few belongings, and depart within the hour."

He rose from the chair and leaned heavily on his walking stick. "Thank you, Mr. Conroy, you are a gentleman and I confess to a personal enjoyment of your company. It is indeed a pity that you are not of better lineage; you would do it great credit. And these actions would not be necessary."

The compulsion to leave lessened, an all but done deal. In its place I felt his relief and a genuine sadness. None of it could reach through to manipulate my behavior. I watched him walk from the room and smiled to myself. The old man had really liked me. More importantly, he loved the Baroness. It was disturbing to see how much.

Years of working third-rate lounges had taught me the discipline of traveling light. I switched into fresh clothes and stuffed everything else into a single carpetbag. On the way out I scooped Reggie up under my right arm. A limousine was waiting to whisk me to the city. I lingered only a moment in the grand foyer of the embassy to pen a quick note of apology to the Baroness and entrust it to one of the staff, slipping him a fifty cred note at the same time. Then I left to look for a hotel.

Like most mercantile worldlets, Brunzibar played host to a lot of industrial high rollers. It catered to them with an assortment of five star restaurants, luxury hotels, and extravagant conference centers. The manager of the Brunzibar Star gazed in amazement at Reggie, confirmed my credit rating, and personally escorted us to the penthouse. The accommodations were remarkable, but I couldn't help thinking how much better they'd be if Calinda were there to share them.

Reggie skipped across the room in a blur of tight dark curls and laid claim to a richly embroidered throw pillow. I wasn't sure if he planned to eat it or sleep on it and I didn't much care. I just wanted a shower. Call me fussy, but I like to start each day with a dousing of hot water and a bar of soap, something I hadn't had time for on my way out of the Traken embassy. The penthouse had three bathrooms and the one in the master bedroom contained the sort of huge and richly appointed plumbing that makes you think of parties at Caligula's palace. I hung my clothes safely out of Reggie's reach (just in case the pillow didn't satisfy his hunger) and surrendered myself to the pleasures of hot water and rich lather.

The police chose that moment to break down the door.

Chief Miles himself was there, with a dozen uniformed police trailing behind, a small throng of hotel staff, and curious onlookers following after. He calmly strode into the master bathroom and announced "This is the police!" I turned off the water, wrapped a towel around my waist, and emerged from wet opulence to see what was up. He tossed a pair of electro-static cuff gloves at me. I caught them and managed not to drop my towel.

"Mr. Conroy, you're under arrest for the murder of Lord Ramilon Nerkt."

My first mistake was in not looking surprised. An announcement of murder is typically something of a shock, and the innocent are supposed to be astonished. But I've spent too many years on stage making people say all kinds of outlandish things. My professional reflexes kicked in and kept any reaction from my face. Besides, Nerkt had already demonstrated himself to be a first class bastard. Plenty of people had to want a man like that dead.

"Chief Miles," I said, "there must be some mistake."

"If there is, it will be sorted out down at the station. Now you can come along easily, Mr. Conroy, or you can be difficult. What's it going to be?"

"Do you plan to parade me through the hotel buck naked, or are you going to allow me to dress first?"

Miles signaled an assistant, who stepped forward and pulled my clothes off the hook, giving them a once over. Under the watchful eyes of the local police, hotel staff, and a few guests, I slipped into my clothes, zipped and buttoned and buckled, and then ran a hand through my wet hair. Miles gestured toward the gloves he'd given me and watched as I slid them on. He pulled my hands behind my back, waited as I laced my fingers, and then activated the gloves. A charge ran through them and turned the flexible fabric into unyielding metallic mesh. Then, gripping my left bicep with one hand, he guided me out of the bathroom.

On the way out I caught the gaze of the hotel manager. "I'll be keeping the room. Look in on my buffalo dog, if you don't mind," I said. "I expect him to be happy and whole and here when I return." Reggie had eaten a large hole in his pillow, pulled much of the stuffing free, and curled up inside it for a nap.

The ride to the police station was uneventful. I'd been arrested plenty of times before, but never made to feel like a guest. The cuff gloves were infinitely more comfortable than the traditional metal-on-wrist variety, and Miles's men showed me courtesy and professionalism, as if they'd all had a refresher course on police etiquette. The civility unnerved me.

Politeness aside, the police on Brunzibar processed suspects no differently from anywhere else I've been. I put all of my belongings into a polyfiber envelope—my watch, Calinda's medallion, my belt—and sealed it. Then I was searched, photographed, x-rayed, and scanned. They compared the data with the details encrypted into my travel visa and deposited me in an interrogation cell as comfortable as an apartment, if you made allowances for the ugly green paint and overly harsh lighting. I took inventory: several large chairs, a sturdy table, and a dirty gray carpet. Matthew Miles sat in one of the chairs, reading a datapadd. He set it on the table as I entered. I caught a glimpse of the word "murder" and a distinctive logo on the screen. I recognized the logo; it was from a popular series of notes used by students going through police academies, a sort of "procedures made simple" collection.

"Boning up?" I asked.

Chief Miles blushed, scowled, and slapped the off-switch on his datapadd.

"We don't have violent crimes here, Mr. Conroy. In fact, we have almost no crime at all. This is a business world and crime is bad for business. Our legal system, and more importantly our penal system, provide vigorous and effective deterrents. Justice on Brunzibar is swift, whether you cooperate with us or not."

I thought about that. During my years as a hypnotist I'd spent more than one night as an innocent man in jail. Innocence wasn't always enough. But Miles hadn't arrested the Amazing Conroy; he'd arrested the CEO of Buffalogic, Inc. I wasn't a two-bit stage performer any more. I could afford as many lawyers as I needed to get me off. Innocence combined with money made a big difference. I tried not to let lack of anxiety show. Miles was just doing his job; judging by the datapadd he hadn't had a lot of experience at this aspect of it.

"Why do you think I killed Lord Nerkt?" I asked.

"The killer wasn't a professional; it was messy, amateurish. Murder isn't as straightforward as they make it seem on the vids. The victim was stabbed repeatedly with a sharp implement, probably a knife. There was a great deal of blood. The killer no doubt cleaned himself up right away, but the experience lingers in the mind. I've seen it before. First time murderers become fastidious for days after the killing."

I tried hard not to laugh. For a cop interrogating a murder suspect he was awfully chatty. I doubted he'd had time to do more than skim the datapadd. "You think I did it because I was taking a shower?"

"Hardly, Mr. Conroy. Though that is an extra bit of consistent information, isn't it? Let me ask you a question now. Where have you been since you left Spencer Novato's party yesterday? If you have an alibi for the last twenty hours now would be a good time to share it."

Calinda immediately came to mind, and just as quickly I knew I wouldn't mention her at all. I recalled Vishto's remarks before I'd left the embassy: Protocols of the noble born. It was one thing to consort with commoners for business, and quite another to allow more intimate contact. My Baroness and I had crossed that line. Only Vishto knew of it; no lasting harm had been done, but that could quickly change. Even the risk of hurting her reputation was cause to keep silent. I had a team of expensive lawyers already on Brunzibar who could probably get me out of this jam. Calinda had only me to protect her good name.

"No," I said, "I don't believe I do."

He smiled and picked up his datapadd. He tapped the screen with the business end of a stylus. "Do you remember what you said to me yesterday? Just after your encounter with the deceased? When I asked you if you wanted to press charges?"

"Not especially, no."

He read from the padd. "You said, 'I'll let him have that one, but if he tries it again it will be the last time.'"

"What of it?" I said.

"You don't see that as a threat, Mr. Conroy?"

"Not especially, no. Do you? I'd just been sucker-punched by the man. What should I have said?"

"He'd struck you more than once actually, four times. Three blows to the face, one to the stomach, according to witnesses. Let's be honest: he beat the crap out of you. He did it front of the wealthy and politically connected woman with whom you attended the party. She even had to come to your rescue, to save you. Now, I'm no expert on psychology, Mr. Conroy, but speaking as one man to another, a beating like that, in front of your woman, doesn't do much for the old self-esteem. So, yes, I do consider your earlier remark to be a threat. On other worlds, men have been killed for far less. You come from another world, Mr. Conroy, and you had ample motive to want Lord Nerkt dead. And men of means, such as yourself, are used to getting what they want."

I had to laugh at that, which didn't earn me any points with Chief Miles. I shook my head and said, "I'm sorry, you need to run a better background check. My social status is newly acquired. A year ago my income was probably less than your lowest grade officer. I'm afraid you've got the wrong man,

Chief. I didn't kill Nerkt. I'm not sorry somebody did, but it wasn't me."

As if on cue the door opened and the Baroness stepped into the room. Two sheepish officers stood behind her in the hall. I felt a wave of relief mixed with anger and the desire to stop all this fuss, all coming from Calinda. But it was muted, hollow, and not remotely compulsory.

"We're sorry sir," said one of the officers. "She insisted on seeing the prisoner at once."

"That's fine," said the chief. "The Baroness can be very persuasive. Leave her with me and go back to your duties." He stood and gave her his full attention. "How can I be of assistance, Baroness?"

"Chief Miles, this action of yours is unacceptable." She was slightly taller than him and looked down her nose as she fixed him with a fair imitation of Vishto's patented stare. "I insist that you release Mr. Conroy at once."

"I'm afraid I can't do that, ma'am."

The Baroness frowned. "You do know who I am?"

"Yes, ma'am. That's why I took Mr. Conroy to this specific interrogation room. The walls are equipped with dampers to block the influence of Traken nobility."

Baroness Parmaq pulled herself up straighter. "I have the full authority of an ambassador of Trakus, complete with diplomatic immunity."

"Yes, ma'am."

"I choose to extend that immunity to Mr. Conroy."

"No, ma'am, I'm afraid not." Miles winced. He looked like he was weakening, but not enough.

"What do you mean, 'no?'"

"Baroness, you should know better. Mr. Conroy is not a native of Trakus. Nor is he an authorized representative of your government. Immunity cannot be extended to him. Nor is this the Traken embassy; you are not on sovereign soil and as such the laws of Brunzibar apply."

"But you have no reason to hold him."

"Baroness, please. After yesterday's altercation he's our most likely suspect for the crime. No one saw him since the two of you left Spencer Novato's party yesterday. He has motive and no alibi."

"He has an alibi," said Calinda. "He was with me. We left the party together and returned to the embassy. He was there all night."

"Baroness, I appreciate your efforts, but we've moved very quickly on this. My people have already talked with several members of the embassy staff. I have confirmation that Mr. Conroy was not in his suite last night. The embassy is a large facility. He could easily have returned with you and then slipped away unnoticed."

"No, you don't understand. He couldn't slip away as you say. He was with me. All night. Must I be more blunt?" Her cheeks reddened and she looked away.

"Baroness, no, you don't need to—" I said. I rose from my seat to go to her, but the Chief pushed me back and stepped between us.

"You're saying you were with him, from the time you left Novato's until . . . " He let it trail off.

"Until just past dawn. I had a morning meeting with the Consortium of Aligned Technologies, a discussion of trade futures that couldn't be rescheduled. When I left he was still asleep."

"The coroner placed the time of Nerkt's death at well before dawn," said Miles. "Are you willing to sign a written statement of what you've just told me?"

"Calinda," I said. "We both know I didn't do it. My lawyers can clear me in time. You don't need to involve yourself. The police will find the real killer and let me out in short order. Please, I'll be fine."

But she looked at me, her eyes welling with tears, and I knew that more than anything else my words just confirmed her resolve. A solitary tear broke free and trailed down her perfect face and she turned back to the police chief. "If that is what you require, then I will sign."

Ten minutes later I was taking my possessions out of a polyfiber envelope and signing forms to verify that I'd gotten everything back. Chief Miles was doing his best to soothe the Baroness. I wanted to hurry over and do the same. I slipped Calinda's gift around my neck and only my motivation changed. My desire to comfort her wasn't a result of her need to be comforted any more; it was something I wanted to do all on my own. I stuffed the remaining items into the pockets of my slacks and hurried over to her, taking her hand in mine. She turned to me and I leaned close and whispered, "Everything's going to be fine."

Almost on cue two of Miles's officers rushed into the room, strong-arming a disheveled and dazed Spencer Novato between them. Novato's once elegant suit was soaked in blood.

"We went to his home to take his statement like you told us, Chief," said one of the cops. "We found him in his car, asleep. We also found this." He held up a transparent evidence bag containing a bloody polyblade. "He claims he doesn't remember anything."

Novato lifted his head and seemed to realize where he was. His eyes widened as he looked at Miles. I could almost smell his panic. "Matt? What's happening?"

"Sir, we used the field analysis kit on the way in." The second officer eagerly handed Miles a datapadd. "It's not conclusive, but the preliminary results show the samples on both his clothes and the knife are consistent with Traken blood."

Calinda's fingers tightened on my arm and waves of shock and disbelief rippled from her, infecting Miles and his officers. "Murderer," she said. "Was it for money? Did you take a life over some business disagreement?"

Miles jerked his head at one of the officers and pointed at us. "Get them out of here." He took Novato's arm, shaking the man to get his attention. "Spencer? I'm placing you under arrest for the murder of Lord Nerkt . . . " The rest of his words were lost to us as the officer ushered us out.

I exited the police station arm in arm with my Baroness and returned to the hotel a free man. The murderer was in custody and Brunzibarian justice would be served. The whole affair with Chief Miles had taken several hours and both Calinda and I were drained. When we arrived at the penthouse Reggie was still sound asleep in the hollow of his pillow. I sat on the floor to be at his level and roused him with a vigorous head scratch. He woke, yawned, and rewarded me with a few licks of his coarse tongue against my wrist. Calinda knelt alongside me and took my other hand in both of hers.

"Come with me to Trakus," she said. "We can leave at once. My personal yacht is waiting at the spaceport."

"I don't think your Chancellor would appreciate that." On the way over I'd given her an edited version of my chat with Vishto to explain why I had left the embassy.

"Vishto is a fool. A dear sweet fool to be sure, who has only my best interests at heart. I love him like a favorite uncle, but that's not the kind of love that fills me when I am with you. He'll come to understand in time; I know he will. Ever since I was a little girl I've always gotten my way with Vishto."

I frowned. "Doesn't all this mind manipulation get a little boring? I can't imagine an entire planet like that."

She laughed and pulled me in close for a kiss, half crushing Reggie between us. "Not all Trakens have the gift, only the noble bloodlines. And we're immune to it ourselves, except among the closest of us. It's a mutation, my love. The rest of the population is as ordinary as dirt."

"You mean, like me," I said.

"You're far from ordinary. You're clever and warm and you make me tremble with just a touch. Vishto may dismiss it as mere infatuation, but I know my heart. I knew you were my destined love almost from the moment we met. You are the chosen consort of a baroness. And, if you'll accept it, you can be the husband of one as well."

Seventeen separate alarms sounded in my head. I pulled back and stared at her angelic face. "Husband? Did you just propose to me?"

Right then and there I had one of those compressed moments of insight, when time hangs suspended and you practically watch as everything drops into place like the first snowflakes of winter falling in front of your eyes. Calinda loved me, and not just because I was the first man in a long time who wasn't interested in her wealth or position. Nor was it simply because in her eyes I was an exotic stranger. These things had helped, had let me get close to her, had allowed her the opportunity to fall in love with me. I could feel it. Protected by the medallion she had given me I could read and understand her emotions rather than being manipulated by them. She loved me, wanted to protect me, wanted to be with me. And in that moment of understanding my own defenses fell and I realized I felt the same way about her.

I took her hands in mine, pulled her up as I stood and drew her close. We kissed, a long lingering kiss. When our lips parted I stared into her eyes and said, "I've always wanted to visit Trakus."

I swiftly stuffed my few possessions back into my carpet bag and called down to the front desk. Yes, the rooms had been fine, yes, the service exquisite, no, nothing was wrong with the hotel, just a change in plans and would you please have a limo brought up for me thank you very much. Then, with one arm around my baroness and Reggie tucked under the other, I departed the Brunzibar Star and headed for the spaceport and Calinda's private yacht.

The police were there ahead of us, waiting to arrest me. Again.

"The guilty always run," said Miles as he pulled my hands behind my back after I'd put on the cuff gloves. We were in a tiny room adjacent to the customs area, a spot usually reserved for searching suspected contraband traffickers and other detainees. The police chief had shoved me in there to escape the gathering crowd. As I was learning, arrests were cause for spectacle on Brunzibar.

"I wasn't running; I was leaving. People are allowed to have other reasons for their actions," I said.

"Of course they are, Mr. Conroy, but when a person is responsible for murder we tend to see his 'reason' as part of a traditional pattern of criminal behavior." The chief activated the cuffs and spun me around to face him. "You almost got away with it too. If you'd gone back to the embassy, or gotten onto that ship, we wouldn't have been able to touch you. But you slipped up, and now you're going to held accountable for the murder of Lord Nerkt."

"We've already been through that," I said. "I was at the Traken embassy all night, I couldn't have killed Nerkt."

"We know that. Spencer Novato did the actual violence. You were there when he was brought in. And I'll give you credit, Conroy, you're a cool customer. You didn't even blink, didn't give a thing away."

"Chief, you're not making sense. What are you talking about?"

"That was Nerkt's blood on Novato. The lab's already confirmed that his polyblade was the murder weapon. Odd though, he had more reason to want Nerkt alive than dead. Their business dealings had worked out to Novato's advantage, but under Traken law the contract becomes instantly voided when either principal dies. Spencer might not have liked Nerkt, but he's too good a business man to let that get in the way of the deal."

I shook my head. "But you just said that Novato committed the murder."

"He did. But he doesn't know why he did it. He claims to have no memory of any of it, that he woke up where my men found him, in his car, dazed, with the dead man's blood all over him and the murder weapon by his side. What does that sound like to you, Mr. Conroy?"

"What, you think I hypnotized him to kill Nerkt?"

"You tell me. You're the expert. You're the one who told him you could convince someone to follow any instruction. Who else should I suspect? You had motive and means. A hypnotically conditioned assassin allows you not only opportunity but an alibi."

"That's a compelling scenario," I said, "but there's only one problem with it. I didn't kill Nerkt."

"We'll see. Even now Spencer Novato is being counter-conditioned by police psychologists. He's remembering more and more. I think he'll be able to provide convincing testimony, and that's the last piece I'll need to see you convicted. Let's go."

He pushed me toward the door, and armed officers flanked me as we left the room. Several more police were holding back the growing throng. Calinda had apparently contacted Vishto immediately and the Chancellor stood beside her. He was clearly trying to comfort her but my Baroness would have none of it. Tears streamed down her face as she clutched Reggie in both arms. "Conroy! My love!" she called out, but the police hurried me away.

I turned to look back at her, tried to show her an encouraging smile, but I don't think she saw it. My heart ached, and I felt its echo radiating from Calinda.

I was being hustled toward Miles's waiting squad car when another police cruiser arrived. Sirens wailing, lights flashing, the vehicle aimed straight for us and crashed into Miles's car. The driver's door flew open and Spencer Novato all but fell out. Gone was any semblance of the dapper mega-industrialist. In his place was a twitching, wide-eyed madman. He rushed forward and pointed at us. One arm extended, one finger jabbing repeatedly at the air in my general direction, he shouted over and over again "You! You! YOU!"

A hand touched my shoulder. Somehow Calinda had used the confusion to break the police line and come from behind. Vishto had moved up with her and the two of them were radiating fear and confusion. The crowd was on edge; their emotions were escalating. I stood there with my hands cuffed behind my back.

"Chief, you're going to have a riot in a minute," I said. "Get us out of here."

"You made me kill him!" Novato was closer now, staggering slowly nearer and sobbing hysterically. "His blood, it's on your hands, not mine. Not mine. Yours!"

"Chief, either get us out of here or uncuff me, now." Reggie had started barking; Calinda's hand tightened on my shoulder and I knew she was preparing to interpose herself between Novato and me. Her fear wasn't for herself; it was for me. Vishto's fear was another matter. He was afraid of Novato, afraid for himself; fear poured out from him. It didn't make sense. I could feel him desperately wanting Novato to be stopped.

Novato didn't stop. Vishto's desires meant nothing to him. Like me he was immune to Traken influence.

Chief Miles had no such advantage. Vishto's need was overpowering. The chief drew his sidearm, possibly for the first time in his career, raised it in a two-handed grip, and aimed down the length of his arms at Novato, his best friend and star witness. All around us the police and onlookers were being compelled to act, all converging uncertainly on Novato.

"You're going to pay," screamed Novato, oblivious to everything but the people directly in front of him. "Your tricks won't help you any longer. I remember everything!"

As if in reaction, raw terror washed over almost everyone. The baroness shoved me, maybe to push me out of harm's way. As the police chief fired I stumbled into him, causing him to drop his gun. It had been loaded with sound charges; the sonic burst took Novato in the left shoulder and spun him like a weather vane. The crowd panicked; some surged forward to pile on Novato, more simply fled in fear. Chief Miles pushed me away and I fell to the tarmac, my hands still behind me. I scraped and banged one knee and smashed my head. My vision went black for a moment and then came back, blurry but serviceable. Then Calinda fell on top of me, dropping Reggie in the process. The buffalo dog squealed and farted copious amounts of oxygen.

"It's Vishto," I yelled, my voice all but lost in the cacophony of the moment. The Baroness stared at me, her panic stalled by confusion. "It's Vishto," I repeated. "Help the Chief. You've got to help him." And she understood.

Her hands slipped under my shirt and grasped the intricate chain. She gave it a hard yank and the medallion was gone, leaving me awash in the telepathic flood coming from Lord Vishto. Not even the influence of my Baroness could save me; his emotions drowned hers. I wanted to die, I wanted to escape, but most of all I wanted Spencer Novato silenced for now and always and I sobbed and cursed myself for my inability to do any of those things.

The Baroness meanwhile had regained her feet and pressed the medallion against the Chief's neck while the man searched for his dropped gun so he too could put an end to Novato. The Chief's eyes cleared of confusion and pain and he understood. He grabbed the medallion, pulled back from the mass of bodies that had converged on Novato and whirled to stare at Lord Vishto. Two paces closed the gap between them and Miles slapped the elder noble brutally once, twice, and then a third time, desperate to distract him. With each blow my panic lessened. My desire to harm Novato evaporated, replaced by a desperate need to save myself. The remaining mob and half a dozen police responded with flight. I lay on the ground, trembling, while Reggie licked my face. Novato had somehow gotten to his feet. He staggered forward.

"Bastard," Novato shouted at Vishto, and swung that same powerful right that he'd used to deck Lord Nerkt just a day before. It had a similar effect now. The waves of Vishto's projected emotion ceased and all I felt were Calinda's desires to have me released and to take care of me, sentiments that I quite agreed with and would have echoed if I hadn't picked that moment to pass out.

I awoke back in the Traken embassy, lying on my back in the Baroness's bed. A minty fragrance floated in the air. Reggie lay curled up on a cushion at my feet, snoring comfortably. Calinda stood over me, lightly dabbing my head wound with a cool compress. She smiled at me and I felt her relief and her love and realized that I was once again wearing the medallion.

"You gave us a scare at first," she said, "but the physician says it is just the most minor of concussions."

I smiled and tried to sit up. The room began to swim so I changed my mind. "Vishto?" I asked.

"He confessed," said Chief Miles as he stepped into view, puffing on one of Novato's cigars. "Apparently Spencer Novato has a similar medallion to yours, a source of some contention, stolen by his grandfather from the previous Lord Vishto decades ago. It also provided the perfect cover. He'd been the only human on Brunzibar immune to Traken influence, making him the ideal tool for a Traken to use in a murder. Turns out Chancellor Vishto has had a dabbler's interest in hypnotism for years. You just happened to be in the wrong place at the wrong time.

"The way I see it, Spencer's reliance on his medallion made him overconfident in all his dealings with the Traken. Vishto seized the opportunity and used hypnosis to manipulate him. The Chancellor had no need of Traken abilities, just the techniques he'd been studying ."

"But why?" I said. "Why did Vishto want to kill Nerkt?"

"Traken politics?" said Miles. "I don't know for sure. We know Lord Nerkt was not well liked. We know that much of the Traken nobility take a dim view of capitalism and found his business success unbecoming. Maybe there's something more there that we haven't found yet."

"I don't believe you'll discover anything further, Chief," said the Baroness, diverting her gaze all the while. "My people tend to keep such matters within the blood. It is not for open discussion."

"What will happen to Chancellor Vishto?" I said.

"He's already gone," said Miles. "Diplomatic immunity. One protected personage killing another and all of it taken right out of my hands. He's halfway back to Trakus by now with a slap on the wrist and an injunction from ever returning to Brunzibar. Meanwhile I have a desk full of paperwork to do. I just wanted to see you were all right, Mr. Conroy, and to make sure there were no hard feelings between us. I was just doing my job."

"I understand, Chief. All in a day's work."

He nodded. "Oh, and here, Spencer wanted you to have this." He handed me a box of Infinity Smokes. "I hope you don't mind— I took one for myself while we were waiting for you to wake up. I can find my way out. Goodbye."

Calinda watched him leave in silence and turned back to me. Her gaze was tender and her face like an angel's. "We can still go to Trakus. Nothing is changed. I still want you as my husband."

"Calinda, I know why Vishto did it."

"What do you mean?"

"He didn't approve of Nerkt's interest in you, did he?"

She blushed and I could feel her embarrassment.

"Ramilon was . . . crude. An oaf. He wanted my title and the greater leverage it would bring him. When I finally realized it I despised him."

"How did he respond?"

"He threatened me, tried to influence my decision like I was a commoner. But he couldn't. And I knew his threats were hollow; he couldn't harm me or my family. He used the same bullying tactics with me that he used in business, as if I was an acquisition he could barter for."

I reached out and took her hands in mine. "And that made you angry."

"Livid. When I told Annaran about it he had Ramilon banished from the embassy." She paused and smiled. "That was just after you came into my life. I was so desperate for distraction, I might not have met you at all if not for Ramilon's foolishness."

Once again she radiated love at me. I desperately wanted to reciprocate but I held my ground. "And Vishto, he knew how you felt? He knew you were angry at Nerkt?"

"I'm sure he did. He was with me constantly after that. You've seen how protective he can be. I still can't believe he made Novato into a murderer. I've known Annaran since I was a little girl. I can't imagine him capable of violence of any sort."

"I don't think he is, at least not on his own. You made him do it."

"What are you saying? I never asked him to kill Ramilon."

"Didn't you? Isn't that what you wanted?"

"No. Well, yes, maybe at that time, in the heat and anger of the moment.

"If you felt that way, then why didn't the staff at the embassy carry out your wishes? Why didn't they try to kill Nerkt."

She laughed then, a surprisingly cold sound. "Nerkt wouldn't have let them. They'd have come within range of him and been unable to harm him."

"I think that's what happened to Vishto. You projected your own anger and intent onto him and he took it for his own."

"That makes no sense, my love. The ability of the noble born only effects those of other blood."

"You told me there were exceptions, that when two Traken are very close, they can influence one another," I said.

She still didn't see. "What of it?"

"You've known Vishto all your life. He's always been there for you, a second father. Your anger and resentment, your feelings of betrayal, all of that got through to him. So he acted, out of love, in order to protect you. Novato may have done the actual murder, but you really killed Nerkt. Maybe not consciously, but your desire pushed him to it. Vishto was your instrument just as Novato was his."

Calinda's eyes widened and she backed away from the bed. She understood, it showed in her eyes, but I could see that she was doing everything possible to deny it, to convince herself otherwise.

"I couldn't," she said. "Annaran did it of his own volition."

"He probably believes that. I doubt it would occur to him that his own actions could be manipulated, but we both know better. A man like Chancellor Vishto doesn't become a murderer after a lifetime of peace." I tried to sit up again, and managed with just a slight spin to the room. I got out of the bed.

She stepped back. "Everything will be fine when we're together on Trakus," she said. Her eyes shone, close to tears. The medallion let me feel her wants, her anxiety, her fear, and it let me ignore them. I shook my head.

"I can't go to Trakus with you. An innocent man is dead, another's been left with blood on his hands, and a third has had his reputation destroyed, and all by accident." I looked away. Even with the medallion I couldn't bear to see her cry.

"It's not my fault," she insisted, her voice quivering. "You! You inspired Annaran with your hypnosis. It was just his harmless hobby before you inspired him. He got the idea from you."

My smile was tight, forced. "I imagine he did, and he turned it into a weapon. But you aimed the weapon. You fired it." I stepped closer; I reached out and held her by her shoulders. "I can't marry you, Calinda. It wouldn't work. I can't live in a world where everyone is projecting their unconscious wants and desires on everyone around them. Even if this medallion keeps me safe from it, I'd still see it everywhere, everything they wanted, everything they imposed on the world around them. No matter how much you deny your responsibility I'd know the truth each time I looked into your eyes. I'm sorry."

"No! You can't leave me. I love you," she cried, and grabbed the chain around my neck, wrenching it free. "You'll stay with me. I need you to love me. I know you do."

It was true. I knew it deep in my soul. I couldn't leave. I needed to stay. I loved her, both on my own and because she wanted me to. Even though I knew why it was happening I couldn't alter the way I suddenly felt. I took her in my arms and held her tightly, nuzzling her perfect neck. I was staying with her, I told myself, staying. I softly kissed my way up to her ear and whispered her trigger phrase.

"Pistachio Isis"

She slumped against me, deeply entranced, and the emotional barrage vanished. I carried her to the bed and looked at her. I was tempted. I could have left her with a suggestion that she accept responsibility for what had happened, and maybe it would have worked. But if I've learned anything over the years it's that in the long run you can't really change another person's mind. We do it ourselves or not at all. She was wealthy and beautiful and powerful and exercising her conscience didn't fit in with her lifestyle.

So I took the easy way out. I left my Baroness with the suggestion to sleep deeply and to think about the events of the past days when she awoke. Maybe she'll surprise us both. Then I took the medallion from her fingers and slipped it into my pocket, gathered up my buffalo dog and headed for the spaceport and the next transport off Brunzibar. I spent the next few weeks convincing myself that my time with Calinda hadn't been the real thing but was just a cavalier fling. And why not? She didn't have a monopoly on denial.

THE MATTER AT HAND

One of the problems I've had with writing the Amazing Conroy goes back to the first story. Conroy's a rogue; well-meaning, good-hearted, but happy to take advantage of a situation when it presents itself. He's a good guy who's been working in some pretty seedy venues, waiting for his big break. By the end of the story, he's had that break, and he's on his way to being a gazillionnaire!

The problem of course is finding new conflict for the character, because making him filthy rich has removed all of the obstacles of his past life. I eventually solved this problem for good, but for that you need to read the novel *Buffalito Destiny*. In the meantime, one of my short term solutions was to give Conroy some other characters to play off of, and thus was born Left-John Mocker. I really like the Mocker, and not just because he works so well as Conroy's straight man, but because he's a fully realized character in his own right. Little of his backstory is revealed to the reader in this story, but because I had to work it all out for myself, he brings a certain verisimilitude to the tale that allows Conroy to reveal a bit of his own depth. I'll always be grateful to the big lug for that.

Never play cards with a telepath. Quarter-ante poker once a week with the boys is harmless, even fun. But the game takes on a very different feel when the stakes involve a half-billion credit contract and your opponent can read your mind.

A week ago I'd been sitting at the head of a boardroom table; a dozen lawyers down either side ignored me as they haggled and bickered over the fine points of a complex contract. The sound of it gave me a headache, but I didn't dare leave. I sat there, my eyes half closed, and fed bits of delicate fractal pastry to Reggie, the pet buffalo dog on my lap. It was that classic Terran tableau, a man and his dog. Well, almost. Buffalo dogs aren't dogs at all, but incredibly valuable alien lifeforms, far too expensive to have as pets. Reggie was the exception, possible only because I had a monopoly on the creatures throughout human space. That's why the lawyers were there.

Half worked for me. The rest represented a Taurian archaeological consortium from Arcadian space. In between bits of pastry I tried to follow the three or four simultaneous exchanges of legalese bouncing from left to right faster, and in more dead earnest, than any championship tennis match. I understood maybe one word in ten. Maybe. My head throbbed, and I was already regretting my promise to Betsy that I'd sit in for her.

While I'd come a long way from my days as a stage hypnotist, I'm not really equipped to run things at my company. I usually leave that chore to Dr. Elizabeth Penrose, a woman with more talent in her big toe than I have in my whole family tree. Ordinarily she'd be the one sitting in on this kind of meeting, right in the thick of it, squeezing concessions and favorable terms out of the opposition until they begged her to stop. There'd be no begging this time. An outbreak of Skurlian influenza had left her stranded in a temporarily quarantined spaceport on the other side of the solar system. The meeting couldn't be rescheduled. Instead, she'd sent me a curt note instructing me to go to the meeting but keep my mouth shut.

My initial excitement about learning a bit about how my business actually worked quickly faded when the lawyer babble began. Even Reggie had tired of all the blather. In desperation I'd started entertaining myself by trying out the new gizmo the guys down in Security had given me. I wore a thick gold ring set with tiny dials on my left pinkie, a surveillance jammer that could block all data transmissions in a ten-meter radius. About ten minutes into the meeting, when the lawyer prattle had saturated my boredom filters and Reggie had started to fidget, I turned it on. Several of the lawyers on both sides twitched and shot to their feet, glancing about furtively. I continued petting Reggie with an expression of total innocence honed from years performing in some pretty seedy establishments. I don't think I fooled any of them. With nary a grumble they adapted, downgraded to legal pads and ink sticks, and resumed their intense negotiating.

Tiresome as it was, I knew why Betsy had wanted me to sit in. Dealing with Taurians is tricky; maybe it's just human projection, but the bullish-looking aliens tend to be both stubborn and hot-tempered. It had taken months to get their lawyers this far, and with the end nearly in sight Betsy expected some last minute trick and wanted someone with authority there just in case. Regrettably, that someone was me.

The voices of the lawyers drifted in and out of my consciousness as they argued about leasing buffalo dogs. The thing you have to keep in mind is that buffalo dogs can eat anything. At first glance this might not seem a particularly marketable talent, let alone one that had made me a fortune in just a couple of years, but it was just what the Taurians needed. Their consortium was trying to excavate priceless artifacts buried beneath tons of toxic waste. The effluvia had proven too corrosive for conventional hardware and too deadly for traditional field operatives to extract. They'd already lost time and equipment and personnel trying.

My company offered them the perfect solution. In a few weeks time we had trained a trio of buffalitos to not only enjoy the taste of the noxious soup, but to eagerly lap up the mess, and delicately nibble their way down through more than ten meters of the stuff, and then lick the artifacts clean without harming them in the slightest. The relics reclaimed during the demonstration had dazzled the consortium and all that remained was for the lawyers to finalize the contracts. The Taurians wanted to lease one hundred trained buffalo dogs over a five year period. It should have been a simple matter after that, but the lawyers seemed to want at least as much time for their negotiations.

Suddenly, three little words cut through the miasma of lethargy that engulfed me. "Everything is satisfactory," said the Taurian spokesperson for the consortium's team. I blinked repeatedly, like a condemned prisoner in disbelief upon hearing he's been pardoned. My heart sang, this exercise in boredom was finally coming to and end. Then, just as quickly, the song soured as the Taurian continued. "If you agree, then Seljor Thu wishes to add a single condition."

I sat there, numb. The fractal pastry fell from my fingers. Reggie bleated in annoyance, his lips nipping at my fingertips. Seljor Thu ran the Arcadian consortium. He was my opposite number, but unlike me he knew what he was doing. I set Reggie on the carpet so he could get at his snack and leaned in, giving all of my attention to the lawyers.

"Seljor Thu is an accomplished player of cards. He wishes to play a single hand of Matter with your CEO." The Taurian spokesman nodded to me, and then returned his attention to my lawyers. "If he wins, instead of leasing the buffalo dogs to our consortium you will sell them outright for the same price. If he loses, the consortium will lease by the terms you have offered, but will also provide testimonials and documents of introduction to no fewer than fifteen alien concerns currently leasing buffalo dogs from your competitors, the Arconi."

My lawyers' stunned silence lasted several seconds, followed by an explosion of dismissive remarks and comments about irregularities, absurdities, and questionable alien senses of humor. When they quieted down again the consortium's spokesperson quietly added, "Seljor Thu has instructed me to tell you this is, as you say, a 'deal-breaker'."

And right then and there I had one of those moments of total clarity where time seems to stand still. You know what I'm talking about, the kind of instant normally reserved for situations where something horrible is about to happen or when you suddenly realize you're looking at the one true love of your life. The particulars were different, but the magnitude of the situation was the same; I was at a choice point. My company, my life, could be irreversibly transformed by what happened in the next instant, if I could only figure out the right thing to do.

I only knew one thing for certain: Taurians didn't bluff.

It wasn't about the money; being wealthy was still new enough to me that none of it seemed real anyway. Losing would hurt the company, possibly even cripple it. Even with litters of five or six buffalitos, replacing and training one hundred of them would be a tremendous strain on a young company's resources. Hell, filling this five year contract was going to be a tremendous strain on our resources. Which is why I felt certain that Betsy, smart pragmatic Betsy, would consider the risk too great and step away from the table. Thanks, but no deal.

But I wasn't Betsy. I couldn't stop thinking about the unparalleled opportunity. The contract with Seljor Thu established a precedent. His consortium had approached us with our first contract outside human space. There'd been feelers before, from other races, other conglomerates and corporations, but dealing with the first humans in the buffalo dog trade made them skittish. They all wanted what we offered, but none of them wanted to go first. The contract with the Taurians held the possibility of opening up markets beyond the limitations of human space. Seljor Thu knew that, and his offer to provide introductions to other alien corporations would launch Buffalogic, Inc. to stellar heights. Suddenly I was grateful Betsy'd missed her ship. She'd have walked away from such high stakes, but there was no way I was going to let the potential windfall slip through my fingers because of a card game.

I slapped both hands flat on the table, startling all the lawyers and causing them to look my way. "Make the deal," I said. Then I scooped up Reggie and exited the room as quickly, before I could second guess myself. Betsy was going to kill me, but it would all be over, one way or the other, long before she got back.

The game was called 'Matter' because of the four states of play, but the professional gamblers I knew liked to call it Telepath's Poker. It was a complicated game, or more accurately four games in one. Imagine a traditional game of High-Low Poker in which you're trying to make both the best high hand and the best low hand you can, using your cards and, if you dared, the cards in a dummy hand common to both players. Now imagine that instead of just high and low you're trying for four good combinations, based on four different sets of rules, criteria, and objectives, arbitrarily named *solid*, *liquid*, *gaseous*, and *plasma*. To make things trickier, although you could express a preference among the four modes of your hand, the end result depended upon what your opponent declared for his hand, as well as the value of the common cards.

The game had one other kink. Beyond the rules of play there were no rules. None. It was one of the few games of chance in the galaxy open to telepaths and they flocked to it. Knowing your opponents' hand and/or the mode of play wasn't a lock, the complexities of the game and the luck of the draw kept it interesting, even among telepaths.

As often happens with such things, the game had become something of a fad, a badge of status, among certain captains of industry, particularly those with one form or another of telepathic gifts. I possessed no such gifts, but I had other resources available to me. Ten minutes after leaving the boardroom, Reggie and I were seated in the back of the company limo on our way to Newer Jersey. I had a favor to call in.

*   *   *

"You're asking me to teach you how to cheat?" Left-John Mocker glared at me from across the back corner table of the Golden Turtle Palace. He loomed even while sitting, more like a bear than a full-blooded Comanche. His features looked carved in red sandstone, a large hawk-like nose, deep-set eyes beneath a thick broad forehead. His lips formed a tight, accusatory scowl.

I ignored the question and instead focused my attention on the bowl of fortune cookies halfway around the spinnable inner table. I reached out, gave the lazy-susan a half turn, and helped myself to a prophetic dessert.

YOU HAVE A NATURAL TALENT
FOR MAKING PEOPLE DO WHAT YOU WANT.

I crumpled the fortune in my hand and looked up. Left-John hadn't moved. "I'm not asking you to teach me how to cheat. I'm asking you to teach me how you play."

"So you're saying that *I* cheat?" The tone of his voice contained a warning. I ignored it.

"John, we're not talking about Stud or Hold'em. This is Matter. Everyone who plays it cheats. And you've not only played it, you're one of only seven ranked human players."

That mollified him. He leaned back and his features moved from hostile-neutral to simply neutral. It made me wonder just how many poker faces the man had.

"What's in it for me?" he asked and gave the inner table a spin, bringing the fortune cookies within reach. He selected one, broke it in half and unfolded the fortune as he chewed the fragments of the cookie.

Reggie lay curled up on a nearby booster seat. He had polished off a huge plate of Quizzical Shrimp Suspense that Left-John had thoughtfully had waiting for him, and then fallen asleep. Tiny whistling snores played in the background of the conversation.

"I'm prepared to pay a reasonable fee," I started, but John cut me off with a sweep of one hand.

"I don't want your money, Conroy. We go back a long way, and you should know me better than that. I'm a gambler. I don't work for a living. Don't insult me again by suggesting otherwise."

I shrugged. "Sorry. Throwing money at problems is a new habit I've picked up. Betsy's been trying to discourage me from it too. Okay, so, um, how about doing this for me because you owe me?"

He laughed at that, laughed with his whole body. It was like watching a grizzly bear laugh. Right before it knocked your head off with the swipe of one massive paw.

"You're going to try and hold that little incident on Canopus over me?" He smiled as he said it, but I knew his smile could mean anything.

"That little incident cost you a broken arm and the affections of a very talented hat-check girl, as I recall. Not to mention my losing four performances and a month's pay when I had to sneak you onto a freighter."

Left-John had picked up another cookie. He crushed it at my reply and his face went cold again. "Are we back to money?"

"No," I sighed.

"Good. Because you ended up with that girl after my freighter took off."

He had me. I didn't know how he'd found out what had happened after that freighter had left, but I'd been more than repaid at the time. I was down to my last reason. "How about you just do it, as a favor to an old friend?"

Left-John Mocker opened his fist, letting bits and pieces of cookie fall to the table. He gazed at the fortune and then looked up at me. "Did you rig the fortunes?" His tone made it clear, he was asking a question not making an accusation.

I shook my head. "You picked the restaurant," I said. "I've never been here before."

He grunted once, and pushed the fortune from his first cookie to me.

YOU HAVE A TALENT FEW MEN POSSESS. SHARE IT.

"One of the things you learn as a gambler," he said, "is to shut up and listen when the universe is trying to tell you something." He crumpled the other fortune in his hand and tossed it at me. I caught it and unfolded the slip of paper.

AN OLD ACQUAINTANCE WILL SEEK YOU OUT. AID HIM.

I couldn't keep myself from smiling. "Timing is everything," I said.

"Ain't it the truth."

*   *   *

Every night for the next week I met with Left-John Mocker at the Golden Turtle Palace. It turned out he was part owner. He'd won a quarter share in the place during a card game the year before, and made a point to eat there whenever he was on Earth. Over plates of Imperial Cashew Decadence, Drowning Man's Beef, and Flaming Duck of Good Fortune I learned the basics of Matter. I'm a quick study, and my teacher grudgingly admitted that in time I might be able to hold my own against other human, non-telepathic players. The praise was small consolation for the twin facts that the game was mere days away and my opponent was an alien.

All week long I'd studiously ignored the daily clamor of Betsy's interplanetary memos urging me to "ABORT ABORT ABORT." Meanwhile, my staff had compiled information on Seljor Thu. Telepathic gifts of one kind or another show up in nearly one percent of all Taurians, but so far none of the information I'd received indicated if my opponent was just an executive game fancier or had the ability to pull the cards from my mind. I mentioned my concern to John, but he just shrugged it off.

"Telepathy is overrated," he said, dealing out the cards again. "I've been playing cards my whole life. It's what I do."

"You took first prize in a tournament that included several known telepaths. They *knew* what you were holding, knew what mode you were going to declare. How could you beat them?"

"Two parts," he said, holding up two fingers. "First, I prevented them from knowing what mode I was going to declare, despite their telepathy. And two, I knew what cards they were holding."

"How? How did you block a telepathic probe, and how did you read their cards?"

He grinned, really grinned. It was the first time I'd ever seen that kind of warm expression on his normally stony face. "I cheated," he said and gestured for me to concentrate on the game.

I considered my cards, and made my play. He did the same, and we both revealed our hands and modes. We'd both declared *liquid*. I had the better hand in that mode, but the game's other factors turned the winning configuration to *solid*, and John's *solid* hand easily won over mine.

A young waiter came and refreshed our tea and then went away. Left-John leaned across the table toward me, reached one hand up to his left eye, and popped the orb from its socket.

"I lost it in the war," he said.

"What war?"

"That's not important. What's important is I've got a cybernetic implant. I can receive visual input from a variety of self-contained prostheses like this one, switching between them at will."

"So?" I still didn't get it.

"So they're small and easy to disguise. I can leave a dozen of them scattered about the room before the game, and flick my input from one to another of them to see what my opponent's holding."

"That's cheating," I said, smiling.

"No such thing as cheating in Matter," he said. He held up the eyeball for my inspection. "This beauty can discriminate seventeen bands of infra-red. Even if someone's playing his cards close to the vest I can still usually read them through the backs by the differing heat signatures of suits and values. It's like playing with a marked deck."

"Isn't that a one shot trick?"

"Only if they figure it out. Most telepaths are so arrogant about their talents that they just assume I must have similar gifts, and a better mental shield to hide them."

"Very handy," I said and held up my left hand, wiggling my pinkie to display the small gold ring set with tiny dials. "Remind me to use this if I'm ever in a game where cheating isn't allowed."

"You have a surveillance jammer?"

I shrugged. "It keeps private business meetings private."

John laughed and rolled his single eye. "Have you really gone that corporate? What's become of the mesmerizing rogue I once shared a jail cell with?"

"He's trying to keep his company in the black and expand it beyond human space," I said. "So, you explained about knowing his cards, but how could you keep your opponent from seeing your intended state of play."

He nodded and popped the eye back into its socket, squinted to get it to set right, and then looked up at me. "You know about all that left-brain right-brain stuff?" he asked.

"Sure, I passed intro-psych," I said. "Left side of the brain controls the right side of the body, has the language centers, all the empirical thinking. Right brain gets the left side of the body and does the more holistic thinking."

"That's the crux of it as I understand it," he said and began shuffling the cards again. "In most folks the two sides talk, signals passing back and forth through a bundle of brain fibers called the corpus callosum."

I nodded. The name didn't mean anything to me.

"I don't got one."

"You don't have what?"

"A corpus callosum. Mine got severed. Long story, happened during the war."

"What war . . . " I started to say, but he cut me off.

"So it's like I got two brains in one body and both of them look at the cards but they have different styles. Each side plans the strategy of play, how many cards to claim from the third hand, the state of matter to declare. But they do it differently. Only the left-brain has language, and that's the only side a telepath picks up. I use my left hand to select my mode token and to point to cards in the third hand, all right-brain strategy. Telepaths get caught flat-footed every time."

I whistled in appreciation. Several of the waiters glanced our way, frowning.

"That's an impressive trick," I said. "But it's not going to help me."

"Nope," he agreed. "It's my trick. You got any of your own?"

"Maybe," I said. "But I've got to get better at the game before they'll have a prayer of working. Deal the cards again."

Seljor Thu agreed to hold our game at the Golden Turtle Palace after I'd sent him the menu. Who knew that minotaurs liked Chinese food? According to his assistant, Seljor Thu was particularly interested in sampling the Bamboo With Steaming Virgin Goddess. Taurians have a very similar physiology to humans, once you get past the bullish configuration of their skulls. Beyond that, they're remarkably like humans, good and bad, psychology and appetites.

At my request, Left-John Mocker had reserved the entire restaurant for our use. Regular patrons were given coupons for a free dinner on another night and turned away at the door. The lawyers from both sides arrived early. They came armed with multiple copies of two different versions of the final contract and happily helped themselves to one of the best dinners they'd ever had. When Seljor Thu arrived, he and I would share a light meal, get to know one another a bit, and then play our single hand of Matter. I had it all planned.

The plan hit a snag when he strolled in twenty minutes later, accompanied by the last of his staff. Never say that Taurians don't have a sense of humor. Seljor Thu wore an authentic matador's jacket and pants, tailored to his tall and broad physique, all bright red silk and metallic embroidery. The rest of his immediate group, Taurians all, had dressed as picadors in somewhat more muted colors. His lawyers, already well into their meal, were dressed nearly identically to my own, which is to say, like lawyers, nondescript and interchangeable suits dripping with legal expertise. Seljor Thu paused by the door to speak with one of his people. Left-John looked over at him and seconds later his elbow was nudging me in the ribs. "You've been set up," he said.

I'd been standing to one side, mentally reviewing the hypnotic programming set in place that morning. Reggie was tucked under my left arm, squirming to get free every time another waiter passed by with a tray of food. I scowled at John. "What are you talking about?"

"I recognize him. He's on the Matter circuit. A pro. When he plays in human space he goes by the name 'Digger.'"

I stared at him, counted to ten in my head, and managed to keep my tone of voice conversational despite a sudden desire to strangle my tutor. "I'm playing against the Taurian head of an archaeological consortium, and you don't think to mention that one of the professional Matter players is a Taurian named 'Digger'?"

John shrugged. "It's worse, he's a rated telepath."

I swallowed hard. My plan was unraveling. "Do you know his range?"

"Just under two meters, more than enough to pick the cards from your mind across the table. You want to bail? It's only money."

I shook my head. "Money is the least of it. This is a power game, and always has been."

He nodded. "The best card games are. So, what's the play?"

"We go ahead as planned. I want you to try and stay out of his range. Keep your ears open and wait for my signal. If necessary, we go to Plan B."

"You got a Plan B?"

"Of course I've got a Plan B."

"The last time you said that to me, we ended up sharing that jail cell. Is this plan going to end any better?"

I swallowed half a dozen retorts and just shrugged. "One way or another, we'll find out real soon." I took hold of Reggie with both hands and passed him to the gambler. Then I went to meet my adversary.

As I crossed the room Seljor Thu broke away from his staff and turned to greet me.

"Ah, so, this must be the Amazing Conroy," he said, using my stage name from a hundred spaceport lounges. I acknowledged it with a slight bow.

"And you must surely then be the famous Digger," I replied.

Seljor Thu chuckled. "Not so famous as some." He glanced in the direction of Left-John. "I am not yet perfectly skilled at distinguishing between humans, but I was fairly certain that gentleman you were speaking with was the Mocker. Has he been coaching you? I had not thought you would be able to hire such a distinguished tutor."

I shrugged. "Oh, Left-John's just a friend. We go way back, former roommates." I gestured and a hostess appeared to lead us toward the private table in the back of the restaurant that had been my study hall for the past week.

We sat at the same table where John and I had met when I'd first asked him to teach me the game. A dozen waiters began arriving, placing platter after platter of exotic cuisine before us. Seljor Thu and I spun the inner table back and forth, sampling each dish, comparing impressions, and sharing light dinner conversation. He was witty, I was charming, and if not for the game looming large at the end of the meal I would have surely enjoyed myself quite a bit.

After a delicious repast the dishes were cleared away and we both helped ourselves to fortune cookies. The Taurian popped his into his mouth whole, chewed, and then extracted the paper fortune from between his lips.

"On my world, there is a group of people, island dwellers, who have a similar custom. At the start of each season they gather all their young people together and randomly pass out small minty wafers, dark ones for the males, lighter ones for the females. One of each bears a small pictograph inside, the symbol for eternal happiness and union. The two youths are matched and mated then and there. They are said to be selected by the gods to form a perfect union."

I smiled. "I don't know where the tradition began here, but nowadays it signifies nothing more than the end of a pleasant meal. The fortunes are generally viewed as little more than a silly game."

I opened my own cookie and stared at the slip.

YOU CANNOT PLAN FOR ALL FUTURES.

Shit. Even the cookies were against me.

"A pity," said my opponent. "This one seemed quite apt. *Amazing defeat awaits those born in the Year of the Dog.*"

I flushed. "Some defeats are more amazing than others."

"Very true," he said. "Shall we proceed then, and learn which kind awaits one of us?"

I nodded. Left-John Mocker temporarily handed Reggie to a waiter. He stepped forward and offered a sealed deck of cards to the Taurian for his inspection.

"With your approval, I have asked my friend here to deal for us."

"As long as he only deals," said Seljor Thu, barely sparing a glance at John. "The game is between us. You may not have the Mocker act as your proxy."

"Of course not," I said. "I think I'm capable of winning on my own."

Seljor Thu laughed, a surprisingly kindly sound without a trace of animosity. "Neither of us believes that, but if it pleases you to say so I won't argue the point." He broke the seal on the box, examined the cards, and returned the deck to John. "You may shuffle at your leisure, Mocker. I defer the cut to my opponent and host."

John rearranged the cards with the dexterity and ease of long practice, his movements simple and efficient. He was not so much shuffling as stacking, gazing off abstractly into space as his hands did the work. How he managed it with the two halves of his brain mute to each other, I can't imagine, but he'd practiced it in front of me just the day before and the results had been impressive. We were still running on Plan A. Both Seljor Thu and I would be dealt good hands, identical hands, in fact. It was the only way I'd come up with to neutralize his greater experience. It wasn't much use against a telepath, but it wasn't my only trick.

Left-John dealt out the cards, retrieved Reggie, and backed quickly into the corner. I left my cards face down upon the table.

Seljor Thu smiled, a big, bovine grin of contentment that made me think of that bull in the children's books who was always sniffing flowers. "Are you conceding already?" he said. "Won't you even look at your hand?"

"Do I need to?" I replied, managing a smile myself. "Don't you already know?"

"I do," he said. "The answer is there in your mind for any with the talent to read it. You expect your hand to be the same as mine. A different suit here and there, but it balances out I'm sure. Very clever of you, Conroy." He paused and bowed his head toward John. "And my compliments to you, Mocker. I never saw you work the trick, not in your hands and I didn't think to seek for it in your mind. Most impressive." He turned back to me. "So you've learned my cards without need of telepathy. But I know yours too, and once you actually look at your cards I'll know what mode you plan to call and choose my own accordingly. And I'm still the better player."

"The proof is in the playing," I said, "and our comparable hands are just the first stage of my plan. Are you ready for the second?" I reached for my cards, gathering them up but still didn't look at them.

The Taurian looked amused, confident. "And what is stage two?"

"Raspberry Gong De Tian," I said softly, and triggered the post hypnotic suggestion I'd given myself that morning. I slipped into a very light trance, and a thin layer of my sensory reality took a sudden detour. "A flavor and a deity. More specifically, my favorite flavor and a Chinese god of luck. I doubt the two have ever been spoken aloud together by anyone else."

I looked at my cards. Across the table from me Seljor Thu began to frown. "What have you done?" I could hear astonishment and perhaps a hint of admiration in his voice.

"I've altered my perceptions. The suits and values that I see on the cards are randomly changing every few seconds. They may have little or no resemblance to what the cards really are."

Seljor Thu rewarded me with a look of puzzlement. "What could you possibly have to gain by such manipulation?"

I shrugged. "It occurred to me that the advantage a telepath has in this game is knowing what his opponent is going to do, what suits and values he has, what state of matter he'll declare. It's an interactive game, but since I don't know what I have, I can't make an accurate call, which means telepathy won't help you make an accurate prediction."

Seljor Thu threw back his head and laughed. "Oh, well done, Conroy. I see how you come to be called Amazing."

"I'm glad you approve," I said.

"I more than approve. This is exactly why I wanted to play against you. How better for me to take the measure of the Terran who wrested control of buffalo dogs from the Arconi? Now, what do you say to a further test of your mettle? What's the expression in your language, 'care to make it more interesting?'"

"What did you have in mind?"

"Double or nothing," he said. "If I win, the buffalo dogs are mine for free. And if you prevail, my consortium will pay you twice the fee and I will personally introduce you to no fewer than thirty corporate leaders of my close acquaintance and recommend to them they lease their buffalo dogs from you instead of the Arconi. Well?"

I'd said it wasn't about the money, but one hundred trained buffalo dogs represented more than half my inventory, and a half-billion credit loss wasn't something that my company could readily absorb. And yet, this was still a game about power, not simply money. I tried to focus on the opportunities and complexities represented by thirty successful contracts outside human space. Either way, Betsy was going to kill me.

"Done," I said and waved a hand to John. "You don't mind if I pat Reggie's head for good luck, do you?"

Left-John frowned and stayed where he was. "If I come any closer, he'll know what cards I put in the dummy hand and have the advantage again."

I smiled and waved him over again. "That's why we had our

little session this morning. Trust me, it's my ass on the line not yours."

John stepped forward and I took Reggie from him. Seljor Thu's eyes twinkled but I couldn't tell if it was delight or disappointment. I gave my buffalo dog a thorough scritching just under his woolly chin and was rewarded with a contented bleating.

"I'm not a telepath," I said, "but I know what you're thinking. Even though to me, my hand keeps changing, you think you know what it is. You think it's the same as your hand. Knowing that, and knowing now the cards available in the third hand, you think I've blown any slight edge I might have had from random chance. You think you've won. But what if you're working from a false assumption? What if my friend here didn't stack the deck as you believe?"

The Taurian grinned. "Why should I doubt my own perceptions? I see the truth clearly in his mind."

I shook my head. "You see only what I put there. Watch closely and I'll take it away. Coyote rhubarb."

John staggered slightly as the hypnotic trigger took effect, and the false awareness of what he'd dealt faded from his mind. Seljor Thu gasped in wonder. "He only knows half the cards."

I nodded. "Only the ones shuffled by his right hand. Coincidentally, those are the ones he dealt to you. His earlier memory of what he dealt both to me and to the third hand might be false. You can't rely on what you see in his mind, and you can't trust what you see in mine. All you know for certain is what you're holding."

Seljor Thu pounded the table with one beefy hand. "Hah! You are wasting your time heading your company. You should let the Mocker take you out on the gaming circuit. You'd make several times your fortune with all these tricks."

I did my best to look inscrutable and simply bowed my head at the compliment. "You're welcome to concede," I said. "I respect an opponent who knows when he's beaten. There's no need to take things further."

He chuckled at that. "But you forget one thing, Conroy. Even left with just the knowledge of my own cards, I'm still the better player. And you are playing completely blind." Ignoring the dummy hand, he placed his cards down on the inner table, then picked up the token that indicated his mode of play. He rolled it around in one hand a moment, and placed it alongside his cards, his hand lightly blocking my view of his choice.

I handed Reggie back to John and watched as the gambler retreated to the corner again. Seljor Thu stared at me, a faint whuffle of air emerging from his bullish nostrils. I could feel the Taurian's eyes on me, and I imagined his gaze penetrating my skull and probing deeper.

"I've left you an opening, Conroy. Will you use the dummy hand without me?"

It was an obvious lure to further muddy the outcome, bringing into play the added complication of interactive rules that would have helped me if we were evenly matched in other respects. I doubted that was the case.

"I wouldn't put myself at that kind of disadvantage. I'll play the cards I was dealt." I whispered another trigger to myself ending the perceptual dance and the shifting cards in my hand settled into place.

Across the table Seljor Thu slapped the table in one-handed applause. His cards were down and he was committed. I studied my own cards, trying to choose the best configuration for all four possible modes of matter. I tried to remember everything John had taught me, everything he'd told me.

I sighed and laid my cards down on the inner table. I picked up my token, John's lessons racing through my mind. I set the token *plasma* side up, covering it with my hand, though I knew full well that Seljor Thu saw the choice in my mind.

"You have played well," he said. "A far better game than I expected of you. With a bit more practice you might have beaten me. I almost feel bad about taking the contract for free, but a wager is a wager." He pulled his hand away from his token and reached to turn over his cards.

A professional gambler admits when he's over-matched and knows how to accept defeat gracefully. I'd seen John do just that on those rare times he lost. But I've always been more of a kick-the-table-over type. Instead, just before Seljor Thu touched his cards, I twisted a tiny dial on the ring on my right hand.

Left-John Mocker screamed.

"John?! Reggie?!" I shouted, shoving my chair back and rising to my feet, one hand pointing over Seljor Thu's shoulder to the corner where Left-John Mocker stood. The big gambler had dropped my buffalo dog. He clutched at his left eye with both hands; wisps of smoke drifted from between his fingers. Reggie tumbled to the floor, bleating in panic. He bolted to me for safety. I scooped him up with relief.

Seljor Thu caught my concern for my pet in my mind. He turned to look at John, only for an instant. It was all the time I needed.

I spun the inner table one hundred eighty degrees. My cards and token now lay in front of Seljor Thu, and his rested before me. Seljor Thu turned back to regard me silently. I tried my best to look apologetic.

"Sorry, John. I must have accidentally activated the surveillance jammer in my ring." I took my seat and turned the cards face up on the inner table. I looked over to the Taurian. "Shall we finish our game? All that's left is for you to reveal your hand."

Seljor Thu laughed. "This may be my hand, now, but they are not my cards. I have underestimated you again, Conroy."

I shrugged. "This is Matter. Beyond the rules of the game, the game has no rules."

"Just so," he said. "I will have my staff draw up a new set of contracts. The entertainment and education I've received tonight more than justifies the added cost. As for the introductions, I have some appointments to attend in the next few days, and then if it pleases you, we can meet again to compare schedules and arrange those meetings."

I bowed my head. "Thank you. I'm sure you'll be happy with the results of our arrangement. It's a pleasure to deal with a professional who knows how to accept a loss."

"Oh, I haven't lost, Conroy. Today, perhaps, but this is just one battle. We will play again, some day, and I will be better prepared for your tricks." He stood, still smiling, and walked away, summoning his staff with a curt gesture. Papers flurried, and moments later the Taurians, their lawyers, and my lawyers had all left the Golden Turtle Palace. I let out a sigh and hugged Reggie close.

John pushed away from the wall. He scowled at me and rubbed his eye.

"Does it hurt much?" I asked."

"Nyah," he said. "Just stings a bit. Mostly it just scared the hell out of me. Worth it though, to see you surprise a telepath." He reached for Seljor Thu's cards and turned them over. "He lost," he said. "How did you know? Between the stacked deck and the hypnotic tricks you pulled, and with neither of you pulling from the dummy hand, you had a fair chance of winning against another player by calling *plasma*. What made you spin the table like that?

"I didn't think Plan B was going to work, and that was the best Plan C I could come up with on the spot. You said he was a pro, and he kept boasting about being the better player. I just took him at his word." I glanced down at the winning hand I'd acquired from Seljor Thu. "Looks like he was right." I sighed again. Thirty introductions to alien corporate leaders. I'd just overextended my company by an order of magnitude and more. Betsy was going to kill me.

YESTERDAY'S TASTE

I met Colin Harvey at the 2009 Worldcon in Montréal. We'd known each other for years as members of Codex, an online writing community, but Colin lived in the UK and I'm in the US. That long weekend in Canada was our first time face-to-face and we really hit it off. Some months later, Colin informed me he would be editing a new anthology from Æon, a small press out of Ireland, and asked me if maybe I would submit something for it. The requirements of the anthology lined up with an idea I'd been tinkering with in the back of my mind, one that involved Conroy, a gourmet chef, and certain concepts of memory that I'd dabbled with back in my professor days. And the timing of it corresponded with an anonymous competition being run by that same online community, Codex. As such, the first versions of the story lacked any mention of buffalo dogs, and the protagonist had a different name. After I washed out of the contest I added Conroy and Reggie and it all worked. The result was "Yesterday's Taste." I emailed the story to Colin late at night in April of 2011. When I woke up in the morning and checked my email, a note from Collin was waiting for me, telling me he loved the story and offering to buy it for his anthology. The following August I was in Reno, Nevada running the eighteenth annual conference of the Klingon Language Institute, a couple days before the start of another Worldcon, when I received word that Colin had died suddenly of a stroke. Colin's publishers honored his contracts and *Transtories* came out a few months later at the end of October. I'm very fond of this story, because it always makes me think of Colin Harvey, who was taken from us far too early.

When Dugli, the most powerful and feared food critic in the galaxy, invited me to join him at a restaurant so exclusive even billionaires like me have to wait two years for a table, I didn't stop to ask why. I packed a bag, scooped up my buffalo dog, and headed for a planet so far off the trade routes that Dugli had sent his private shuttle to ensure I'd come.

Bwill is not a tourist destination. The people smell, the air tastes funny, and the local language will make your ears bleed. But alongside other more common sea creatures, its oceans team with *lithic ichthus*, a species of silicon-based fish hard as corundum and ugly as sin. Imagine a swimming creature made of rock. Rock fins, rock gills, rock scales. The culinary masterminds of Bwill prepare them using a series of marinades that permeate the minerals of these creatures, and over the course of months render them as tender and delicate as meringue, and exquisitely safe to be ingested by us carbon-types.

Dugli's shuttle delivered me to Bwill, and a waiting sloop took me from the splashport straight to the dock of *Stone Fin*, a restaurant created by master chef Plorm. A crowd of Bwillers—with a handful of offworld foodies—loitered in front, waiting for their reservations. I was probably the only human on Bwill and Dugli the only Caliopoean. A dark, otterish pelt covered him from crown to heel, with tiny flaps where humans would keep their ears and a whiskered nose that gave him an astonishing palate. We spotted each other at once.

"Conroy!" Dugli's webbed hand pulled me from the sloop and before I could say a word he had frogmarched me past the outraged stares of would-be diners and into the restaurant. Reggie, my buffalito, clattered after on tiny hooves, desperate not to be left out. We were expected. Plorm herself took us through the curtained maze typical of Bwill style and seated us at an elegant table of polished onyx and chalcedony.

I settled Reggie into a booster seat intended for Bwillian toddlers. Dugli waited for the chef to return to her kitchen before speaking. His dark eyes gleamed in the restaurant's candlelight. "So, Conroy, what's it been? Three years?"

"Life is good, Dugli. How's the galaxy been treating you?"

"Truth to tell, I've been despondent of late. But a few months back, I heard a whisper of a hint of a rumor that turned out to be true, and now I'm the happiest man alive. Or I will be soon. That's why you're here."

I smiled, waiting for the catch. "If feeding Reggie and me a fine meal makes you happy, who am I to argue?"

Dugli snorted. I knew he didn't approve of feeding fine cuisine to pets, particularly given that buffalitos were capable of ingesting literally anything. Moreover, he knew that I knew it, but he didn't bring it up. That should have been my second clue that he wanted something.

"It won't be a good meal, Conroy. It will be a *great* meal. Plorm studied under Nery, the greatest chef this world ever produced."

"I know. I'm looking forward to her stonefish."

His head bobbed in agreement. "Exquisite. The second best meal ever found on Bwill. But . . . What if I said you could have the *very* best served alongside it? Nery's seven cheese cribble puffs!"

"That's crazy. The secret of Nery's cribble course vanished with him twenty years ago."

"I assure you, I'm completely sane."

"Then how? Nery's dead. Everyone knows that."

"What everyone *knows* is a lie. He's been lost all this time, not dead."

"Lost?"

Dugli grinned like an otter. "And I've found him!"

At dawn a groundcar waited to take Reggie and me from our hotel. We shared the road with pedicabs and bicycles but passed no other motorized vehicles on our way to the fish market. Picture a series of cracked and stained piers where the denizens of the local fishing industry—which is to say every third person on Bwill—had tied up their boats. I'm normally good at distinguishing among members of an alien race, but that morning I would have sworn my limo driver was the same Bwiller who had bussed our table the night before, having just changed clothes and gone on to his second job.

We arrived amidst a cacophony of scavenging seabirds and whirring cargoloaders. The pierworkers' shanties sounded to my ear like an orphanage's worth of two-year olds in a nursing home of cheek-pinching grandmothers. Even worse than the noise was the smell! The piers reeked of decay, the boats stank from a local sealant made with the rotting remnants of seaweed, and the pungent citrus scent of hardworking Bwillers filled in any olfactory gaps. The fisherfolk of Bwill have an ironic avoidance of bathing that has them banned from traveling offworld; imagine fermented limes and tangerines blended with the funk of human body odor and you'll get the idea. With Reggie trotting after me, I exited the limo reluctantly, limited by having only two hands and desperately wishing I could cover my nose and both ears simultaneously. Dugli strode toward me, one delicate, webbed hand broadly plastered over his whiskers. He had his aural flaps sealed tight.

"Conroy! Come on, if we hurry we can catch the last bit of the performance."

We rushed down the length of one of the older piers, it's shattered and crumbling surface held together by layers of graffiti and little else. At its far end a group of Bwillers milled about with their backs to us. Dugli pulled me toward them.

The natives of Bwill are humanoid, same as you and me, but on average a head shorter. Their complexions are a bit craggy—though many an adolescent boy on Earth has endured worse acne—and range in color from sunset red to crayon orange. Dugli shoved his way through the throng of locals and yanked me after him. Reggie scampered underfoot, dodging shoes and the thorny toenails of bare Bwiller feet. I muttered apologies, but no one noticed. Everyone was focused on the old man at the edge of the pier who sat chanting in a voice as raspy as sea salt. I could see him easily over the heads of the others, but Dugli pushed us to the front with the determination of a man whose outlook on life includes the certain knowledge that his opinion is infinitely superior to yours.

"There he is, Conroy. The fish poet. His name is Rhine."

I nodded. The oldster was tall for a Bwiller. His burnt orange skin had achieved the clear complexion of the elderly. He wore only a dirty overall, patched and mended beyond its years and possessed a full beard, which on Bwill generally denoted poverty or at a minimum a healthy disregard for money. Wielding a knife in each hand he balanced, juggled, flipped, and methodically sliced away bits of an enormous, marinated stonefish, all while intoning sonnets with a voice like sandpaper. Fish poetry. Beautiful to watch and painful to hear. I don't get it, and I probably never will.

"Dug, you could have sent me a vid," I raised a hand to pinch my nose shut as a wave of fish art wafted my way, breaking through the other odors that I was becoming inured to. "What's so special about this guy?"

"He's Nery," said Dugli, his face lighting up like he'd just tasted the best Eggs Montrachet on four planets, and for good reason if he wasn't wrong.

"Why are you so sure he's not dead?" I turned away, my head ringing from phonemes and tones that I couldn't begin to parse, as a smell thick enough to elbow its way down my throat threatened to push my gorge back along the way it had come. The crowd of art-loving Bwillers parted as I pressed through. I kept walking.

Dugli followed. "The Bwill government doesn't permit physical death as punishment, not since the transpersonal faction took power. Instead, they wiped away the man he was and sent him back into society. Nery became Rhine. Rhine the fish poet was once Nery the master chef. The man who invented the legendary seven cheese cribble puff is still alive, and I've found him."

We were nearly to the limo with its promise of scentless silence. I faced Dugli and shook him by his shoulders. "He was also Nery the master spy. When he wasn't cooking, he was stealing industrial secrets and selling them to the highest bidder, right up until he was caught, convicted, and killed. The body may be the same, but the mind is gone. Nery doesn't live in that man's head any more. The only person home is Rhine. All I saw on the pier was a broken-down fish poet."

"Well, sure," said Dugli, grinning like a young otter caught with one hand in a fishy cookie jar. "Why do you think I brought you here, Conroy? Because your buffalo dog business has made you rich? Nonsense! I know plenty of people richer than you. But you're the best hypnotist I know."

"I'm the only one you know. What do you expect me to do?"

"Regress him."

"Excuse me?"

"Don't be coy. You've done this for me before. Remember that woman on Kaftan's World? You hypnotically regressed her back to childhood until she remembered a day when she watched her grandmother preparing fireweed kreplach. We recovered the recipe."

"Dugli, she hadn't been on the wrong end of transpersonification. It's not the same!"

"You don't know that. The Bwill medical establishment has never heard of hypnosis. The techniques they employ here may not be proof against your own methods. Just imagine it, Conroy, by this time tomorrow we could be enjoying seven cheese cribble puffs!"

The mere idea of the possibility set my mouth to watering like an old Russian dog. Dugli had rung my bell. "I'll try, but I make no promises."

Dugli hurried off to 'make arrangements'. I picked up my buffalito and wondered if anyone would bother to ask the fish poet what he wanted.

Reggie and I spent the rest of the day in our hotel suite with the windows sealed tight and the air controls turned up to full. It wasn't just to give us a reprieve from Bwill's aromas. A buffalito's unique ability to eat any and all matter is eclipsed only by its talent for converting whatever it consumes into flatulence of pure oxygen. I could have kept Reggie from farting by limiting his intake, but there were so many new things for him to taste on Bwill it didn't seem fair. Instead I'd ordered a variety of small plates from the extensive room service menu, and a steward who could have been the twin of my limo driver delivered them, along with a special bottle of stonefish liquor sent compliments of the manager.

I scattered the small plates across the floor, pausing just long enough to transfer a small portion of each onto a platter for my own enjoyment. Reggie wound his way through the culinary slalom, sampling a bit before moving on, repeating the circuit several times until he'd consumed every morsel. I finished my own meal before he was halfway through and turned my attention to the unexpected booze.

It takes months to make stonefish edible, but it takes decades to make it drinkable, and then just barely. The good stuff—and I had to assume the bottle in my hands represented such—could take centuries. The rumors I'd heard back in Human Space spoke of a smoky elixir that put the best single malt scotch to shame, but I'd never been able to verify them. The government of Bwill refused to allow even so much as a single drop of their precious liqueur offworld. A visiting diplomat from the Gilman colonies had tried to export a flask in a diplomatic pouch and the ruckus had cost them their embassy. She'd also been relieved of the flask.

And here I was with a full bottle.

I cracked the seal and wafted the opening under my nose. The smell was . . . primal. Antediluvian. It made me think of the sea and things that might be found in its deepest depths. Of darkness and tastes predating history.

Reggie pranced over, happy and proud for having licked every plate clean. He climbed onto my chair, crossed onto my lap, and navigated up my chest to shove his face next to mine for a sniff of the bottle. I don't know if it brought primordial oceans to his mind, but he yipped in interest. I reached for one of his freshly cleaned plates.

"Dugli's dreams of cribble puffs will probably never materialize, but at least we get to sample the mysteries of liquid stonefish." I poured a portion onto the plate and set it on the floor. It resembled a miniature oil slick, viscous, with a sickly, greenish tinge. Reggie gave it a tentative lick. He barked, jumped back from the plate, and barked again.

"Not to your liking, boy?" He advanced on the plate, gave it another lick, and backed off again. Weird. I considered taking a swig right from the bottle, then got up to fetch a glass instead, the better to appreciate it.

That's about the time the remains of the oil slick exploded!

Reggie went flying, horns over tail, and landed on the other side of the suite. The blast knocked me off my feet, but I managed to hold onto the bottle. It sloshed a bit but not enough for anything to splash its way up and out of the neck, let alone mingle with the air or whatever else had produced such volatile fumes. I scrambled back to where I'd left the stopper, jamming it into place. To do this I'd had to maneuver around a crater in the floor that looked down into the suite on the level below.

Reggie scampered back, none the worse for being a cannonball. He peered into the hole and barked at the Bwill couple that were now looking up, twin expressions of confusion on their orange faces. My own expression didn't look half so calm.

Someone from the hotel took the bottle away. Then someone else escorted Reggie and me out, and not into custody as I'd feared but into an even nicer suite. A third someone must have contacted Dugli because he arrived soon after in the company of the hotel manager who assured me nothing like that had ever happened before and couldn't apologize enough.

After the manager had groveled sufficiently to allow him to exit I confronted Dugli.

"Someone just tried to kill me."

"Don't be absurd. You probably had some residue on your clothes that interacted with the liqueur. Something you brought in from offworld. I understand if you're a little on edge after the accident, but that's all it was. Flukes happen."

"Maybe. Or maybe someone doesn't want Nery brought back."

"Conroy, there are probably a hundred people on Bwill who don't want Nery back. Do you have any idea how many he betrayed? The man was a legend. He had the culinary powers of a god, the athletic prowess of a planetary champion, and a list of romantic conquests that included every Bwill female with any real political power, wealth, or beauty. He used his talents to worm his way into people's confidences and then stole them blind!"

"So you're saying someone did try to kill me?"

"Not at all. Only that someone might, if he knew what we're attempting. But nobody does. I told you, I'm the only one who knows that Rhine was Nery. If I thought otherwise, I'd be shoving you and your pet back onto that shuttle, and climbing in right behind you, and getting offworld before the fireworks started."

Reggie chose that moment to bump against my leg for some attention. I scooped him up and stroked the fur on his hump. He closed his eyes and pressed his head against my chest. I said nothing, content to glare at the Caliopoean.

Dugli sighed. "Look, if it will make you feel any better, I'll shift some other people around and make it look like you're still staying here. Meanwhile, I'll secretly move you to a different hotel, and in the morning send Rhine to you so you can do the regression there. Okay?"

"If you don't believe there's a threat, why are you so quick to humor me?"

"What I believe doesn't matter, Conroy. If you think you're in danger, you're not going to be focused on the task at hand. I need you at the top of your game. We'll probably only get one chance at this."

"Why's that? You said no one knows Rhine was once Nery."

"No, but people are going to start asking questions soon enough, and if I could figure it out, once they know where to look, others will too. Before that happens, I want us both on my shuttle halfway back home."

"With a big basket of seven cheese cribble puffs, I assume?"

Dugli smiled. "Two baskets. One for each of us."

*   *   *

215

Dugli's driver took us to a different hotel on the opposite side of town. The driver went in and registered a room in the name of the Bwill equivalent of John Smith, and Reggie and I moved in as unobtrusively as the only human and buffalo dog on a planet full of ruddy, smelly, craggy people can manage. My buffalito has a long history of being able to curl up and sleep anywhere. Somehow, I followed his example, because I was awakened hours later by Dugli pounding on the door to my room. Wiping the sleep from my eyes, I had the room's security console visually confirm the person who had yet to stop knocking, and let him in. He entered, escorting the familiar figure of an aging fish poet.

"Why are you here so early?" I double-locked the door and followed my 'guests' into the room.

"Early? Don't be insulting, Conroy. We've been up for hours. Fish poets wake before dawn to meet the new catch at the docks. They find it inspirational. Now, let's get started. Where do you want us?" Rhine had changed into clean overalls since yesterday's performance at the pier. He moved with a limp. Dugli seated the Bwiller on a low couch, securing him all around with throw pillows.

"I want you gone. This isn't a stage performance, so I don't need an audience. Besides, you've got some misdirection to be managing. Leave me and, uh, Rhine here. We'll be fine. Come back later, and bring brunch."

The food critic glowered but left. I dropped into a chair across from Rhine and Reggie took it as his cue to leap into my lap. We both looked at the fish poet who sat staring at his bare feet.

"So, Rhine? Please tell me you speak Traveler, yes?"

He nodded. "Some. They taught us in school, back when I was a boy." His voice rasped much as it had the day before, and his accent rang with an overlay of tones that might have been a critical part of his native language but had no place in the pidgin speech used by this part of the galaxy.

"Great. And you know why you're here?"

"Your friend thinks I used to be someone else, and that you can make me remember who. I told him he's wrong, that I've always been me." He lifted his head and smiled. His eyes were a pale mint green. "He was very certain though. When he was done I was half convinced he was right."

"But only half?"

"Mr. Conroy, look at me. Look at my hands. See all these scars? They're from a lifetime of handling stonefish. I've worked with them all my life, fishing and netting and mongering and versing. These aren't the hands of a lover or a champion caster. I've had my share of tumbles in and out of beds, and as a fry I cast discs with my friends, same as everyone else. But my life's been hard work. The man your friend wants me to be didn't do menial work like that. If he were here, his hands would be manicured, not rubbed raw by life."

I studied his outstretched hands and the crisscross traceries of too many scars. Were any of them more than twenty years old? Were some of them caused not by catching stonefish but from cooking them?

"Well, like you said, Dugli can be pretty insistent. Since we're both here, and he won't be back with brunch for a while, why don't we humor him and give this a try? Just sit back, close your eyes, and listen to my voice. Let the room fade away and picture yourself back at the pier. Imagine the sounds and smells of the place, the taste of the air, the feel of things."

I continued building a familiar sensory tableau and eased him into a suggestible state. Then I created a two word trigger that instantly plunged him deeper each time I spoke it. Then up again, then deeper. Which answered the first of Dugli's unasked questions: the natives of Bwill could indeed be hypnotized. I took my time, reinforcing the trance over and over, until I was having a conversation with a part of his subconscious mind. Everything to this point had been preamble and stage setting. It was time to get specific.

"Do you know who Nery was?"

He snorted, eyes still closed, slumped over but alert despite his posture. "Everyone knows Nery. He was famous. Dead too, for about twenty years now."

"Think about him for me. Imagine everything you know about him is arrayed before you, like silvery fish in a net."

"I see them."

"Good. Now, grasp a fish, the one that represents your earliest memory of Nery. What is it?"

"When he came from nowhere and won the world title. I'd just gotten back from days at sea, been working as part of a five-man crew and we had a hold full to bursting of stonefish, twice what we'd hoped to bring in. The whole crew had landed in a bar at the dock and was celebrating, and there on the vid was Nery, hitting every target on the range with his disc, ricocheting it off pillars and beams with precision casting like no one had ever seen. It was poetry watching him . . . " He fell silent, and his hands, which had been clenched tightly around an imaginary fish as he spoke, fell open and empty again.

"Take up the next fish in the net," I said. "What's that memory."

"A story I heard from a bedmate. She was going on and on about some actresses in the tabloids, fighting over which of them was having a fling with him . . . "

"And the next?"

"Delivering a fresh catch to one of his restaurants. Just missed meeting the man himself. I was dropping off a cage of gargantua crabs. One of the other chefs signed for 'em. Nery was out front, hobnobbing with some diners and serving up cribble puffs . . . "

We went on like that for most of an hour, one gleaming fish of memory at a time. Each sounded flat, like a news clipping from Nery's life tied to a bit of episodic memory from Rhine's, up to and including where he'd been when Nery's death sentence had been announced.

"That's when I took up my knives and words. It just didn't make sense no more, that someone larger than life like that could be brought low. Just cause my life didn't matter wasn't excuse to snuff out his. That was my inspiration. That injustice gave me voice, and these hands that had caught and hauled began to carve and slice, and the poems just came out of me from nowhere."

This last memory convinced me. The fish poet had been born when the master spy had died. Rhine and Nery were one and the same. But knowing that wasn't the same as being able to do anything about it. I couldn't regress him back to his other self. The transpersonality techniques had installed a past into him. Whether it was fictitious or borrowed or constructed from a template didn't matter. It was whole and complete unto itself. I tried to slip past it, sneak into Nery's memories by some backdoor association, via primal emotions, even through base sensations of pain and delight, but I couldn't. There wasn't anything to sneak in to. His memories hadn't simply been erased.

Rhine's had overwritten them. Nery was dead, and only the fish poet remained.

I eased Rhine back to full consciousness, leaving him with the suggestion that he'd feel relaxed and well rested and with no ill effects from his hypnotic experience.

"Did it work? Am I really Nery, like your Caliopoean believes?"

Reggie jumped into Rhine's lap and butted his head against the fish poet's stomach demanding to be petted. "No. And yes. I think he was right, but those memories, the person you were, if any of that still exists I can't reach it."

"Good." His fingers worked through the ringlets of Reggie's wooly head.

"You wouldn't want to be famous?"

"I do sonnets about people who are larger than life. They always end tragically. It's better to be a fish poet. Sure, I live on charity, but people think I'm lucky. And the hours are better."

My smile was interrupted by a rumble from my stomach. I hadn't had breakfast and it was well past time for lunch. Dugli still hadn't returned and I wasn't willing to wait any longer. After yesterday's experience, room service was out of the question.

"Are you familiar with this part of the island? Any place you'd recommend for a good meal? I'm buying."

Rhine set Reggie aside and stretched. "Have you ever had Nyonya?"

"You have Indonesian food here on Bwill?"

"We have a culinary exchange program with several planets, yours among them. Every year we send some of our best chefs offworld for a year. Many return and open fusion restaurants. There's a woman who went to Malaysia and came back with a cargo of leaves and spices. Her place isn't far, but we can't get a pedicab this time of day. Do you know how to ride a bicycle?"

I smiled. "It's been a while, but I'm sure it will come back to me."

He limped to a comm unit on the wall and called down to the front desk. "They'll have a pair of bicycles waiting for us by the time we get downstairs. You'll probably want a basket for yours if your friend is coming."

Reggie yipped. "I wouldn't dream of denying him a taste of Nyonya-Bwill fusion."

*   *   *

It's true what they say about riding a bicycle. I hadn't been on one in decades, but after a wobbly beginning that startled Reggie, my body remembered what to do and I was traveling smoothly down an avenue on a sunny, noxious day. Rhine peddled effortlessly alongside. After twenty minutes of brisk, below-the-waist exercise we were deep in the corporate sector of town and guiding our bicycles down canyons formed by hundred-storey walls of capitalistic zeal, all gleaming ceramo and hurricane-proof glass that was as different from the poverty of the docks as day from night. A doorman dressed in a loose tunic, trousers, and sarong took charge of our bicycles and welcomed us to *Nyonya Baba*. The restaurant was one of several in the building that catered to the robber barons responsible for running things on Bwill. The lunch rush had come and gone. The maître d' didn't look twice at me, but practically bowed to Rhine as she escorted us through the maze and past a dozen empty tables before seating us by a window.

"Don't take this the wrong way," I said, "but this doesn't strike me as the kind of place you could normally afford."

"It's not. But it's considered lucky to have a fish poet in your establishment, provided he can afford the fare. You're still paying, aren't you?"

I nodded, and we ordered three servings of the day's special, a variation on traditional otak-otak made with stonefish wrapped in a locally grown banana leaf. Whether a result of the exercise getting here or the exquisite meal, Rhine became loquacious. While Reggie and I ate he unwound an introduction to the intricacies of fish poetry with commentary on everything from the complex pairing of vocal pitch and stress with angle and speed of knife strokes while juggling/slicing a marinated stonefish within the strictures of a sonnet's fourteen lines.

As we topped off our meal with kuih, brightly colored cakes made from the Brill equivalent of glutinous rice, he brought his lecture to a close. "Ultimately, it's a lot like the bicycle."

I paused with a mouthful of cake. "Sorry?"

"Once you know how to do it, you don't worry about it any more. I don't have to think about the movements of the knives or the rhythms of my voice. That's automatic. All of my focus is reserved for the new part, the words I'm using for that specific poem. Everything else my body already knows how to do."

Reggie chose that moment to let loose with a long stream of otak-otak inspired flatulence, which in turn triggered an epiphany for me. I knew the solution to Dugli's problem.

When it came time to pay the bill, I asked the waiter to send the manager over. From her flawless pumpkin complexion she had to have been older than Rhine. Her long, lustrous hair was as black as the shimmering pajamas she wore. She addressed Rhine first, speaking in a local language. He waved her to me and she switched to crisp and flawless Traveler.

"You found your meal satisfactory, sir?"

"No, I found it incredible. I've had the pleasure of dining in Singapore and Malacca many times, and your otak-otak was the finest I've ever sampled."

"I will pass your words on to our chef. Please, how else may I be of assistance?"

I'd hoped for more of a reaction, but I hadn't praised the food to soften her up. "This is going to sound very odd, but I would like to rent out your restaurant for the rest of the day."

"Sir? I am sorry, but if you wish to host a dinner party here, you would need to give us at least six days notice."

"You misunderstand. I don't want dinner. I want the restaurant. Actually, just the kitchen. But everyone can go home. Everyone *has* to go home. I want to pay you for the use of your empty kitchen and have you close your restaurant. Just for the next few hours."

"What you ask is not possible."

"Normally, I suppose not. But it's your lucky day. I'm traveling with a fish poet of some renown." I took out my credit chip, keyed in the cost of lunch, moved the decimal point three places to the right, and handed it to her. "Possible?"

She stared at the chip long enough to confirm the number. Then she pulled back a sleeve to reveal a standard comm bracelet and clipped my chip to its transaction port before I could change my mind. As she handed back my chip she spoke to her wrist, a rapid singsong of instructions. In the next instant she was gone.

Rhine stared at me. "She just ordered her staff to tell all the patrons there's been a small fire in the kitchen, apologize, and ask them to leave, while inviting them to return for a complimentary meal any time in the future."

"Excellent!"

"What are you doing?"

Before I could answer our waiter returned. "If you will follow me please?"

"To the kitchen?" She nodded. I stood and tucked Reggie under my arm. "C'mon, Rhine. Time to make history."

"We're making history?"

"No, just me. You're making seven cheese cribble puffs!"

The kitchen staff was leaving as we came in. Reggie began scampering around ready to wreak havoc but calmed down once I built him a bed of dish towels. Rhine seated himself on a tall stool near a walk-in freezer. With Reggie napping, I forced an apron and the Bwill equivalent of a toque on the fish poet.

"What's the point of this? You said it yourself, I'm not Nery. I'm no kind of chef. I can carve stonefish, but I can't cook."

Instead of replying, I positioned him in the middle of the kitchen, right where an executive chef would stand to command his sous-chef and the various station chefs below. But no, that wasn't right. Nery had never allowed anyone in the kitchen with him when he made his cribble puffs. Which meant he'd had to be able to reach and do everything by himself.

Those legendary seven cheese cribble puffs had defied classification. A braised entree that was also a fish dish that nonetheless had the delicacy of the finest pastry. I moved Rhine to a spot midway between where *Nyonya Baba's* poissonnier and rôtisseur would have stood, a quick step would take him to either spot. The pastry chef's station was a bit further but still near.

"Mr. Conroy, what do you expect me to do?"

I stood directly in front of him, and caught his gaze. "Ride a bicycle," I said.

"What?"

"Hestia Ambrosia." Rhine responded to the trigger I'd installed and slipped instantly into trance. His eyes closed and he swayed in place. "Listen carefully now. Let your mind go blank. I don't want you to think. You don't need to think. It doesn't matter that you don't remember anything of Nery's life. You don't need his mind to

222

be a master chef. The memory of how to cook is in your muscles and reflexes. Your body knows everything Nery knew. In a moment, you're going to open your eyes. You won't need to think. You wont' be able to think. You'll just respond to the needs of the *wont'* situation. Your body knows what to do. Let it do it. Just go with it. If you understand, let your mind sink deeper, surrender yourself to the situation, open your eyes and let your body respond."

I stepped back out of his line of sight. Rhine opened his eyes, tensed and waiting.

"Order in, chef," I said. "Seven cheese cribble puffs!"

Nery flew into action. It was the same deliberate movement I'd seen on the pier when the fish poet's knives had juggled and carved a massive stonefish. He grabbed bowls and pans, opened cupboards and cabinets, sought and discarded ingredients and spices. *Nyonya Baba's* kitchen had everything he needed, and I watched as he prepared the signature dish that had died with him twenty years before. Seeing the intricacy of it, the elaborate construction of the entree, made me understand why it had never been duplicated. It was culinary complexity that made fish poetry look like throwing together a peanut butter and jelly sandwich by comparison. And then, after an eternity that passed too quickly, he was done. Nery placed several circular pans into a pre-heated oven and set a timer. Then he stepped back, tensed and waiting once more.

"Both of you, step away from the oven doors. Now!"

While I'd been absorbed watching Nery, another Bwiller had entered the kitchen. Her voice sounded familiar, and when I turned toward the entrance and saw Dugli standing in front of her, soaking wet and with a chef's knife at his throat, the pieces all fell into place. It was Plorm.

"Why couldn't you leave him to his sonnets?"

I eased Rhine/Nery away from the oven, positioning one of the station chef's tables between us and the others. "You knew who he was all along."

"Of course I knew. He was the sun to me. A pair of overalls and beard couldn't blind me to him. He made me all that I am. But cooking wasn't enough for him. For years after his death his students suffered the shame of his crimes. Now my name burns brightly on its own, no longer tainted by his. But you wanted to bring him back."

I could have kicked myself. "You tampered with the bottle in my suite. The steward who brought it was the driver, who was also a busboy at *Stone Fin*.

"My son," said Plorm.

Dugli sobbed. "He tried to drown me, Conroy! He drove me into the sea."

Plorm shoved Dugli in my direction, freeing her other hand and drawing another knife from her belt. "This ends now. I didn't set out to hurt anyone. Your mad quest for Nery's recipe will destroy everything I've rebuilt. But you've conveniently arranged for everyone to be gone from here tonight, and every chef knows how dangerous a kitchen can be. A trio of tragic but fatal accidents."

The bell on the oven dinged. Reggie woke up and barked. Plorm shifted her glance for an instant to my buffalito. Nery snatched up a circular pan and flung it into the air.

Plorm ducked, but it wasn't necessary. The pan flew wide and high, passing harmlessly over her at great speed. She laughed once and took another step toward us, brandishing both knives.

With a clang the pan hit the wall, ricocheted off, struck the adjacent wall, bounced again, and caught Plorm in the back of the head with sufficient force to knock her to the ground senseless.

The authorities took Plorm away to a forensic hospital to test for a concussion, and sent someone to pick up her son back at *Stone Fin*. They took Dugli to the hospital too, just to check him over. Other officials suggested that Rhine and I leave the kitchen-turned-crime scene, sooner rather than later. I agreed, but asked the fish poet to get Reggie for me. As he did, I found a clean, cloth sack and emptied the contents of two cooking pans into it from the oven.

We left the restaurant and walked a while. Office workers coming off shift flooded the street around us, and if these worthy Bwillers found anything unusual in the sight of a human, his buffalo dog, and a transpersonified fish poet they had the good grace not to let it show. After several blocks, a pedicab stopped in front of us and the operator invited us aboard in broken Traveler. We set off for my hotel.

Rhine hadn't said a word, even after I brought him out of trance. The only sound was the cabby's feet slapping against the street. I considered using his trigger again, to understand and try to ease his obvious pain, but I didn't have that right. Instead I said, "Rhine, talk to me."

He looked up at me and reached for Reggie, pulling my buffalito into his lap and cradling the animal tenderly. That simple gesture broke something open in him. "I could have killed her. How did I do such a thing? How is it possible?"

"You didn't do a thing. That was all Nery."

"No, you said you couldn't reach Nery, that he was gone. That leaves only me. I did it."

"Rhine, were you ever a champion disc caster?"

"What? No, I told you, I just fooled around with it as a kid."

"That's right. But Nery was the best on Bwill. He trained at it, burned the knowledge into his muscles. When the situation called for it, the body remembered how to do it, and was able to do it because I prevented *you* from being there to interfere. Do you see that?"

"I . . . suppose."

"And another thing. Plorm was never in danger for her life. She'd been Nery's protégé; he'd never have hurt her. I don't know if some part of him still resides in you and knew her or not, but consider the cast that took her down. A double ricochet to catch her by surprise? Nery was that good. If he'd wanted to do more than knock her out, do you have any doubt it would have happened?"

Rhine looked down into Reggie's soulful brown eyes and managed a smile. "You're almost as convincing as your Caliopoean."

"I'll take that as a compliment. Now, what do you want to do?"

"How do you mean?"

"You're not Nery, but I could help you to recover some of the things your body remembers. You could recreate his recipes, maybe even become a competitive disc caster if you like."

He passed Reggie gently from his lap to mine. "No, Mr. Conroy. Those skills belong to someone else. I told you, I'm content to be a fish poet."

There was nothing left to say and the pedicab continued on in silence again. I offered Rhine the sack and he reached in and helped himself to a puff. I took two, one for myself and one for Reggie.

They were still warm. I bit into mine and it burst in my mouth like a succulent explosion of savory delight. Beside me I heard Rhine gasp.

"Oh my! I think I finally understand what brought you and Mr. Dugli to Bwill."

"Yeah. Nothing else like it in the world. On any world."

"May I have another? For inspiration? I think there are sonnets that need to be written about these things. What did you call them?"

"Nery's legendary seven cheese cribble puffs. Sure, have as many as you like."

He laughed. "I don't dare. There wouldn't be any left for you or Mr. Dugli."

"Good point. He'd better hurry back if he expects to get some."

About the Author

Lawrence M. Schoen holds a Ph.D. in cognitive psychology, spent ten years as a college professor, and when not writing currently works as the chief compliance officer for a series of mental health and addiction treatment facilities. He's also one of the world's foremost authorities on the Klingon language, as well as the publisher behind Paper Golem, a speculative fiction small press serving the niche of up-and-coming new writers as well as providing a market for novellas. In 2007, he was nominated for the John W. Campbell Award for best new writer, and in 2010 his short story, "The Moment," was nominated for a Hugo Award. He's probably best known for the short stories, novelettes, and novels, all concerned with likable rogue and stage hypnotist, the Amazing Conroy, and Reggie, Conroy's alien companion, a buffalo dog that can eat anything and farts oxygen. Lawrence and his wife, Valerie, live in Pennsylvania.

182 touch → touched
186 effects → affects
197
211 //

223
209, 215, 219, 225   Is "Caliopean" rel to
                     "calliope"? 2 Ls?
224

CPSIA information can be obtained at www.ICGtesting.com
Printed in the USA
BVOW071900211112

306198BV00001B/10/P

9 780984 967087